The Pleasure Was Mine

The Pleasure Was Mine

TOMMY HAYS

St. Martin's Press

New York

www.stmartins.com

Excerpt from "When You Are Old" reprinted with the permission of Scribner, an imprint of Simon & Schuster Adult Publishing Group, from *The Collected Works of W. B. Yeats, Volume 1: The Poems, Revised,* edited by Richard J. Finneran (New York: Scribner, 1997).

Library of Congress Cataloging-in-Publication Data

Hays, Tommy.
    The pleasure was mine / Tommy Hays.
        p. cm.
    ISBN 0-312-33932-1
    EAN 978-0312-33932-6
    1. Widowers—Fiction. 2. Older men—Fiction. 3. Fathers and sons—Fiction. 4. Loss (Psychology)—Fiction. 5. Grandparent and child—Fiction. 6. Alzheimer's disease—Patients—Fiction. 7. South Carolina—Fiction. I. Title.

PS3558.A875P57 2005
813'.6—dc22   2004051311

First Edition: March 2005

10   9   8   7   6   5   4   3   2   1

In memory of Tom Hays
and in gratitude to Marguerite Hays

And as always for Connie, Max, and Ruth

Contents

Acknowledgments

Writing a novel is a more social process than the lone writer might realize during the time he's writing it. But looking back, I am struck by how many generous and thoughtful people played a part in the evolution of this book.

Abigail De Witt, Kathy Sheldon, and Mark Swanson patiently read and critiqued early drafts of the novel. Reynolds Price, who has been supportive of my work in so many ways, helped shape a later draft. George Singleton also gave important suggestions toward the end of revision. Valerie Leff stepped in with encouragement, as well as critical counsel at a crucial time. Steve Baker, Dale Davis, and Nanette Johnson offered much-needed moral support.

I am thankful for the camaraderie of the generous faculty and students of the Great Smokies Writing Program at the University of North Carolina at Asheville. I appreciate UNC-Asheville's support, especially from Director of Creative Writing Rick Chess and Director of Special Academics Elaine Fox, as well as her assistant, Leanna Preston.

I want to thank Malaprops Bookstore, especially owner Emoke

B'Racz and manager Linda Barrett Knopp, for supporting my work and the work of other writers in the Asheville community. Also I want to thank Duff and Margaret Bruce, owners of The Open Book in Greenville, South Carolina, for all their help over the years.

Finally, I want to give deepest thanks to Neeti Madan of Sterling Lord Literistic, who wholeheartedly represented the manuscript, and to my editor, Diane Reverand, and her assistant, Regina Scarpa, who artfully and painstakingly made it a book.

But one man loved the pilgrim soul in you,
And loved the sorrows of your changing face. . . .

—William Butler Yeats, from
When You Are Old

The Pleasure Was Mine

One

Newell's Request

My wife has gone. I can't say that I blame her. After fifty years, Irene had probably had enough of keeping up my end of the conversation with family and friends, while I slipped outside to weed the garden or drove over to Pete's for a piece of pie and a cup of coffee and talk that didn't send my blood pressure through the roof.

She had probably had enough of my temper, my dark moods, my foul mouth, my all-around disagreeable self. She had probably had enough of me coming home reeking of turpentine and flecked from head to toe with latex or enamel. She had probably had enough of what most everybody wondered and some, over the years, were rude enough to ask: How in the world did a tall, thin, fair-skinned beauty and one of the most respected high school English teachers in all of Greenville County, in all of South Carolina for that matter, wind up married to a short, dark, fat-faced, jug-eared house painter—a high school dropout, who when he first heard about semicolons, figured they had something to do with digestion.

Not that she ever complained. Never once did she even hint at being sorry about that muggy July night back in '52 at Pete's, when it was still a drive-in, when she said yes to me between bites of a slaw burger all-the-way. Over the years, whenever she mentioned anything about us, it was always how glad she was she had married me, what a good fit we had been, and how easy we had had it compared to most couples. I could have said all that back to her and meant every last word, but I never got around to it. Maybe she'd had enough of that, too.

I don't mean Irene wished for this. If she had had any say about her demise, losing her mind would have been about last on her list. It is hard on an English teacher to forget her words. It's hard on a woman who prides herself on order to have the objects of the house mutiny against her, like the time she couldn't find the iron, and I came across it days later in the freezer, or when her missing watch turned up in the sugar bowl.

The doctor agreed that the sudden death of our daughter-in-law might have brought it on, but he also said she probably would have come down with it eventually. He said it was hereditary, even though neither of her folks lived long enough to come down with it themselves.

Still, I can't help thinking if I had not been such a cranky bastard, if I had taken her to the pictures or out to the S&W Cafeteria more often, if I had gone along with her on her evening walks, or if I had just sat around with her at night reading or watching a little TV, things might have been different. If I had worked harder at keeping her company, her mind might have not been so quick to wander.

The doctor prescribed medicine that was supposed to slow it. I managed to keep her home for a couple of years, when she was forgetting telephone numbers or where she set her glasses or how to sign her name. But it wasn't long before she forgot bigger things like how to drive, how to cook, how to take a shower. One time I came home late from a job. It was already dark when I pulled in front of the house. I saw her through the window. The shades were still up and the lights on, and she was sitting in the living room watching TV in her underwear for all the world to see, like she had started to get ready for bed but forgotten midway. She would have been mortified if she had been in her right mind. That was when I hung up my brushes for good and shut down my little painting company. I was afraid to leave her alone.

Then in December, the day after Christmas, the phone rang at three in the morning. I felt for the receiver in the dark.

"Who is this?" I asked, keeping my voice down. Irene had had more and more trouble sleeping, and once she was awake, she was awake for hours, wandering the house.

"It's Mildred." Mildred Smeak had been a math teacher at Greenville High and was a friend of Irene's. She lived up the street. Irene and Mildred had both retired five years ago.

"You know what time it is?" I whispered, reading the glowing numbers on the electric clock by our bed. Then I remembered she had called like this in the middle of the night once before, when her husband had his first stroke. "Is it Herman?"

"Irene is sitting at my kitchen table."

"What?" I turned on the light, and my heart dropped when I saw Irene's side of the bed empty. I hadn't even heard her get up. "What's she doing there?"

"Wants to borrow a couple of eggs, at least that's what I finally figured out. She kept saying she wanted some of those things in which chickens are involved. Says she's making a cake. Says it's somebody's birthday."

"I'm sorry, Mildred," I said.

"It's all right, we have been having a good talk." Then Mildred lowered her voice. "Except she might think I'm her mother."

"I'll be right there."

"Bring her overcoat and shoes."

On a nineteen-degree December night, Irene had walked barefoot down to Mildred's in her nightgown.

"It's nobody's birthday," I had said as I drove Irene back home. This was when I still believed that as long as I kept the facts in front of her, she had a fighting chance.

"It *feels* like somebody's birthday," she said, looking out the van window. I had wrapped the coat around her, but her teeth were chattering.

"Even if it was somebody's birthday," I said, "and even if it wasn't the middle of the goddamn night, we have two whole cartons of eggs in the frigerator." I knew, because I had been doing the cooking for a good while. And what I cooked was eggs, so I made sure we had plenty on hand.

"Whose . . . residence is this?" she asked, as I turned into our drive.

I thought she was pulling my leg, the way she used to. But when I looked at her, her face pale and blank in the streetlight, I saw she didn't know where she was.

"I want to go home," she said, sounding lost like a child.

"We *are* home," I said.

"This little . . . dwelling?" she asked, looking toward the house. "Where's the big porch? Where's the man who takes care of me?" She was talking about her father and the house she grew up in on Crescent Avenue.

"Mr. Blalock has been dead for forty-five years," I said. "This is where you and I live, where we always lived."

We passed nearly half a century in that house—alone together, with our boy, Newell, and then alone again. Its crumbling brick, sagging joists, and cracked plaster were the sum of us, and for

Irene to not recognize it was like a plug had been pulled and our lifetime together was draining away.

When I came around and opened the van door for her, she didn't move. "This isn't my house," she said.

"Of course it is," I said.

"I'm not going in," she said.

"You can't just sit out here all night," I said. "You'll catch your death."

"This is not . . . where I'm from," she said, sitting back in her seat, folding her arms, and looking straight ahead. By the porch light, I could see her breath make little clouds in the cold night air. She looked like a lost little girl sitting there.

I felt a wave of tenderness toward my wife. "Now, Irene," I said in a softer voice, "we need to go inside and warm you up." I started to take her arm.

"Let go of me, you son of a bitch!" She slapped me.

I raised my hand to my stinging cheek. In all our years together, Irene had never hit me. Yet it wasn't the slap that shocked me so. What really shook me up, what really told me we had entered a world I did not begin to understand, was her cursing me the way she did. Never in our fifty years had she cursed me. I'm not saying she hadn't been aggravated with me plenty over the years, but never had she called me anything worse than a stubborn old goat.

I stood there in the freezing cold, wondering what to do. I couldn't leave her where she was. I looked around the neighborhood, not a light on anywhere up or down the street. I didn't want to have to wake neighbors; besides, I didn't want them to see Irene in such a state. I could handle this on my own. I considered starting the van back up, turning on the heater, and waiting out the night with her, but I worried about carbon monoxide.

My ankle ached, so I sat down on the porch step. "What are we going to do?" I asked aloud.

Irene looked straight ahead, like she was traveling somewhere, keeping her eyes on the road.

"We can't stay out here all night," I said.

Irene didn't budge, didn't even blink.

I sighed and crossed my arms against the cold. I could drag her inside, but I hated to think of the struggle she might put up, and all the commotion might wake the neighbors. I wondered if maybe Mildred might still be up. Her house was too far down the street for me to make out if her lights were still on. Maybe she wouldn't mind coming over to help get Irene inside. I started into the house to call Mildred and was in the kitchen dialing the number, when I heard the van door slam and footsteps cross the porch. When I went into the front room Irene was closing the door behind her. "It's freezing out there," she said, rubbing her shoulders. Then in a voice sounding like her old self, she asked, "Why'd you leave me out there?"

I looked at her. She wasn't kidding.

"You didn't want to come in," I said, helping her out of her coat.

She yawned. "I'm exhausted," she said, and headed back to our bedroom. I followed her, helped her into bed, and pulled the covers over her. She fell asleep as soon as her head hit the pillow. Now I was the one who was wide awake. I went back to the kitchen and fixed a cup of instant coffee and sat there till dawn, hearing again and again an Irene I did not recognize call me a son of a bitch and mean it. That was scary enough, but then to have her come inside a couple of minutes later like nothing ever happened—well, that shook me to the core.

The doctor put Irene on an antidepressant, and it did even her out some. She didn't become as frustrated, although every now and then she still cursed me. More than once, she scratched me when I was trying to get her out of bed in the morning. A couple of times she drew blood. It wasn't her temper that finally did us in. It was her wandering. I had put in dead bolts so she couldn't roam the neighborhood at night, but short of strapping her to the bed, I couldn't prevent her from wandering through the house. One night, I woke to a loud crash and found her sprawled on the living room floor. She had tripped over a throw rug.

I took her to the doctor the next day. He said she hadn't broken anything but that she might if we didn't take more precautions. He said it was time to consider a "facility." He said this to me and to Newell, who had come down from Asheville, which was sixty miles away, for the doctor's appointment and was now sitting on the other side of Irene.

"I'm keeping her at home," I said.

"Daddy, we've been over this," Newell said.

"It's going to become too much of a strain," the doctor said.

"Are you saying I couldn't handle it?" I said.

"Not at all," the doctor said. "I hope I'm in half as good shape as you are when I reach seventy-five." Bill Chandler, our family doctor, a young man about Newell's age, leaned on the corner of the examining table.

"Mrs. Marshbanks's condition is deteriorating gradually," the doctor said, "and it has been my experience that it's best for the patient and their family if the patient makes the transition to a facility earlier rather than later."

"Listen to him," Newell said. He glanced at his watch, and it wasn't the first time. I knew he was in a hurry to get back to Asheville.

The doctor took Irene's hand. "Mrs. Marshbanks, how would you feel about living somewhere else?"

A worried look crossed her face. "Are you going to . . ." She paused. "Are you going to leave me out in the woods?"

The doctor shook his head. "It would be a place where people can take care of you. I don't think Mr. Marshbanks can care for you by himself much longer."

"I see," she said, squinting at me, like she saw some weakness she hadn't noticed before.

"How would that be for you to live somewhere else?" the doctor asked her.

She kept looking at me, but something in her eyes changed like she was seeing beyond me.

"She doesn't need to live anywhere else," I said. "I can take care of her at home." I jumped out of my chair and, having nowhere to go in the tiny examining room, stood there, pissed off.

"She needs to be in a place where somebody can keep an eye on her twenty-four hours a day," the doctor said. "What if she falls again, and you're not around?"

"I'll hire somebody to sit with her."

"What if she wanders out of the house?" the doctor asked.

"I'll put in one of those alarms."

"It's not just Mrs. Marshbanks I'm concerned about," the doctor said.

"He's right," Newell said. "You need to take care of yourself."

I turned on Newell. "You just don't want to have to worry about her!"

"I don't want her to get hurt again," Newell said, looking at Irene, then back at me. "And I don't want you to get hurt caring for her." He glanced at his watch again.

"Why don't you go on home, Newell," I said.

"It's just that I have a class to teach later today," he said. "But I still have some time."

"The thing to keep in mind, Mr. Marshbanks," the doctor said, "is that the patients are usually pretty content." The doctor smiled at Irene, who smiled back at him. "It's hardest on the family members who have to watch it."

My ankle ached, a sure sign it was going to rain. I sat back down on the stool. "I'm not putting her in one of those homes as long as I live," I said.

"It will be all right," Irene said, looking me in the eye. She didn't know what we were talking about. She just saw I was upset.

"There are some good nursing homes in town," the doctor said.

"I'll help you find a good place," Newell said.

"You can visit her every day," the doctor said.

"And I'll come down more often," Newell said, "and bring Jackson." He yawned, his eyes had big circles under them.

"I'm not putting her away," I said, taking Irene's hand.

"Mr. Marshbanks," the doctor said, "you will be no good to her if you're laid up with a bad back or a broken hip or some other injury that you're sure to get if you continue to care for her."

"You will do fine," Irene said to me, patting my hand, like it had been me we had been talking about. "You will do just fine."

Rolling Hills had wide halls with nice carpet, fancy little chandelier lights outside the rooms, gold-framed old-fashioned English prints of dogs, cats, and children. For weeks, Irene thought she was in a fancy hotel, that is when she didn't think she was on a cruise ship. Most of the residents were dressed, clean, and shaved, and seemed content enough. Unlike most of the other places Newell and I looked at, it didn't smell of urine. The nurses and aides didn't seem so down in the mouth.

I stayed with Irene every day from midafternoon till bedtime.

Some days I took her to ride or to get ice cream, but I always had her back by four-thirty, when they started getting them ready for supper. Every day I rolled her into the dining room. Her walking had become less steady, so we had had to buy a wheelchair. She sat at a table with three other residents. Dot was a quiet old woman who mostly fiddled with the buttons on her blouse but would run away every now and then, sometimes making it several blocks before the aides caught her. Decatur Dixon was a smart, alert man in his sixties, wore an eye patch, had had two strokes, and liked to joke, "Doc says three strikes and I'm out." Mr. Greathouse was a ninety-year-old retired peach farmer who always wore a tie and who whipped out his harmonica each night after supper and played "Oh Susannah" or "Turkey in the Straw." Decatur and the old man usually did most of the talking while Dot fiddled with her buttons.

After supper I would roll Irene back to her room, and if she wasn't too tired, we would sit and watch TV for a while. It was a little like old times or how old times should have been. Irene often put out her hand for me to hold, as she used to do when we first went to the Carolina Theater downtown.

The hardest thing was leaving at night. I waited till she was tired, then I would ask an aide to help her into bed. Every night she would ask, "Are you going down to work in the shop?"

Every night I would say, "Just for a little while."

"You come to . . ." She paused. ". . . to the place where we lie down."

"I'll come to bed soon," I would say. She had usually closed her eyes by then. I would slip my hand out of hers and stand there a minute wanting to crawl in next to her. But an aide would come in to check on her or one of those bed rail alarms would go off down

the hall or Dot would click by on her walker, in training for another escape attempt.

One evening, about five months after Irene went into Rolling
Hills, I was late getting home. Irene had had trouble falling asleep.
Being the end of May, it was still light on my drive home. I had
stopped by the Kentucky Fried. I didn't eat at Rolling Hills. I was
too busy helping Irene eat. She couldn't feed herself too well. Her
hands were so shaky she couldn't get the fork or spoon up to her
mouth.

I had seen those dining room ladies eye us. The rule was that
you could eat in the dining room as long as you could feed yourself. Otherwise, you had to eat in your room, and that was an iffy
proposition. If you ate in your room, they would bring your tray
sooner or later, but if the aide had too many patients, she might
spend five minutes trying to get you fed when you needed someone there an hour. I was beginning to see that this was the way of
a lot of things. The less you could take care of yourself, the less
you were taken care of.

Part of the problem was George Mercer, the sorry excuse for an
administrator. Mercer, who always wore a coat and tie, was a pale,
big-assed fellow with praying mantis arms. Decatur Dixon called
him The Mercenary. He didn't do a damned thing except stroll
the halls, smiling, and saying how he liked to keep in touch with
the residents, but he never stopped to speak with them.

I had thought about moving Irene to another home, but stories
about other nursing homes made Rolling Hills sound like a stroll
in the park. I also considered bringing Irene back home, but I
knew Bill Chandler was right. I couldn't manage her at home. She
didn't have many angry outbursts anymore. But with her walking

deteriorating, it made it tricky just getting her in and out of the car to take her for a ride. Some days she could walk just fine. Other days she could hardly stand.

All I could do was see that she was bathed, had clean clothes, and ate a good supper. Even though I was only out there four or five hours, I drove home as beat as if I had been stripping paint from dawn till dusk.

When I pulled into the drive and heard the phone ring inside, I hoped it wasn't Rolling Hills. Sometimes Irene would wake up after I left, and I would have to drive back across town. I made them agree that if I would come sit with her, they wouldn't give her sleeping pills. The pills kept her groggy the next day.

I grabbed the box of chicken and hurried inside, flipped on the light, and answered the phone.

"Yeah?"

"Everything all right?" It was Newell, calling from Asheville.

"I thought you might be the nursing home," I said, catching my breath. "Your mother is having a hard time falling asleep."

"I tried calling earlier," he said. "You should get an answering machine. You're probably missing a lot of calls."

"If it's important, they'll call back," I said.

"How is Mama?" he asked, deciding to change the subject.

"Fair to middling."

True to his word, Newell had helped me pick out a nursing home, had helped me get her moved in, and had visited when Irene had first gone into Rolling Hills. His visits had petered out, and he hadn't called in a couple of weeks.

"I meant to get back down there," he said. "But I'm teaching four classes this semester, plus two studios, we're just finishing exams, and I have a stack of a hundred and fifty art history papers to grade. I had a commission due a month ago I haven't even begun, and Jackson is playing soccer this year, so I take him to practice twice a week, then to a game on Saturdays." He paused. "You know how it is, with all you have to deal with."

"To tell you the truth," I said, "it's easier since she went in the nursing home." I tried to think of something else to say but couldn't. I had never liked phones.

"One reason I'm calling," Newell said, "is that I've been invited to be artist-in-residence up at Penland this summer for six weeks."

"Penland?"

"An art school outside of Spruce Pine. They would give me a place to stay and free meals. And I could just paint."

"Sounds good," I said.

"There's one catch." He paused. "Jackson can't go with me."

"Where's he going to stay?"

"That's why I was calling." He paused again. "I was wondering if I could impose upon y'all."

Irene's two cats, a black one and a gray tabby, rubbed my pant legs. Like me, they were probably hungry as hell. I nudged them away with my leg. "Go on, get out of here!"

"Bad idea?" Newell said, like I had been talking to him.

"I'm talking to your mama's goddamn cats! They won't give me any peace."

"What do you think?"

"About what?" I asked. The cats rubbed my pant legs hard. I kicked at them and sent them tearing out of the kitchen and down the basement stairs. Irene would have had my hide for that.

"I wondered if Jackson could spend the six weeks with y'all?"

"No 'y'all' to it," I snapped. "It's just me now." I was astonished that Newell would want me to take the boy. "Doesn't Jackson have friends up there in Asheville he could stay with?"

"None that I feel comfortable asking for such a long period," he said. "I could come down from Penland and visit him now and then. And maybe y'all could come visit up there."

"He was always more partial to your mama," I said, doubting the boy would want to spend the summer with me. I never knew what to say or do with him. He was a solemn, quiet boy, and he had become more that way since his mama died. "He'd be bored," I said. "I'm at the nursing home most of the afternoon and part of the evening."

"Mama would understand if you didn't come every day."

"Irene doesn't understand dirt at this point."

"Jackson could go with you," he said. "He's good at entertaining himself. Maybe a little too good."

"What's that supposed to mean?"

"He has been quiet lately," Newell said.

"The boy has always been on the reserved side."

"He's quieter. I've been so busy I haven't had time or energy to try to get him out of it. I thought it might be good for him to be around you and Mama for a while."

The cats were back at my legs. It was all I could to do to keep from drop kicking them to Timbuktu. The truth was I had gotten used to living alone and didn't want a nine-year-old boy around.

"I don't think it'd work," I said.

"I understand," Newell said, and from his tone I could tell he did. I could also tell he was disappointed.

Then I imagined Irene saying, Look how hard Newell works at his job and raising a boy all on his own, and it hasn't been that long since he lost Sandy. Irene would have pointed out that Newell wasn't asking for a summer vacation, that he would work as hard at his paintings as he did at everything else. She would have also said how much she would love having Jackson around her at Rolling Hills.

I sighed. "Tell the boy it won't be summer camp around here," I said.

"Are you sure about this?"

"When you bringing him?"

"Penland starts in two weeks," Newell said, suddenly sounding excited. "That Friday would be his last day of school. What if I bring him Saturday?"

"All right."

"I was wondering if you might like to get out. You could meet us at Jones Gap."

"I haven't been up that way in years," I said.

"I've been telling Jackson about how we used to fish. I would like for him to see the place, if you think you're up to it."

"I'd have to be back at the nursing home by four-thirty." Jones Gap was a state park at the tail end of the Blue Ridge Mountains, about forty-five minutes north of Greenville. Irene and I used to take Newell up there when he was a boy, and we would picnic, fish, and swim in the Middle Saluda. Irene and I had continued going up there until she got sick, but I hadn't been with Newell since he was a teenager. I was surprised that he remembered the place.

"Jackson could ride home with you, and I'd go down to the nursing home, visit with Mama, even get her fed supper so you wouldn't have to go over, then would head up to Penland." He had thought this through.

"You could spend the night at the house," I said.

He hesitated. "We'll see," he said. "What do you think?"

"I reckon that'd work," I said, warming to the notion of getting up into the mountains. "I'll bring the fishing gear."

"I'll bring the food," Newell said. "I can't tell you how much this means to me."

"Don't," I said.

Newell paused for a moment. "Noon okay?"

"That's fine."

"Good night," he said.

"Night." I hung up, wondering what in the hell I had gotten myself into. What would I do with a solemn nine-year-old boy for a whole summer? I almost picked up the phone and called Newell back, but the cats were at my legs again.

"All right, all right!" I opened a can of cat food and spooned it out into the tin pans Irene had always fed them in.

Irene took in strays. At one time we must have had ten or twelve around the place. Outdoors mostly. I never cared for cats. Still, they kept the moles and the rabbits out of my garden. And since Irene was always asking about the cats, the least I could do was feed the two we had left.

I sat down at the kitchen table to my Kentucky Fried meal. Though the chicken was cold and nowhere near as good as Irene's, it wasn't bad. I took an apple out of the bowl of Granny Smiths I kept on the table, peeled it with my pocketknife, and cut it into wedges. It was an old Case knife my daddy gave me before he died. It was worn on the sides, but I kept the blade oiled and sharpened. I never went anywhere without it. In fact, I had cut Newell's umbilical cord with it.

I thought about my boy. He was a real painter, not a house-painter like me, but the artist kind. At six years old, he could draw a bird or a dog or a tree better than I could. By the time he was ten, I had him working afternoons and summers painting trim and doing detail work. He could lay down a truer line than most of the men I had working for me. *Brilliant* was the word his art professors at the University of South Carolina trotted out. After he graduated, he made a real living painting pictures of the outdoors mostly, landscapes. Folks sometimes paid him as much for one of his little paintings of a meadow or a field or a forest as what I charged to paint a two-story house.

Newell met Sandy at an opening of his at a gallery in Charlotte. An emergency room nurse, Sandy was smart, levelheaded, and the first girl who could compete with Newell's first love—painting. They married. Newell was offered a good job teaching art up in Asheville at the college, made a very good living, had Jackson, and was a good father. Sandy and Newell tried having another child, but it wouldn't take. They went to several of those help-it-along doctors, even drove down to Atlanta to see some world-famous doctor at Emory, but none of it did any good. A couple of years later, long after they stopped trying and after they had stopped seeing all those doctors, guess what?

Sandy was seven months with child when they had come down for an Easter Sunday visit with us. Irene had an Easter egg hunt for the boy, and I had never seen the three of them so happy, like they were getting ready to start a whole new part of their lives. On the way back to Asheville, a confused old Florida bat driving a Lincoln Continental turned the wrong way down an exit ramp and ruined it all. Sandy and the baby were killed instantly. Newell and Jackson walked away with hardly a scratch.

We worried Newell might fall apart. Sandy had done most of the work of keeping house and home together. But he threw every ounce of what he had left into the boy, who was broken up about his mother. He had always kept a lot to himself, which made it hard for Newell or anybody else to read him. Newell took him to a counselor. The counselor played cards with Jackson and had him draw pictures and went on walks with him. A hundred dollars an hour to play cards and go on walks with kids. Nice work, if you can get it. Maybe it was the walks or maybe it was time, but after a while, the boy seemed better, at least as far as anybody could tell.

Irene worried so much about the both of them and was always trying to get them to come down for the weekend. She spent long afternoons with Jackson, having tea or reading to him or just sitting on the front porch. Sometimes he would help me in the garden or around the house. Mostly he liked to be with his grandma. I didn't blame him. Who in their right mind wouldn't rather be up in the kitchen, eating homemade ginger snaps and listening to stories about Cuba and China and other exotic places with a pretty, sweet woman like her, than down in the garden on their hands and knees, wrestling crabgrass and dandelions out of the ground with an old coot like me?

Wasn't long after Sandy's death that Irene started forgetting where she set her sewing basket or what book she had been in the middle of or the names of neighbors we had known for fifty years.

After supper, I went out to water the garden, walking up and down the rows with the hose, soaking the corn, the tomatoes, the okra, the lima beans, the mustard greens, the broccoli, the peppers, and what all else I had planted. Every year I planted a large garden, and Irene and I enjoyed fresh vegetables deep into the fall. This spring it wasn't till I had the garden planted and the sprouts were pushing their bowed heads up through the broken ground, that it hit me— who was I growing all this for?

"How was Mrs. Marshbanks today?" I looked up to see my neighbor, Billie Athens, leaning on the split-rail fence that ran between our backyards. In her early thirties, she was a dark, strong-jawed girl with thick eyebrows and bright, watchful eyes. Hers was a face full of feeling, and one that, for me, had always been hard to look into.

"Irene is having trouble sleeping," I said, setting the hose down among the tomato plants and kneeling to pull a few weeds.

"I'm planning to go by on Sunday," she said. Billie had been visiting Irene ever since she went into Rolling Hills. She had moved next door a little before Irene's illness really took hold. She would come over, and the two women would discuss books or art or other educated things. Billie even took her to the symphony. When Irene became sick, she shopped for us at the grocery store or kept an eye on Irene if I needed to run an errand. Billie and I had never had much to say to each other. Seemed all we had in common was Irene. Ever since Irene had gone into the nursing home, Billie had made a point of talking to me. I couldn't help wondering if Irene, in one of her lucid moments, had asked her to look out for me. Or the girl felt sorry for me. Either notion irritated me.

"What's Newell working on these days?" she asked. Billie was a first-grade teacher and a potter on the side. Before she had ever met Newell, she had noticed his painting over our mantel. It was of early dawn on a pond somewhere around Clinton, South Carolina—mostly water and grass and sky with a few clouds. She said she had a painting of his, and the way she went on about his work, I realized she knew more about him than I did.

"He's spending his summer at some art place up above Asheville," I said, pinching back the new shoots on the tomato plants and pulling off the dead leaves.

"Penland?" she asked.

"That's it."

"Is his son going with him?"

"Jackson's staying with me," I said, unable to keep the irritation out of my voice.

Billie had spoken with Newell and Jackson a few times, when they came to visit, and had even run into them out at Rolling Hills.

"You don't sound excited," she said.

"Not sure what I'll do with him."

"You'll think of something," she said confidently, which for some reason flew all over me.

"I don't want to think of something," I snapped. "I don't have the energy to think of something. I have gotten used to the way things are. I have gotten used to being *alone*."

"I'm not sure that's something one should get used to," Billie said.

I started to say something else, something I would probably regret. Instead, I jerked up a big milkweed plant growing next to the fence, knocked the dirt clod against the post, then tossed the plant onto the pile of weeds in the garden path. Then I pulled up a couple more. When I finally looked up again, I was relieved to see the girl was gone.

I worked a little longer, pulled a few more weeds. As I turned off the water and rolled up the hose, I saw the light on in Billie's little pottery studio. She and a couple of her women friends had built it in the back of her yard. Irene had me help hang the windows. Sometimes now if I got up to get a drink of water I would look out the kitchen window and see her working over there.

I glanced at her shed a couple of times, feeling a little guilty for the way I talked to her. When she first moved here from Atlanta, she had come off a messy divorce. Irene said the fellow had not treated her right. She told Irene she had had her fill of men. Now here I was snapping at her. Irene had been right—I was a son of a bitch.

Back inside, I eased myself down on the couch in the den and propped my leg on the coffee table. My ankle ached. I had broken it seven years ago, when I fell from a ladder, painting the eaves on a two-story house. It didn't bother me, except in rainy weather or if I was on it all day.

I picked up a worn copy of *Jude the Obscure*, a book I had read more times than I could count. I had always been a reader. When I was a little fellow I startled my folks by being able to recite every single nursery rhyme in Mother Goose. In church, there wasn't a Bible quote I couldn't throw right back at those Sunday school teachers. All I ever cared about in school was the library and getting to read biographies about Robert E. Lee or Davy Crockett or Teddy Roosevelt. By the time I had grown and married Irene, about all I read were dime-store novels and the sports section of the *Greenville News*.

Irene introduced me to Jane Austen, George Eliot, Dickens, Hemingway, Steinbeck, and the long-winded Thomas Wolfe. Writers like those made me see the world in a little different light. Ever since Irene had gone into the nursing home, I found myself rereading Thomas Hardy, especially *Jude*. I read it to keep from feeling pitiful. I mean how could anybody feel sorry for himself after reading about the miserable life that poor boy led?

I read until my eyelids started getting heavy. I went to the back door and called the cats and they came running up through the dark garden. The light was off in Billie's studio. Some nights I would watch her through the big window, sitting at the wheel, hunched over it like she was protecting something. As I started inside, it hit me how dense I had been this evening, how quick I had been to take what she said so personally. When Billie had said to me she wasn't sure living alone was something one should get used to, she had been talking about herself.

I thought of Irene alone in Rolling Hills. She hadn't been calling me by name as much. In the past couple of weeks, when I walked in her room now, she wouldn't smile right off, like it was taking her longer to place me. She had called me "Daddy" a few times, and the other day she had sat on her bed, kicking her legs like a little girl, and asked, "When's Daddy coming home, Mills?" like I was her brother. Slow but steady, she was pulling away from me. All she seemed to know for sure was that I fell within that circle of men who had mattered in her life.

I hauled myself back to the bedroom, got undressed, brushed my teeth, took a couple of ibuprofen for my ankle, and crawled into bed. I lay there for a good while, worrying about what I was going to do with Jackson. I guessed he would sleep back in the guest bedroom where he and his father and Sandy used to sleep when they visited. Then I had the idea of fixing up Newell's old room upstairs, a room that hadn't been used in years. It would be a lot of work, but maybe the boy might like to stay in his father's old room. I thought about that a while. It would need to be painted and fixed up. I had a couple of weeks.

A car screeched by outside. Some kids out too late. Then the house was quiet. Irene would be asleep in her narrow bed with rails to keep her from rolling out, and her door would be open onto the hall, and the shaft of light would cut across her sweet, gone face.

I turned out the bedside lamp. As on many nights, I had to remind myself I could scoot on over, that I didn't need to leave room.

Two

Out of the Picture

The day before I was to meet Jackson and Newell up at Jones Gap I took Irene on our regular afternoon ride. We were driving through the north Greenville countryside, or what was left of it. What hadn't been eaten up by the strip malls, the Walmarts, and the Home Depots. Then we got into fancy developments—developments with big brick entrances and names like Millard's Farm or Swire's Creek or Wykle's Woods that had sprung up. They had kept the names, but they had lost the places. Probably a lot of the old-timers had been forced to sell their land to pay off the nursing homes. Rolling Hills my ass. More like Rolling Bills.

The quality of the scenery didn't seem to matter to Irene, as long as there was some. I could have ridden her around the same block for an hour, and she would have been as entertained as if I drove her to California. She enjoyed going to ride, even though she wasn't always real clear who this ugly old coot was who took her.

"Newell and Jackson are coming tomorrow," I said. "Jackson's spending the summer." I had been telling her this ever since Newell had called. Some days she heard me. One day she even

said, "Put clean sheets on the beds." Today she just sucked on the
straw to her iced tea and looked out the window.

"Newell wants some time to himself. Probably a good idea,
don't you think?" I glanced over at her. "With all that he's been
through."

She looked out the window.

"But the boy," I said. "I'm not sure what I'll do with him."

She set her iced tea in her lap and reached for the door handle
for about the nineteenth time, but I had taken it off. A few weeks
ago, she had unlocked the door and opened it while we were going
sixty miles an hour and would have rolled out into traffic if I
hadn't caught her arm. So I took off the inside door handle.

I became so busy perseverating on Newell and Jackson coming
that I stopped paying attention to where I was going. Lightning,
followed by the crack of thunder, brought me to my senses. I was
driving down a road I had never seen before in my life. I had managed to get us out into the country all right. We were driving beside a big pasture, and there was nobody around except a couple
of jerseys. And it was clouding up.

I drove to the end of that road, thinking I would come out
somewhere familiar, but I didn't recognize the road name. The next
road I turned onto wound through woods I had never seen before.
I thought I knew every nook and cranny of Greenville County.

It was nearly four-thirty, when I was supposed to have her back
for supper. The dining hall ladies would be fussing. They liked to
get the residents in and out of there so they could go home. I
looked for somebody to ask directions, but there wasn't even a
house around. Just woods, giving way to fields, then more woods,
which were dark in the first place, but then it had been getting
darker till it was almost like nighttime. The lightning flashed, and
the thunder sounded on top of us. It was fixing to pour.

"I'll be goddamned," I whispered. "We're lost, Irene." I looked over at her as she was taking the top off her iced tea. "I wouldn't do that . . ."

A little spilled into her lap. Mostly ice. The way she cried out and tried to jump up out of her seat, you would have thought a snake had fallen into her lap.

"It's all right," I said, pulling to the side of the road, putting my flashers on. "It's just a little tea." I swept the ice out of her lap and dabbed at her dress with my handkerchief. She clenched her teeth and shook her head, tears welled in her eyes.

"It won't stain," I said.

But she wasn't looking at her dress. She was looking out the window. She made a low, eerie moan, a sound I had never heard her make. Then she looked back at me, and for a moment she was her old self, seeing what her new self had become.

"Worried about getting lost?" I asked.

She shook her head.

"I'm so sorry, Irene." I took her hand. "I wish there was something I could do."

She opened her mouth to say something like she knew what I could do, and a sound came out, but it wasn't a whole word. She raised her eyebrows and smiled sad-like and put her hands in her lap, like she gave up. A big drop of rain hit the windshield, then another and another, and pretty soon it began to pour. I cut the engine, and the sound of the rain on the roof drowned out all other sounds. Now and then it would thunder and lightning, but that didn't bother Irene. At home she used to get me to sit with her on the piazza whenever a thunderstorm came up. When we were young, she used to walk right out into storms. So we sat there, holding hands, looking out, unable to see a thing for all the water sliding down the windshield. It was like we were the last living people on earth.

I began thinking how we had met the summer she had graduated from Agnes Scott and come home to be with her father, who lived in a big rambling house on Crescent Avenue, the richest street in Greenville. Irene's mother had died when she was six years old, giving birth to a stillborn boy whom they buried in the same coffin with Irene's mother in Springwood, the downtown cemetery. And Irene's younger brother, Mills, was down in Columbia at law school. So Irene's father, J. K. Blalock, lived alone. He had hired me to paint his house. It was the biggest job I had had and took me a good part of the summer.

Irene was a tall, slender girl with soft eyes and full lips. People compared her to Grace Kelly. With Mr. Blalock at his law office downtown most of the day, I used to steal glimpses of Irene when she would sunbathe in the backyard or when she worked in the flower bed or when she sat on the front porch and read. I scooted my ladder over to her vicinity. Sometimes, she brought me iced tea and cookies. After a while she began to make lunch for the both of us, and we would sit out on the porch and eat cream cheese and pineapple sandwiches.

What surprised me was how she talked to me, like a regular person, not like some big lawyer's daughter who had been off to college and back and who knew way more than I ever would. She never made me feel stupid.

Some days her father would come home, and the three of us would sit out on the porch and have a long lunch. Mr. Blalock, a heavy man who drove a Cadillac and wore a Panama hat, would offer me a cigar and launch into some good long story. One of the things I liked about his stories was that if he was ever in them, it was to make fun of himself.

One day after lunch, I had gone back to painting at the back of the house while Irene walked with Mr. Blalock to his car. I heard Irene scream. I jumped from the ladder, tore around to the front of the house, and found her bent over Mr. Blalock, who was sprawled on the drive, his hat beside him on the cement. He was unconscious.

"Call an ambulance," I said. As Irene ran back to the house, I dropped down on my knees and put my head to his chest. He had stopped breathing. Not knowing what else to do, I pushed on the old man's chest, where I hoped his heart might be. I pumped, wondering what in the hell I was doing. I don't know how long I pumped his chest. I remember blue jays jeering overhead, like what in the hell did that idiot painter think he was doing?

His chest started to rise and fall. He was breathing. His eyelids fluttered, and Irene was back standing over us. "He's coming to," she said as he opened his eyes.

"Damn!" her father said, wincing and rubbing his chest.

We were helping him lean back against the Cadillac when the ambulance showed. They had him in the ambulance in no time and Irene climbed in, too, and they tore out of the drive. I was left standing there, shook up. I didn't paint anymore that day.

Turned out to be a little heart attack, the doctor called it a warning. Mr. Blalock was back at his law practice within weeks. He lost weight, quit the cigars, and took up going for long walks around the neighborhood. And I stretched out that painting job as long as I could. Even when I was done, I kept thinking up excuses to come back—some of the trim I had overlooked or stairs I hadn't sanded enough. I couldn't get enough of Irene. Finally, when I couldn't think of any more excuses to drop by, I called her one afternoon when I knew Mr. Blalock was at the office. I dialed the number two or three times before I let it ring. I had rehearsed how I would ask her, how I would keep my cool, and how I would slowly work my way to the reason for my call. When she answered the phone, all that went right out the window.

"This is Prate Marshbanks," I said, my throat tight. "Would you go out with me on Saturday night?"

There was a pause on the other end.

"I know it's real sudden and all," I said, "and if you have other plans . . ."

"Sure," she said. "I'll go out with you."

It was my turn to pause. "Just like that?" I said, beads of sweat rolling down the inside of my shirt.

"Just like that," she said.

"What about Mr. Blalock?"

"I don't think he would want to go along," she said.

"I mean don't you need to check with him?"

"I'm twenty-two," she said. "I'm old enough to decide with whom I'll go out."

"What about his heart? Mightn't it give him another attack when you tell him you're going out with me?"

"You underestimate my father."

"If I was him," I said, "I wouldn't let you go out with me."

"He likes you," she said. "And it doesn't hurt that you saved his life."

"Don't make any difference. A daughter is a father's treasure, his pride and joy. He don't want you going out with an illiterate so-and-so like me."

"You're far from illiterate," she said. "Anyhow, Daddy doesn't usually test my dates' reading skills. At least not on the first date."

"You know what I mean," I said.

"Did you call to talk me out of going out with you?"

"Well, no . . ."

"So what time?"

"What time?"

"What time on Saturday do you want to go out?"

"Seven?" I pulled that out of the air, not having given time any consideration, figuring I wouldn't get this far.

"Where are we going?"

"The pictures?" I pulled that out of the air, too, and was thankful she didn't ask me what was playing.

"See you then," she said, and hung up. And the whole rest of the week I bought the paper first thing, turning to the obituaries, fearing I would find Mr. Blalock's death notice.

Finally, Saturday night rolled around. I pressed my good shirt and pants, shined my Sunday shoes, and checked my hair in the mirror for the umpteenth time. I had gotten a haircut that afternoon at B.Y's Barbershop on Augusta Road, and I looked to me like a jug-eared Mickey Rooney.

When I pulled up to the house, I felt light-headed, like I had given blood. I walked up the steps and managed to ring the doorbell. I heard heavy footsteps, the door opened, and there was Mr. Blalock. He looked thinner but older, his face hollowed out and frail. He smiled but looked puzzled.

"Hello, Prate," he said like he was surprised to see me. "Didn't you get my check for the bill?"

"Yes, sir, I did, Mr. Blalock."

"Wasn't it for the correct amount?"

"Yes, sir, you paid me exactly right."

He screwed up his brow. "Well, how can I help you then?"

"Didn't Irene tell you?"

"Tell me what, Prate?"

I cleared my throat and found myself staring at the back of my hand, which had tiny flecks of paint all in the hairs. I could never get out the tiny flecks no matter how hard I scrubbed. "Well, sir . . ."

"Yes?"

I looked down at my feet. "I'm thinking this porch floor might need one more coat, especially with all the foot traffic it gets." I bent down, rubbing my hand over the floorboards.

"Are you going to charge me for it?" he asked in a gruff booming voice, one I bet he used in the courtroom against some poor defendant.

"I'll do it for free," I said, standing back up.

"Is that why you came by? To tell me the porch floor needed another coat?"

"No, sir. I mean, yes, sir," I said, starting to back up. I knew it had been wrong to ask Irene out in the first place. We were from two different worlds and didn't have any business mixing. "Good night, sir."

"Daddy, that's enough." I heard Irene's voice somewhere behind him.

"Are you sure that's all you came for, Prate?" asked Mr. Blalock. He let the door swing wide. There she was standing in the foyer in a red dress and high heels, wearing pearls and earrings and looking even more like Grace Kelly. She was pulling a sweater over her shoulders. She kissed her father on the cheek. "Don't wait up."

She took my hand and led me, stunned and wordless, down the steps and out to the car. In her heels she was even taller, and I felt as ridiculous as Mickey Rooney taking Grace Kelly out on a date. By the time we reached the car, I had gathered enough wits to open the door for her. I stumbled around to my side and got in when Mr. Blalock came down to the car and stuck his head in my window.

"Prate?" he said, sticking his face nearly right up in mine, sounding gruff again.

"Yes, sir?"

"No monkey business tonight."

"No, sir." My voice cracked.

But he was grinning, and Irene was laughing, and said, "Leave him alone, Daddy."

When we pulled away, he was standing in the middle of the driveway with his hand raised to us like he knew what was next, like he knew that it wouldn't be but a few months before I asked to marry Irene, like he knew he would say, "At least she isn't marrying a lawyer," like he knew he would be all alone in that house for good, like he knew we would bring him Newell, a boy grandchild he could dote on for the four good years that stood between him and the day he was to join wife and baby in the cemetery downtown.

It wasn't ten minutes before the rain let up and rays of sun cut through the dripping trees and mist was rising from the road. I leaned over Irene, who was staring out the window, and fished the map out of the glove compartment. There was a tap at my window. My heart nearly jumped out of my throat when I saw this black fellow in a yellow raincoat, motioning me to roll down my window. I thought we were being held up till I glanced in the rearview and saw his BellSouth cherry picker parked behind us. With all the rain, I hadn't even heard him pull up.

I rolled the window down.

"Saw you had your flashers on. Are you all right?" He sounded whiter than me. I knew he wasn't from the South.

"I was taking my wife for a ride from the nursing home," I said, "but got us lost." I held up the map.

"Which nursing home?"

"Rolling Hills."

"Wow, you have strayed."

"You know the place?"

"My mother used to be over there." He straightened, pulled the hood from his head, and looked back down the road, like he was trying to remember directions, but then he said, "I've got a little time. Why don't you follow me?"

"I don't want to put you out," I said, wishing I could get the directions and be done with it. "If you could point me the right way."

"The easiest thing is for you to follow me," he said. Before I could say another word, he had hopped into his truck, pulled around me, then waited for me to pull out behind him. I followed this big old cherry picker driven by this black Yankee phone repairman for nearly half an hour down more roads I had never been on in my life. I was beginning to think he was leading us somewhere else, somewhere farther away, like he was playing a joke on these old white people. Then we popped out on the very road Rolling Hills was on, and I followed his truck into the nursing home parking lot.

Rolling Hills was a single-story brick building not ten years old, with four different wings, making a square, and a courtyard in the middle. A sidewalk circled the outside of the building. Sometimes in the afternoon I pushed Irene in the wheelchair all the way around, but if the sun was out, it was a brutally hot walk. The only shade was from Bradford pear trees, which bloomed white in the spring but kept their limbs to themselves, giving hardly any relief from the heat. The longer Irene was at Rolling Hills, the more I understood that the place was like those trees, pretty but lacking in substance.

I tried to pay the phone man for his troubles, but he frowned when I pulled out my wallet. He helped me lift the wheelchair out of the back of the van, helped me get her in it, and started to push her in for me, but I said, "I can take it from here."

"You sure?" he asked.

"*She's* the one in the nursing home," I said, taking hold of the wheelchair. Don't be rude, I knew Irene would have said if she had been in her right mind. The man drove half an hour out of his way for us. So I said, "I thank you for your help."

"It was a pleasure," he said, sounding like he meant it. He studied Irene, who was looking off into space. I had noticed him watch her before. "My mother had it, too," he finally said.

"I thought you meant your mother had worked here," I said. Most of the aides were black, but there were only a few black residents.

"No," he said, smiling a little impatiently, as if he had seen my thinking, that he was used to that kind of thinking. "She lived here for three years. Died six months ago."

"Well, I'm sorry," I said.

"She died a little bit every day, he said, still looking at Irene. "By the time she actually passed, it was more a matter of vital signs." Then he said, "Of course, she's in a better place now."

"You think they get their minds back in Heaven?" I asked. I wondered if Irene would remember me if I managed to squeeze through those pearly gates.

"I believe they must," he said. Then he bent down and took Irene's hand, and said, "It has been a pleasure to meet you, ma'am."

And I'll be damned if she didn't look him right in the eye, and say, "It has been a pleasure to meet you, sir" like she knew who he was and what he had done for us.

As he pulled away in his truck, I rolled her on inside and into the dining room like we weren't half an hour late. I wheeled her to her usual table, where Decatur Dixon and Mr. Greathouse had already finished up and were drinking their coffee and Dot, her plate mostly untouched, fiddled with her buttons. And even though the dining room ladies—a white fat one and a skinny black one—put up a stink, frowning at the big clock on the wall and saying Irene's food was cold and she probably wouldn't touch it, I held my tongue for once, and they brought her tray.

I unrolled the silverware from the napkin, tucked the napkin in her blouse, then forked up a bite of mashed potatoes and put it into Irene's mouth.

"Mr. Mercer says no one should be in here if they can't feed themselves," the white fat one said, as she cleared Mr. Greathouse's tray.

"What kind of rule is that?!" I asked, my tongue getting the best of me. "As long as I'm in here helping her eat, I don't see how it makes any difference. She likes sitting here with these folks, in this nice dining room."

"A rule is a rule," the fat one said, sliding the tray onto a cart.

"And an idiot is an idiot," I said.

"Listen, Mr. Marshbanks," she said, standing over me, her jowly face getting all red, but she was still speaking real calm-like, "there's no need to get personal."

"I thought we were talking about a person? Isn't my wife a person?" I asked, standing up. "Aren't the folks sitting around here at these tables, aren't they persons?!"

She backed up two steps, not used to people standing up on her. Still she spoke real calm. "If Mrs. Marshbanks can't feed herself, she will have to be fed in her room along with all the others."

"The hell she will!"

About that time, Irene picked up her fork and lifted a bite of mashed potatoes into her mouth. Then she did it again and again.

Mr. Greathouse clapped.

"Right on, Miss Irene," said Decatur.

Dot even looked up from fiddling with her buttons.

For the first time in days, Irene was feeding herself, and she proceeded to eat every damned thing on her plate. I was prouder of her than when she won Best Teacher of South Carolina. I sat back down and shut up, and let Irene speak for herself. Of course I knew she might not feed herself tomorrow, but I had begun to see that the older we became, the smaller the victories, and if we didn't glory in the little ones, then likely as not, we gloried in nothing. And with every bite she took, Irene was telling that frowning dining room heifer, See? You don't know the first thing about the woman I was.

That night the smell of latex greeted me when I opened the front door. I had been repainting Newell's old room upstairs. Paint was a smell I could never get enough of. I know they say it shrivels your brain, and mine probably was good and pickled by now. Still, to me, the smell of paint was the smell of good work done, and I had always loved my work. A lot of people used to ask, Doesn't it get boring just standing there, going up and down, up and down, with a brush all day long? And for fifty years at that? I was never bored with my work. In fact, nothing gave me more pleasure than scraping away the old and laying down the new, time and time again. I felt a little bit like God, bringing life back to old rooms, old houses. When I finished a job, I left people feeling a little better about the place they lived. Painting wasn't one of those jobs, like Irene's teaching, you brought home with you. It was there to do, you did it, you left it. Painting houses was as close to a calling that I ever got. Whenever I dreamed, I dreamed of smooth, prepped surfaces.

Even in retirement, I kept our house, exterior and interior, painted clean. At the first sign of a chip or a peel or fading, I was all over it, scraping and sanding and priming. Irene used to say I was obsessed. The only room she wouldn't let me touch was Newell's old room upstairs. Actually it was the *only* room upstairs. A big room with lots of windows. When I built the house I had intended the upstairs to be our bedroom, but I never got around to putting in a bathroom. So when Irene was pregnant with Newell and having to make all those trips up and down the stairs to the bathroom in her condition, we moved to the back bedroom downstairs. When Newell outgrew the nursery, we moved him to the bedroom upstairs.

Anyhow, after Newell's call about wanting me to keep Jackson, I had gotten to work repainting his old bedroom. It hadn't been painted since Newell went off to the University of South Carolina more than twenty-five years ago, and it was dingy and worn-out-looking. Not a room you would want a child to have to spend his summer away from home in.

Irene never would let me touch that room, because when Newell was thirteen he had painted a mural on the wall of his bedroom. At the time, we knew he had been doing something up there, but we didn't know what. Finally, he invited me up to his room, and when I walked in and saw he had painted a jungle scene *on* the wall, I lit into him, "You ought to know better than painting on the wall!" I told him to march down to the basement, get a brush and a bucket of paint and paint over it. Irene came up to see what all the commotion was and gasped when she saw the painting.

"It's all right. I've sent him to fetch the paint bucket and a brush," I said, "I'm having him paint over it this minute."

"It's a mural," she said. "A beautiful mural of our street."

"Our street?" When I looked again I saw that she was right. It was our street, but with the grass grown waist high, the trees thick and hung with vines, neighborhood flowers grown man-sized. Behind all the jungle vegetation were the houses of the neighborhood. And if you looked closely you saw the people, who were dwarfed by the vegetation and a few tiger-sized cats. One of Newell's favorite books had been Rudyard Kipling's *The Jungle Book*.

"I knew he was good," Irene had said, walking back and forth in front of the mural that had the sharp smell of fresh enamel. She looked back at me. "But this is something else." She saw right then what the art critics would see later on. And maybe I saw it, too. I was just worked up about him turning the walls of our house into his own personal canvas.

So the mural stayed. Long after he went off to college, I was still going up there and sitting on his bed to see what new thing I might notice—a cat hidden in a tree, a brick coming loose in a chimney, a green snake sliding through the grass, a child peeking around the corner of a house. Every now and then the painting let you see something new.

Over the years when I brought up the idea of painting his old room, Irene balked, afraid I might damage the mural. You would have thought it was the damned Sistine Chapel. So Newell's room became dingier, and the mural darkened as time went by. It didn't help that, taking the suggestion of some art collector, Irene closed the windows against the dampness and put up heavy drapes to keep light out.

Jackson's arrival was my excuse. It was like getting to scratch a thirty-year itch. Still I was careful. Several collectors and more than one museum curator had come up here, drooling over this wall. The last fellow, from the High Museum in Atlanta, which already had several of Newell's paintings, had offered about as much as our house was worth. He was a tall, thin fellow with a long face and a worm of a mustache. He wore a coat and a turtleneck. He said the painting needed to be in a "controlled environment." Like because we didn't have air-conditioning, we lived in the Dark Ages.

I asked the curator how they were going to take a wall, a load-bearing wall at that. He said they had their ways, and I bet they did. We could have used the money with Irene starting to get sick, and Newell had said it was ours to do with as we pleased, but Irene told the fellow from the High what she had told all the others—not for sale.

I ripped down those drapes and threw open the windows. It took me one whole morning to get the room prepped—clearing the cobwebs, dusting, scraping, and sanding, then washing it all down. Then over several days, I repainted the walls, the same Benjamin Moore blue they'd been painted twenty years ago. Benjamin Moore was the only paint I'd use, and in fact, I wouldn't take a job if the owner wasn't willing to pay for good paint.

I used a brush. I was afraid a roller might splatter the mural. The good thing was that Newell had painted his picture in enamel, so it cleaned up easy. Course I don't know how the curator would have felt about me cleaning his precious masterpiece with 409.

That night after supper, I went up to put the box springs and the mattress back on the bed frame. I had gotten the bed back together and in its rightful place and was starting on the sheets—washed as Irene had instructed—when the doorbell rang downstairs.

"I don't need more pamphlets," I said to myself, thinking it was

more Jehovah's Witnesses, who had been working the neighborhood. Used to drive me wild how Irene would invite them in,
serve them tea and cookies and give them a little money.

I was wrestling with the fitted sheet when I heard the front door
open downstairs. Whoever it was was coming right on in. Either
the Jehovah's Witnesses had gotten bolder or Newell and Jackson
had showed up a day early.

"Mr. Marshbanks?" It was a woman's voice.

I came downstairs and found Billie in the front room, looking
at Newell's painting over the mantel. "So you're all right?" she
said. Her hair wasn't tied back tonight, but fell to her shoulders,
and she was wearing a shimmery turquoise blouse and a black skirt
and turquoise earrings.

"Today was the last day of school and some of the teachers
went out tonight to celebrate," she said. "When I came home, I
didn't see you in the garden, then I remembered I hadn't seen you
out there the past few evenings."

Maybe it was because I was tense about the boy coming or
maybe I was tired, but before I could catch myself, I said, "I can
take care of myself."

The girl's face went a little pale.

"And if Irene has asked you to check on me," I said, unable to
stop myself, "well, you have done your duty and you can go on
about your business."

"Mrs. Marshbanks hasn't asked me to do anything," she said.

"Well, you don't have to worry about me."

"Listen, Mr. Marshbanks," she said, her voice taking on an edge.
"It's not you I'm worried about. You and Mrs. Marshbanks have
been such good neighbors. Mrs. Marshbanks is already gone. I don't
want to lose you, too, because when you go, some perfect couple
with two perfect little children and a big friendly golden retriever is

going to move in and depress the hell out of me." Her face had gotten all red, and her jaw was working.

"Let me get this straight," I said, still feeling angry. "You would rather have an old man you could feel sorry for, than a family who might feel sorry for you."

"I don't feel sorry for you," she said. "How could I feel sorry for a man who was lucky enough to spend his life married to a woman like your wife."

I sighed and let my hands fall at my sides. "You have a point," I said.

For a moment we didn't speak, and I hoped she would leave. But she said, "I smell paint."

"I've been repainting Newell's old room upstairs, getting it ready for Jackson. He comes tomorrow."

She looked past me in the direction of the stairs.

"Not much to see," I said, but I led her up there as way of apology.

"With all the windows, it's like being up in a tree house," she said when we got upstairs. She hadn't seen the mural yet. She was standing with her back to it.

I looked around at the job I had done. I had repainted the trim with white enamel, which set off the blue walls, although the walls themselves could have used another coat or two. The room hadn't looked this good since Newell was in grammar school.

"When I built the house, this was going to be Irene and mine's bedroom," I said, starting back on the fitted sheet.

"Let me," she said, took the sheet, and shook it open across the bed so that it fell perfect. She slipped it over the corners, then slid the spread on and folded it neatly over the pillow, all in two minutes' time. "I worked as a motel maid at a Holiday Inn one summer," she said fluffing up the pillow. That's when she looked up and saw the mural.

"Oh," was all she said, all she could say at first. I had seen the same blindsided look on a lot of the art people who had come up here. She sat down on the end of the bed and stared openmouthed at the picture. "I never knew about this," she said finally.

"Newell painted it when he was thirteen," I said.

"Thirteen?" She looked at me, then back at the picture.

I walked up to the picture, rubbing my hand across the smooth clean surface.

"It's this street," she said.

I sat beside her on the bed and studied the painting. I was dog-tired. Irene would have said I was overdoing it. It wasn't painting the room that had tired me out. The nursing home was draining me, even if I was only there a few hours. Mostly I worried how Irene was treated when I wasn't around. And there was something wearing about the place itself and the unnatural concentration of so many old and failing people.

A breeze rattled the blinds I had put up in place of the curtains. I was aware of the weight of Billie next to me on the bed, her tanned arm barely pressed against mine. I smelled Jergen's lotion. Irene had used Jergen's.

"What is it like to have a son who is such a fine artist?" she asked, still looking at the painting.

"He's got his problems like everybody else," I said.

"I guess we're all human," she said.

"Oh, Newell is plenty human," I said.

"I know he's been through a lot," she said. "With the death of his wife."

"Everybody has been through a lot," I said, pushing myself up off the bed and walking over to a window. I scraped paint off the glass with my thumbnail and looked back at the girl sitting there on the bed, her legs pulled under her.

She got up and walked close to the mural, then turned and looked at the room. "Jackson will like it up here."

A breeze rattled the blinds again.

"That boy makes me uncomfortable," I said.

"You're not exactly Mr. Congeniality yourself," she said.

I looked at her hard, but it didn't shut her up.

"Think of it this way," she said. "The two of you will have a lot *not* to talk about."

I stared out the window. The last light had coated our street and the houses in a satin finish. I looked at her. "What in the hell will I do with a nine-year-old boy for six weeks?"

Later that night, as I had finished cleaning up the room, I remembered that Irene needed clean clothes, and that I would need to send them with Newell if I was meeting him tomorrow. "Goddammit!" I groaned and headed back downstairs to the laundry room, which was right off the kitchen, and emptied the laundry bag of dirty clothes into the washing machine. I stayed up another two hours, drying and ironing.

When I was finally ready for bed, I stepped out to call the cats and noticed a light on in Billie's bedroom window. Then I thought about my boy up in Asheville. His Sandy gone.

Right after she died, he had kept saying he didn't deserve her. And lately, I had been feeling that way about Irene. After all, I never dreamed I would marry a girl as beautiful or as smart or as kind as she. Still, I never fully appreciated what I had in her. For most of our marriage, I worked, day and night and sometimes on weekends, too. What that did was keep me from spending time with her. It kept me from knowing how much Irene meant to me.

But I knew it now. I knew it every night I left her in her room, in that bed of hers. I knew it as I walked down that long hall of beds, each floating in TV light. I knew it every night I slid between the cold sheets of my own bed, reached over and cut off the light, then waited for the dark to rise and carry me on out into that deep wide river of regret.

Three

The Empty Stringer

It was a relief to drive in any direction besides Rolling Hills. And the thought of getting up into the mountains and casting my line in helped balance some of the reservations I had about the boy. I woke at five o'clock, having gotten into the habit from my housepainting days. I loaded the van with three fishing poles, my tackle box, my cricket bucket, my waders, and a thermos of coffee.

I hung Irene's ironed dresses carefully in the back and set the grocery sack of folded nightgowns and underwear on the seat. Laundry had never been my strong suit, but when I learned that the nursing home charged sixty dollars a week for laundry, I got good at it quick.

I was through downtown Greenville and headed north on Highway 25 as the sun rose. I stopped at a Hardee's outside Traveler's Rest for three sausage biscuits and a cup of coffee, then veered left onto Highway 276, driving up through Marietta and Cleveland. Driving through small towns always lifted my spirits. They seemed real, unlike downtown Greenville. The Woolworths, Ivey's, and JC Penney's of my younger days had been replaced by outdoor cafes, coffee shops, and boutiques.

I turned off Highway 276 where it met River Falls Road and pulled over at Gudger's Groceries there on the corner, a small wood-frame building with a Coke machine out front. I had not been in the store in years. Old Man Gudger was at his usual post behind the counter. He must have been in his mid-eighties. As usual, he wore overalls and a crisp white shirt, and he was sitting on a stool behind the register, reading the paper. And it was never the local paper. Always the *Charlotte Observer* or the *Atlanta Constitution,* sometimes even the *New York Times.* He had a long face with a pointy nose on which perched a pair of black-rimmed reading classes. His skin was parchment.

I didn't see Mrs. Gudger, who was usually sweeping or straightening the stock. A sparrow of a woman, she hopped around the store, making small talk with the customers.

"Hello, Prate," Mr. Gudger said, looking at me over his glasses like it had been four days rather than four years since I had last set foot in the store. He took my bucket and headed to the big cricket box he kept toward the rear of the store.

"I thought you fly-fished." He handed the bucket back to me, full of fat black crickets.

"Fly-fishing aggravates my arthritis," I said, rubbing my shoulder. "I'd rather these fellows do the work for me." I held up the crickets. "I'll need a license, too," I said. And while he filled out the form, I went over to the little produce section and bagged half a dozen apples and brought them to the register. Newell would not bring apples. He didn't like them.

"You know they're not local," he said, looking at the apples. "Way too early for local."

"My system doesn't know the difference," I said.

"That'll be ten-fifty altogether," he said, ringing it up on the cash register. "Where's your wife?"

The question caught me off guard. For the first time in weeks, Irene had slipped my mind.

"Had to put her in a home," I said, taking a twenty-dollar bill out of my worn wallet with little flecks of paint on it and handing him the bill.

"That's hard news," he said. "She was a good woman." Then he handed me my change. "Pretty legs as I recall," he said, raising his shaggy old eyebrows at me. "Very pretty legs."

"They're still pretty," I added, remembering how he used to talk Irene up whenever she came in the store. "She's kept her figure," I said. "It's her mind that's not what it was." And that was true. Her body was about in as good a shape as it had been ten years ago.

"They isolated the Alzheimer's gene," the old man said.

"Pardon me?" I said.

"They're working on a test that can predict whether you are likely to develop Alzheimer's," he said, sitting back on his stool. "Every week there's something in the paper about some new test that can predict how you are likely to expire. They have tests for cancer, heart disease, diabetes, all kinds of blood diseases." He wiped his glasses on his shirtsleeve, then put them back on. "I don't know about you, but I don't really care to know the particulars concerning my demise."

"Amen to that," I said.

"If you ask me, they ought to save all their time and money, and have one test for everybody," he said. "You walk in the doctor's office. They see you're alive, breathing and all. If you're a borderline case, they check your pulse. Then they pronounce you, 'Still with us.' And that's it. You received your test results right there in the office."

"I like it," I said.

"Charge ten, maybe fifteen dollars a pop, but it would be the only test you would ever have to take. It would put most of the medical profession out of business."

"All right by me." I thought of all the tests Irene had to undergo when they first diagnosed Alzheimer's—X-rays, CAT scans, blood tests, urine tests, reflex tests, memory tests. They poked, prodded, and questioned her for weeks, and if she didn't have Alzheimer's in the beginning, she sure did by the time they finished with her.

"So you're fishing solo?" Mr. Gudger asked.

"My boy is driving down with my grandson from Asheville," I said.

"Your son has become quite the artist," he said. "There was even something in the *Times* about him."

"He does good work."

"I remember when he was a little fellow, and you used to buy up all our pads and pencils for him," he said, nodding down the aisle where they kept school supplies. The old man was right. Newell had gone through pads and pencils like some kids went through bubble gum. When we came up to Jones Gap, he would lose interest in the fishing, pick up his pad and pencil, and spend the rest of the morning drawing—a kingfisher hovering over the river, a couple of trout swimming in place against the current, or a crawfish scooting back under an overturned rock.

"Stop by on your way out," the old fellow said, as I put the license in my wallet. "And show me your catch."

I picked up the cricket bucket and the apples and started out the door. I stopped. Something didn't feel right. I turned back around to the old man, who had picked up his paper. "Mrs. Gudger up at the house?"

"Passed away last June," he said.

It was like the breath had been knocked out of me. I set the crickets on the floor and walked back in.

"Be a year ago next week. Stroke," he said. "One minute she was dusting the shelves, the next minute I hear all these cans fall, and I come around and find her on the floor."

"I'm sorry to hear it," I said.

"These things happen," he said, like it was one more thing he had read about in the paper.

"I'm very sorry."

He picked up his paper, like that was all he had to say on the subject, and I said, "So long" and he said, "Good luck" from behind his paper, and I don't think he was talking about my fishing.

I climbed into the van with my cricket bucket and apples and headed on up River Falls Road, feeling foolish for jabbering about my troubles, while the old man had been sitting there with the worst thing. And it *was* the worst thing. I am not saying it wasn't hard to witness Irene fade. Hardest thing I had ever done. Hard to have her look at me, and say, "Don't I know you?" But it did not take a rocket scientist to know that when she died, she would be gone in the biggest way of all. I would lose the sight of her. I would lose the sound of her voice. I would lose the touch of her hand. No matter what the old man said—and I know he was trying to make me feel better—to have your wife die on you would be like being cleaved in two. Maybe it was selfish, maybe she would have been happier already up there, treading the streets of gold, but I did not hope for her departure anytime soon.

I had started down the road when the van nearly pulled itself to the side. What was I doing gallivanting off into the woods, while Irene was back at Rolling Hills, needing me? I would have turned around, if I hadn't told Newell I would meet him. I pulled onto the road. Still, I felt a strong tug at my back.

River Falls Road followed the Middle Saluda for ten miles up into the Jones Gap State Park. The road started out straight in the rich, open bottomland, much of it planted with pole beans and corn, and this year, a lot of red peppers. A good cash crop. The road curved as the river snaked up into wooded hills, then into the mountains themselves. Little cabins and A-frames perched along the river's edge, covered up by beech trees and rhododendron, looking like they were about to topple in.

I started to pass the River Falls Lodge, but decided to turn down the little road that led to it. The lodge was a low, long building with a tin roof and screened sides. Looked fixed up. The roof had been replaced and so had the screened sides. Somebody had been working on it. The old rusted sign out front that said River Falls Lodge had been cleaned and repainted. I had heard that the young people were square dancing up here again.

I parked in front. No one was around. I walked inside. The stage was still there, and the dance floor was the same as ever, with new boards here and there. I used to bring girls up here to square dances in high school and later. Had a pretty mean swing if I do say so myself, made all the girls dizzy. I could clog better than most anybody, my feet spending more time in the air than on the ground. But it was the music I couldn't get enough of. Those old mountain fellows would sit up on the stage, the stoniest expressions I ever saw, but the music that came out of their banjos and fiddles and guitars was pure heart—fast and happy, slow and sad, whatever they played they meant.

I walked outside, looking up the little road that led down from the River Falls Road, and I remembered the night Irene and I first kissed. I had brought Irene here after we had been going out for a couple of months. I had been worried she wouldn't take to the music. It was nothing like the symphonies Mr. Blalock listened to on the hi-fi on Sunday afternoons.

When we pulled up on Saturday night, there were cars parked along the road, leading to the lodge. First thing we heard was fiddle music, then the caller's voice, and the rhythmic stomp of feet.

"If you don't like it, just say the word, and we'll leave," I remembered telling Irene.

"That's about the tenth time you've said that," she said.

"I want you to have a good time," I said.

"I always have a good time when I'm with you," she said, taking my hand across the seat. She had been a lot bolder than most of the girls I had gone with.

"I don't see how that can be," I said, pulling my hand back. "I don't say hardly nothing. I don't *do* hardly nothing." We had gone out several times, but I couldn't ever think of anything much to say or do. I could hardly bring myself even to touch her.

"I like that about you," she said, taking my hand again. "It's refreshing."

"How can a bump on a log be refreshing?" I pulled my hand back again.

"You're not slick like the others," she said. "You don't have any lines."

"You'd think I could come up with at least one or two," I said.

"And you're not always trying to put the make on me."

I looked out the window at the lodge all lit up. My throat felt dry. "It's not for lack of wanting to."

With that, she scooted across the seat, took my head in her hands, and gave me a long kiss. My hands slid down the silky sides of her dress feeling the fullness of her ribs as I pulled her close. And she kissed me deep and long. The closer I held her, the more of a dream she was. Up at the lodge, hoots and hollers rose out of the fiddle music that was going fast and furious. The building shook with all the stomping like it was about to rise up off its cinder-block foundations. Kissing Irene for the first time was as close to a religious experience as I ever got. That night she danced circles around me, and we never even made it to the dance floor.

As I drove deeper into the gap, I breathed in the rich, dank air, a smell that was like coming home, even though I had been raised in the thick, steamy air of the piedmont. I steered the old van along the river, having to take the curves slow, the mountains rising around me. The morning light, which I had mostly left behind, was only now edging down over the ridges, looking like a fresh paint job.

I pulled into the parking lot, which had been regraded and graveled since I had been here last. There was a new shellacked wood sign that read JONES GAP STATE PARK. I walked up a new-mulched trail over a new, arching bridge with iron rails to some new concrete picnic tables. Beyond the picnic ground was a new park office that was closed and a new bathroom, both of them built out of stone. The South Carolina Park Service had been hard at work.

The only folks around were a young couple, who from their grubby looks, had been camping. They sat at a picnic table, cooking a big breakfast of grits and eggs and bacon on a Coleman stove. It smelled good. They looked surprised to see me, to see anybody so early. The fellow nodded, and the woman smiled. She was pretty in a homely sort of way, pale and freckled, with thick lips and a little-too-wide mouth. She had a tattooed bracelet on her wrist.

"Join us?" the fellow asked.

"Brought my own," I said, holding up my thermos and my

Hardee's bag. "But I appreciate it." I walked to the far side of the picnic grounds, finding a table close to the river, where I drank coffee, ate sausage biscuits, and watched the river.

When I glanced back at the couple, I saw they had settled down to their breakfast, scooting close to each other, looking sleepy and satisfied like they were all there were in the world to each other.

After I finished the biscuits, I went to my van to get the rods and slip on my waders. I noticed my little sign on the van door was fading. Newell had painted it a good ten years ago. Maybe I could get him to repaint it this summer. It said MARSHBANKS PAINTING COMPANY. Newell had painted a smiling fellow with big ears, standing on a ladder with a paintbrush in his hand, who was supposed to be me. Underneath the ladder he had printed my motto:

Good work is not cheap.
Cheap work is not good.

I had thought that up myself. I had been painting a little house down in Easley when it came to me. I missed painting houses. I missed the good, tiring work of it, and I missed meeting the people whose houses they were. When you painted houses, especially interiors, you saw people at their most personal. You saw what they lived like. I could look at a wall in somebody's house and tell from the fingerprints, the hairs, the scuff marks, and the holes, if they had kids, if they were young kids or old, if they had dogs or cats, if they were careless or particular, if they were kind or cruel, if they were happy or sad. Walls talked to me, and sometimes I was embarrassed by what they said.

I left a note on my windshield for Newell, saying I was headed to my usual fishing hole. I collected the gear, the crickets, and the apples, and walked up through the picnic tables again. The fellow and his girl were cleaning up from the breakfast. He was folding up his Coleman. When he saw me with my gear and my waders, he said, "Good luck."

I stopped, looked at the girl who was rinsing off the dishes by the spigot, then back at the fellow. "It's none of my business," I said. "But this is the best time of your lives."

The couple looked at each other, like what do we say to that, and I started to walk on off, but the girl came over to me. "Thank you, sir," she said in a real thick mountain accent. She looked over at the fellow like, Did you hear that? The fellow held up his hands like she had won some argument.

I walked on, past the closed office and across the wide footbridge to the other side where the Jones Gap Trail started. The trail, shaded by beech and hemlock, followed the river for a good eight miles, a gradual climb, all the way up to Raven Cliff Falls—a four-hundred-foot falls. Irene and I had hiked to the falls from farther up Highway 276 a few times in our younger days, camping at the foot of the falls. I would make a fire on the little beach below the falls and spread out a blanket after we ate. We would lie back, and as the stars assembled in the night sky, Irene would instruct me on the constellations, her voice almost lost in the sound of the falls, and the firelight throwing shadows high up the rock walls. And it was like we were the only two people on earth, which was fine by me, since Irene was the first woman I had ever been alone with who did not make me lonely.

I looked up from fishing, startled to find Jackson beside me on the boulder, watching. He had always been like that, appearing and disappearing, without ever seeming to come or go. He was a thin boy with brown hair and Irene's blue eyes. He had shot up a couple inches since I seen him last.

"Where's your daddy?"

He pointed back down the trail but kept watching my bobber float on the surface. This little pool, which was about a mile and a half upstream from the picnic grounds, was one of my favorite fishing spots. The big boulder above it made the water still and deep, and a huge, old beech tree—scarred by sweethearts' initials carved over the decades—leaned out over the river, shading pool and rock, fish and fisherman. I glanced up at the sun, surprised to see it so high. It was near noon.

"Check out my stringer," I said, nodding toward the bank.

Jackson walked back across the rocks, found the stringer I had stabbed into the bank at the edge of the water. He looked over at me.

"Pull it up," I said.

He slowly pulled it up, and although he didn't speak, I could tell he was impressed. He had trouble holding up the five brown trout and two catfish.

"Don't let the cats barb you," I said.

He held the squirming fish away from him, then gently set them back in the water and squatted beside them, watching them swim slow in the water.

"You and me are going to have some good eating," I said.

The boy looked at me like he didn't get my drift.

"That's enough fish for several suppers next week," I said.

He looked back down at the fish.

"You want to fish?"

He shook his head.

"I brought a pole for you."

"I haven't ever fished."

"The fish don't know that."

The boy came over cautious-like, and I got another fishing rod.

"It's all set to go. We just need to bait the hook. Grab a cricket out of the bucket." The boy stuck his hand down in the cricket cage and pinned a cricket against the screen and raked him gently into his palm. He cupped it carefully in his hands, looked at it for a minute, then slipped it into my hand.

I pinched it by its legs. "You run the hook up through him," I said, pushing the hook into the cricket's middle. "See him spitting tobacco juice? That's how you know you've done it right."

The boy wrinkled his nose.

"You get used to it," I said. I handed him the rod. "You know how to cast?"

The boy shook his head.

"Mash that button on the back of the reel as you pull the pole back. Hold it down until you cast forward, then you let the button go to let the line out."

The first time he tried, he let go of the button too soon, and the line jerked to the side. The bobber and the hook bounced on a big rock. The second time he let go too early, and the hook and bobber fell to the ground behind him.

"Try it again, but this time let go right as you come forward with the pole."

The boy tried again, and this time did a perfect little cast right into the center of the pool.

"Good job," I said. "Now comes the easy part."

The boy sat beside me, frowning like he wasn't too sure about this fishing business. He kept his eye on his bobber. Newell appeared, walking up the trail with a knapsack on his back. He was red-faced and out of breath.

"You already have him fishing I see," Newell said.

"Check out my catch," I said, nodding to the stringer.

"Man," Newell said, squatting down and pulling up the stringer. "You've been here a good while." He set the stringer back down and stepped across the rocks to where we were.

"Since about six-thirty," I said. "Did you see my note?"

He nodded. "And that couple down at the campground told us you had come by," he said, slipping off the knapsack he had on his back and setting it on the rock. "You made quite an impression. I didn't even have to ask. The girl said, 'You're his son. You look just like him.'"

He took out his handkerchief and wiped his forehead. His face was still red, although he wasn't breathing as hard. "I'm out of shape," he said.

"I thought you jogged," I said. Newell had always been pretty good about taking care of himself and for years had been a big jogger.

"Haven't had time this semester," he said.

Newell watched Jackson hold his rod. "How do you like fishing?"

The boy shrugged.

"I'm a pretty sorry father, aren't I, never taking you fishing."

The boy shook his head like he didn't go along with the sorry father business. Newell and I talked a little while. Even when we tried to include him, the boy kept silent, dutifully watching the bobber.

"You're watching it too hard," I said.

"Really?" the boy asked.

"Act like you're not paying attention," I said. "Look around like catching fish is the last thing on your mind. That's when they bite."

"How will I know when they bite?"

"Keep your finger on the line."

Jackson turned his head, trying to watch the bobber out of the corner of his eye. He still didn't look like he was enjoying himself, so after a while I said, "Your daddy will keep an eye on yours."

The boy handed the rod to Newell, got up and ran over to the bank where the stringer was, leaned down and studied the fish.

"I'm grateful to you for taking him," Newell said, watching the bobber. "I need this break."

Newell looked careworn. His face was puffy, and his eyes had such dark circles under them they looked bruised. The girl back at the picnic tables was right. Newell was cursed with my looks. Although he wasn't quite as short or as stout as me, he had my big nose and my jug ears. The boys in elementary school used to call him Dumbo. What those boys didn't know was that he had also inherited his old man's temper. One day, without warning, Newell turned on the biggest bully, a boy twice his size, and clocked him so hard upside the head that he sent him to the emergency room with a concussion.

"How's Mama?" Newell asked, keeping his eye on the bobber.

"She has good days and bad," I said.

"I'm sorry I haven't been down more," he said.

"You have a lot going on," I said.

He lowered his voice so the boy would not hear, "If you think this will be too much, I could make other arrangements."

I glanced over at Jackson, who was holding up the stringer slightly out of the water to get a better look at the fish. "We'll be all right."

"I'll sit with Mama at the nursing home this afternoon and see she gets supper," he said. "You and Jackson can go on home and not worry about having to visit her today. At least I can relieve you from nursing home duty for one day."

"You don't need to do that," I said, still feeling that old tug from Rolling Hills. "Jackson and I could go on over there directly."

"Let me be useful," he said.

I knew how he felt. I felt like that every day, wanting to be useful, wanting to help in some small way, wanting to believe I still had a purpose as far as she was concerned.

"Be sure the aides change her clothes, including her underwear," I said. "Sometimes they get busy and forget."

"I will."

"When I don't take her for a ride in the van, I usually roll her around outside the nursing home in the wheelchair. So she can breathe fresh air."

"She's in a wheelchair?"

"Some days she doesn't walk well, and the nursing home gets nervous about folks falling. They don't want to get sued. They like to keep them in the wheelchairs."

Newell sighed.

"I roll her out to the courtyard in the middle, under the shade of that little arbor, and she drinks her iced tea. You'll want to stop by McDonald's across the street and get her a sweet tea." I reeled in my line, saw my bait was gone, put on another cricket, and threw it back in. "And when you take her to supper, you might need to cut up her food, maybe even help her eat. It depends on how she's doing. Don't let those dining room biddies give you any flack."

"I'll take good care of her."

"You and I picked that place because it looked good," I said. "And it did look good for the first month or so. I have had to buy three channel changers, because they were stolen from her room, a nice folding chair has gone missing, and a vase Billie gave her has disappeared," I said. "And if people are low enough to steal, they're low enough to do other things."

Newell had set down the rod and was looking into his hands. That was how he listened.

"And some days when I go to see your mama, she seems upset but can't say why, and I ask the aides and they say she's having a bad day, and I thought it was her mind, but now I'm not sure." I sighed. "Her care all depends on the aide she has that day. The good ones burn out because the nursing home doesn't hire enough aides for the number of residents, so the aides are always running around putting out fires. And whenever I complain to Mercer . . ."

"The administrator?" Newell asked. He had met him briefly when we first looked at Rolling Hills.

"Whenever I complain, he appears concerned, says he will look into it and get back to me, but of course he doesn't get back to me. He doesn't get back to anybody," I said. "These nursing homes know how to treat patients good enough to take their money and bad enough to save most of it for themselves."

"Goddamn," Newell said, his jaw clenching. "Maybe I'll give them a piece of my mind."

"That's not a good idea," I said. "If you go around pissing off everybody over there, they will take it out on Irene."

"How would they do that?"

"They have their ways."

"Maybe I shouldn't leave Jackson with you," Newell said. He looked worried now, and I was sorry.

"Jackson and I can manage," I said.

I hadn't intended to tell Newell what I had been thinking about the nursing home. It was just dawning on me what kind of place it really was. Newell had a lot on his shoulders, and I wanted to help out if I could.

"Granddaddy," Jackson said, hopping up on our boulder and pointing at his bobber, which was scooting along the surface. It plunged under the water. Newell grabbed up the pole, jerked on the line to set the hook, then waved the boy over. "Come land this fish." And he handed the pole to Jackson.

The pole started jumping around like it was alive. "Reel him in, son," I said.

"How?" the boy asked.

"Crank the handle." I showed him how to turn it. His eyes widened as he struggled to reel it in, the rod bent double.

"It's hard," he said.

I had to reach over and set the drag so the line would let out when it was getting close to breaking. The line would whine out, then the boy would reel him in a little, then the line would whine out again, and the boy reeled him in a little more.

"Don't let the line go slack," I said. "He'll spit the hook."

I reached back for the net, then eased down the boulder and into the water. It was cold, even through the waders, felt like little pins up and down my legs. When Jackson reeled him in close enough, I reached under and scooped up the fish—a pretty brown trout, bigger than any I had caught that morning.

"It's a nice one," I said, reaching down in the net, taking the fish by the lip. The hook came out easy.

"Your first fish, Jackson," said Newell. "He's a whopper!"

"Want to hold him?" I asked, holding him up to Jackson. I showed him how to smooth the fins down from the front to the back. The boy took the fish, feeling the weight of it. He turned the fish so he was looking it right in the eyes. It opened and closed its mouth like it was trying to speak. Then the fish leapt out of the boy's hands or at least that was what it looked like. The fish flopped a couple of times on the bank, and before I could get to it, flopped once more into the water and was gone.

"Aw, I'm sorry," I said, putting my hand on the boy's shoulder. "I should have kept him in the net."

The boy, not seeming the least bit upset, looked in the direction his fish had swum off. Something was up. I found my stringer coiled neatly on the ground, all of my morning's catch gone.

"What in the hell?!" I picked up the empty stringer.

At first I thought a turtle must have eaten them, but there weren't even any heads left. Besides, turtles didn't coil stringers neatly. Jackson had been messing with the stringer.

Jackson didn't look at me.

"I fished all morning for those!" I felt my face go red. "Why did you do that?"

Jackson didn't speak.

"Jackson!" Newell came over and grabbed him by the elbow and shook him hard. "Answer your granddaddy! Did you let those fish go?"

The boy nodded slowly.

"Why!! Why would you do such a thing!!" Newell shook him again, harder.

The boy didn't speak.

"Do you know how rude it is not to speak when you're spoken to?"

The boy still didn't speak.

"Answer me when I ask you a question!" Then he popped the boy hard on the bottom. Tears sprang to Jackson's eyes, or I thought I saw tears, but they seemed to sink back into his eyes.

Newell paced around the boy, seething. "You think Grand-daddy is going to want to take care of you for the summer if you go around letting his fish go? Well, do you?" He grabbed the boy's arm and shook him again.

"It was just a little prank," I said. I was sorry about losing my morning's catch, but Newell's reaction made me pause.

Newell still had hold of the boy's arm. "Are you trying to sabotage my summer? Is that it?"

"No," the boy said.

I put my hand around Newell's shoulder and walked him away from the boy. "It's just fish," I whispered to him.

"This is the kind of thing he has been doing lately," Newell said, trying to keep his voice down, although I was fairly certain the boy heard. "Never says a goddamned word. Then he does something like let all your fish go without warning."

"He's being a boy," I said. A strange boy, I thought to myself, but a boy nevertheless.

Newell looked like he didn't know whether he was coming or going, then he stalked off up the trail.

Jackson rubbed his butt.

"Your daddy is going through a hard time," I said.

The boy looked at me. "How come when grown-ups go through a hard time, we kids have to go along with them?" He wasn't being smart, he wanted to know.

I felt bad. I had primed Newell's temper telling him about the nursing home, but I hadn't seen this coming. Newell had always had a temper, but I'd never seen him turn it on the boy. "I shouldn't have told him about the nursing home," I said.

"He's been mad a lot lately." Jackson looked off in the direction his father had disappeared.

"He'll be back directly," I said. "You want to fish some more?"

Jackson didn't look at me.

"I guess not," I said.

He went over to Newell's pack, pulled out a paperback and

started to read. I watched him for a minute, then sat down on the rock and picked up my fishing pole, but my heart wasn't in fishing either, so I reeled in my line.

"What you reading?" I sat beside the boy.

He didn't say anything, not like he was ignoring me, but like he was already someplace else. Finally he looked up. *"The Secret Garden,"* he said.

"Sounds like something I might like," I said. "Is it about gardening?"

The boy shook his head and kept on reading. I sat there beside him, listening to the water and the wind in the trees. I wasn't sure I could do much for the boy this summer, but maybe it would be something if all I did was not get mad at him.

Wasn't long before Newell returned. I could tell by his sheepish look that his anger had passed. He couldn't look the boy in the eye, but he did sit down beside him.

The boy kept on reading.

"I'm hoping there's more than books in there," I said, looking over at the Newell's backpack on the rock.

"Good idea," Newell said, getting up. "Let's eat." The boy continued to read.

Newell and I went back out to the big boulder.

"Sure is a big reader," I said.

"He's gotten to be a bookworm." Newell opened his pack and unwrapped ham and cheese sandwiches for him and me. "Like his granddaddy." Newell cut his eyes at me.

"More like his grandmama. He's smart like Irene. Maybe he'll grow up to be a school teacher or a college professor." I nodded toward Newell.

"I don't have anything against reading, but that's about all he does these days," he said, whispering. "He doesn't want to play with friends. I make him go to soccer because it's the only thing he does outside anymore."

"Maybe it's a phase?" That was about as psychological as I got. I unwrapped my sandwich and took a bite.

"When I walked up and found him actually fishing I couldn't believe it," he said. "After my behavior today, he won't want to do *that* anytime soon." He handed me a 7-Up. "I'm hoping a little time away from home will do him good." He paused. "A little time away from me. In fact, I could use a little time away from me."

Jackson's appetite must have gotten the better of him, because it wasn't long before he closed his book and came over and sat down with us.

"Hungry?" Newell held out a peanut butter. The boy hesitated, then took it and started tearing into it like he was starved. Halfway through the sandwich he scooted a little nearer to his father. The three of us sat on the big boulder and ate, three generations of Marshbanks. It came to me that the three of us had never been alone together. Either Sandy or Irene or both had always been around whenever we got together. This was different, the three of us out here in the woods without women, without their talk.

I was about to fetch the bag of apples I bought from Gudger, when Newell reached down in his knapsack and produced two big Granny Smiths, handing one to the boy and one to me. I was surprised. Before Sandy died, he wouldn't have thought to bring apples because he didn't like apples. He had left that kind of selfless thinking to Sandy. I took out my pocketknife and peeled the boy's apple, then mine.

After we finished lunch, Newell lay back on the rock and fell asleep. The boy picked up his book, but I said, "Put that down and follow me."

He followed me up the trail to a flat place where a little creek emptied into the river.

"Here we are," I said.

"Where?" the boy looked around, unimpressed.

"Salamander Heaven," I said.

He looked down at the rocks. "I don't see anything."

"The trick is to find a flat rock that's half in the water and half out." I turned over a big flat rock. We waited for the water to clear, then sure enough, a little speckled fellow was sitting in the pool the rock had made. The salamander didn't move, as if hoping not to draw attention to itself.

I cupped my hands over it and scooped him up as he started to wriggle away. I opened my hand, and there the salamander was. I set him in Jackson's hand. Jackson didn't say anything.

"They always look like they're grinning," I said. "Like they know something you don't."

It wriggled through his fingers and shot underneath another rock. "They're quick," he said. He bent down and turned over another rock. We hunted salamanders for the next half hour, catching them and letting them go. After a while Newell joined us.

"Here's a pretty one." Newell pointed to where he had just turned over a big rock.

The boy, who had developed a foolproof method for catching them, came over, leaned over real slow, his hand just above the water, then, like a snake striking, he grabbed up a big salamander that was spotted orange.

"It's a newt," Newell said. Jackson held it in his cupped hands, and father and boy both looked at it, their heads almost touching, then the boy let it go.

"I'll leave y'all to it," I said, and went back and sat on the boulder. I thought about fishing, but when I picked up the cricket bucket I saw it was empty. Jackson had struck again, but I didn't mention it. Didn't want to set Newell off. I leaned back on the rock. I was dog-tired from staying up so late the night before doing laundry.

The afternoon got away from us. It was nearly four o'clock when I happened to look at my watch and told Newell he needed to get on down to Rolling Hills. "She'll be waiting on me," I said. The three of us walked back down the trail, passing by the shelter where the couple had been eating breakfast. They had packed up their gear and left.

As we walked out to the parking lot, Newell kept looking at Jackson like he was having second thoughts about leaving him. And that caused me to have second thoughts as well. I suppose I hadn't stopped having them. What was I going to do with a solemn, solitary little fellow? I wasn't a counselor.

Newell helped Jackson get his suitcase out of the trunk of their car and put it in the back of the van. Jackson handed me a heavy knapsack full of books. "Man," I said, taking it from Jackson and heaving it into the van. "Did you clean out the Asheville library?"

I gave Newell Irene's dresses and the grocery sack of folded clothes. "Hang the dresses in her closet," I said, "and put the night-gowns in the first dresser drawer and the underwear in the second."

"You do her laundry?"

"Saves two hundred and fifty dollars a month," I said.

"I could pay for that," he said. "I could help you with a lot of the nursing home bills if you'd let me."

"You better get going," I said. "She'll be getting restless, and they'll be wanting to slip her a Mickey."

Newell went over to Jackson, who had been standing off to the side, and gave him a good long hug. "You sure this is all right?"

The boy paused, then nodded and made a brave attempt at a smile.

"I'll come down in two or three weeks to visit," Newell said. But then Newell came over to me and whispered, "Maybe this isn't such a good idea."

Maybe not, I almost said. Maybe we ought to call the whole thing off. Maybe I didn't need this moody, unpredictable, too-quiet, bookish boy shadowing me all summer while I tended my failing wife. I thought of Irene and what she would do in this situation and heard myself say, "Jackson and I will be all right. Won't we?"

Jackson nodded.

Newell took a folded piece of paper out of his shirt pocket and gave it to me. "This is the address and phone number up there, and my cell phone number, too," he said. "Penland is only two hours from here, so I can be down here in a jiffy if you need me."

"Right about now she'll be in the foyer waiting," I said, checking my watch.

Newell gave Jackson one last hug, then got in his car, and, rolling down his window, said, "Thanks for everything."

"If she doesn't know you," I said, "don't take it personally. She doesn't know me half the time."

Newell began to pull away but all of the sudden Jackson started running after the car. "Wait! Daddy! Wait!" He had had a last-minute change of heart, and that was okay by me. But when Newell stopped, the boy ran up to the car saying, "Rudy." Newell reached into the backseat and handed him a stuffed dog—an old stuffed dog Jackson had had since he was a baby. I didn't even know he still had it.

With head down, Jackson walked back to where I stood, and as Newell pulled away, he clutched the dog to his chest and waved. When the Suburu disappeared around the bend, he seemed to go

limp, like a puppet that has had his strings snipped. His face darkened, but he did not cry.

"I won't be a lot of trouble," Jackson said. He was still watching
the bend in the road where the car had disappeared. After a while
he walked around to the van, climbed into the passenger seat, shut
the door, and waited.

Four

Something to Hold

I drove us along the same gravel road Newell had driven down a few minutes earlier. I half hoped the Subaru would reappear, that Newell would change his mind and return for the boy.

"It's nothing against you," I said. "Your grandmother takes my full attention."

The boy looked straight ahead, although Rudy, the stuffed dog, kept an eye on me.

Last time I had seen Rudy was at Sandy's funeral, when Jackson had stood tearless at his mother's graveside, hanging on to that dog for dear life. The dog had lost an eye in the wreck, and later Irene sewed on another, but it didn't quite match. Made it look like Rudy was cutting his eyes at you. Now his fur was worn in big patches.

"Old Rudy has seen better days," I said.

The boy pulled the dog against his chest.

"He's a good dog," I said. "Hell, I'm looking mangy myself."

The boy didn't smile.

I drove us out of the park and along River Falls Road. When we passed the lodge, I told him that I had brought his grandmother there to dance, and everybody had wanted to know who the pretty girl was. The boy glanced at the building, but didn't speak. An afternoon haze had settled over the gap, making everything smoky. How different things would have been if Irene had been with us.

We had reached the main road, and I was about to drive by Gudger's when the boy said, "I have to go."

"Number one?" I asked, figuring I could pull over and he could pee by the side of the road.

"Two," he said.

I turned into Gudger's Groceries. When I climbed out of the van, the boy sat in his seat.

"I thought you needed to go," I said, feeling my face heat up. I saw what Newell meant about the boy's silence working on him. I noticed him looking at where the door handle should have been and remembered I had taken it off.

"Sorry about that," I said, opening the door for him. "Your grandmother keeps trying to get out in the middle of traffic."

We went inside. When he came out of the bathroom, I motioned the boy to come over by the register, where I had been talking to Mr. Gudger.

"Wanted to show you my catch." I put my hand on the boy's head.

Mr. Gudger came around the counter, frowning at the boy over his glasses, looking him up and down. "Whoeee, that's a big 'un. What'd you catch him on?"

"Night crawler," I said.

"Might be a record," the old man said, going over to the ice-cream freezer, taking out a Nutty Buddy, and handing it to the boy.

"Thank you," Jackson said shyly as he peeled the paper wrapping and threw it in the trash can by the door.

Gudger turned to me. "Have you told him about all the houses he's going to help you paint this summer?"

The boy stopped licking his ice cream.

"Thought I'd break it to him gradual," I said.

"You could leave him with me for a week, help me get the stock straight."

"Now that's an idea," I said. The old man and I went on like that, Jackson's eyes moving back and forth like he was following a Ping-Pong match.

After a while, I said we better get on home so I could figure out supper.

"You're not having fish?" Mr. Gudger asked.

I looked at the boy, who was toeing a knot in the floorboard.

"We were strictly catch and release today," I said. "What do I owe you for the ice cream?" I felt the boy relax beside me as soon as he understood I wasn't going to tell on him.

On the drive home, we rode with the windows down. The air thickened as we moved out of the mountains and down into Greenville. Jackson had pulled out his book and was reading. By now Newell would have taken Irene into the dining room, up to the table with Decatur and Mr. Greathouse. While the two men talked about the Braves game, Newell would cut Irene's chicken or spoon applesauce into her mouth.

After a little while, Jackson closed his book, and said, "I couldn't stand the thought of their heads cut off."

"Whose heads?"

"The fish."

"That's why you let them go?" I asked.

"I'm a vegetarian," he said.

"A what?"

"It means I don't eat meat."

"I know what it means." I looked ahead at the road. To my father, the butcher, being a vegetarian was about as un-American as being a Communist. He said people who didn't eat meat were weak-minded and low of character. He said their brains dwindled and that the children of vegetarians had tiny heads.

"Since when did you become a vegetarian?" I asked.

"Since Mama died," he said. I didn't remember Sandy being a vegetarian, but she would have been smart enough to keep something like that from me.

We had passed through downtown and had turned onto Augusta Road, where I had planned to stop at one of the fast-food places to pick up something for supper.

"So no Kentucky Fried?" I asked, as we passed a big sign with the Colonel.

The boy shook his head.

"No Big Macs?" I nodded at the McDonald's on the corner.

He shook his head again.

"No Whoppers?"

"I do like fries and shakes," he said.

"A man can't live on fries and shakes alone."

The boy raised his eyebrows, like he wouldn't mind trying.

"How come nobody told me you were a vegetarian?" I asked, wondering what other things Newell had not warned me about. "What about eggs?" I asked as I turned off Augusta onto Jones Avenue. "You eat eggs?"

He nodded.

"Well then, I guess we're still in business."

I pulled into my driveway and turned off the engine, looked at the house, then back at the boy. He was touching the knob where the door handle should have been. "Why did she try to get out?"

"Brother, I wish I knew," I said. He had to wait for me to come around and open the door. He jumped down and, with Rudy tucked under one arm and his book under the other, walked toward the house. When he used to come with Newell and Sandy, he would sprint up the walk and, meeting Irene on the porch, hurl himself into her arms. Only the cats came to meet him this evening from around the back of the house. He put down Rudy and the book and petted them.

I had gone around to the trunk to get his suitcase. I saw Billie walk up the drive, and my initial reaction was *Why does she have to come over here and make a production out of this?*

"Any luck?" she asked, seeing the fishing poles in the back of the van.

" 'Fraid not," I said.

"I wanted to say hello to Jackson," she said. "Need any help carrying stuff?"

"That's all right," I said.

Before I could stop her she had lifted Jackson's knapsack and lugged it up onto the porch, setting it beside the boy, who was still petting the cats.

"Whew!" she said. "What do you have in there?"

"Books," the boy said.

"Do you mind if I take a look?" she asked.

"That's okay," he said.

She pulled out several books. "Roald Dahl, Madeline L'Engle, C. S. Lewis. These are some of my favorite writers," she said. "This should keep you busy this summer."

"I've read most of them already," he said flatly.

"I see you have a *Redwall* book," she said, holding up a worn paperback with a mouse dressed as a knight on the cover. "What if I told you that I teach elementary school and I have the keys to our school library and that my school has all the *Redwall* books?"

The boy looked up at her for the first time. "Even *The Legend of Luke*?"

"Even *The Legend of Luke*," she said.

"Even *The Bellmaker*?"

"Even *The Bellmaker*," she said. "I'll take you over next week. If that's all right with your grandfather." She looked at me. "I'll be going back to clean up my classroom for the summer."

"We don't want to put you out," I said.

"I'll call," she said to the boy, "and we can go in search of *The Legend of Luke*."

The boy didn't look up or respond at all. A whole summer of this might drive me to distraction.

After Billie left, I took Jackson upstairs. I was excited about showing him Newell's old room. The late-afternoon light streamed through the windows, and the room shimmered. The new-painted walls almost glowed. When I turned to the mural, it looked real, like there was light coming from inside the painting, making it deep and rich like a place you could step into.

When the boy walked in and set the knapsack on the bed, he glanced at the painting and headed back downstairs. I thought, *What an ungrateful boy.* I had slaved away, painting and fixing up this room, so he would have a nice place to stay, a home away from home, and this was the thanks I got. And as I was getting worked up, Irene's voice came into my head saying, Prate, who did you really fix this room up for? She was right. I had fixed it up because I couldn't bear a room in my house going untended. The more I was away from Irene, the more she became a part of my thinking, helping me see the other side, short-circuiting my anger. Irritated the hell out of me.

By the time I was downstairs, the boy had opened a can of cat food and forked it into the cats' pie pans. He knelt beside them, watching them eat. He had always doted on Irene's cats and helped her take care of them. I saw the boy scowl at my .22, leaning in the corner beside the kitchen door.

"I've been using it for the squirrels raiding your grandmother's bird feeder," I said.

"You shouldn't kill squirrels," he said.

"I'm a bad shot," I said.

I started a pot of water boiling for the grits and got out a carton of eggs. The boy watched the cats eat.

"You let those crickets go today, too, didn't you?" I asked.

He didn't answer.

"You can't go around letting everything go," I said, pouring oil into the frying pan. "Remind me never to take you to the zoo."

After supper, Jackson started to walk off, but I asked him where he was going.

"To read," he said.

"First you'll help me clear the dishes," I said.

He came back and helped me carry the dishes to the sink, where I had run water. He started to walk off again.

"These dishes aren't washing themselves," I said.

"Don't you have a dishwasher?"

"Just got a new one," I said, putting a dishrag in his hand.

He rolled his eyes, and I thought he was about to complain. Instead, he stepped up to the sink, plunged his hands into the soapy water, and pulled out a dish, which he began to wipe halfheartedly.

"Put some elbow grease into it," I said.

The boy scrubbed a little harder, rinsed the plate and set it in the drain.

I put away the food and dried the dishes. After we finished, he sat down at the kitchen table with his book, and I went out and worked in the garden till dark. When I came back in, Jackson was still at the table reading.

"Time for bed," I said.

He looked at the kitchen clock. "My bedtime isn't until ten o'clock in the summers."

"Around here it's nine."

"It's only eight-thirty."

"That gives you time to take a shower," I said.

"I take showers in the morning."

"Around here you will take them at night, keeps the sheets clean."

He sighed, closed his book, and trudged upstairs. He came back down with his pajamas and his toothbrush, cutting his eyes at me as he disappeared into the bathroom. He was in the shower when the phone rang. It was Newell. I could tell by the static he was on his cell phone.

"I just left Rolling Hills," Newell said.

"It's pretty late," I said, sitting at the kitchen table. "Everything okay?"

"Took Mama a little while to get sleepy, but she was in bed when I left."

"You had the aides change her clothes this afternoon?"

"And I helped her with supper, although she ate most of it herself. She seemed a lot better than I expected. She even said my name when I walked in."

"She has good days," I said, not wanting him to think that every day was as easy as he had had it. The phone sounded extra staticky.

"My cell phone battery is low," he said.

"You want to spend the night here?"

"I better get on up there," he said. "Sooner I get to work the better." His voice sounded farther away. "How's Jackson?"

"He's in the shower," I said. "Do you want me to get him?"

"I'm losing the connection," he said, his voice coming in and out. "I'll call in a few nights," he said, talking louder over the static.

Jackson came out of the bathroom in his pajamas, his combed hair still wet.

"Hold on, Newell," I yelled into the phone, "here he is!" I handed the phone to Jackson. "It's your daddy. He's on his way up to Penland."

The boy grabbed the receiver. "Hey, Daddy!" He nodded. "I'm okay," he said. "When will you come back to visit?" His smile dissolved, and he handed the receiver back to me. "The line went dead."

"His phone was going out on him," I said. "He promised to call you soon."

He looked at me. "You don't think something happened, do you?" His voice was tight and a little desperate. I realized what the boy had seen in his mind's eye, what he must have seen today when his father drove away or anytime his father drove off to work or on a trip or anytime he arrived late—a car coming the wrong way, bearing down on the only one he had left.

"His phone went out on him," I said. "His battery was low is all."

The boy started up the stairs.

"He's fine," I said, following him over to the stairs, but he ran on up.

I sat in the kitchen, waiting by the phone, wishing Newell would call back. I tried reading my book, but worry was at the end of every sentence. I wasn't worried about a wreck. I worried that he might never get over Sandy, no matter how many masterpieces he painted.

You never stop worrying about your children, and I had started worrying about Newell before he was born. I remembered when Irene was pregnant with him, nearly forty-seven years ago.

Irene's mother had died in childbirth and her grandmother had, too. With modern medicine, Irene stood a lot better chance. Even so I became more worked up with every passing day. Irene became calmer. I thrashed around those nine months, like a lot of fathers-to-be.

I turned to my vocation. While Newell was incubating, I painted the entire house, inside and out. I painted on the weekends. I painted late at night. Whenever I became worried or fretful, which was nearly every spare minute, I broke out my brushes.

The day Newell was born Irene had woken early with contractions. Then they quit. False labor, the doctor called it, said it could still be days. I went on to work, but at lunch I drove home to check on her. As I pulled up, I saw Mr. Blalock's Cadillac parked in front of the house. As I came up the walk, the door swung wide, and there was Mr. Blalock trying to help Irene through the door, her arm around his neck.

"It's time," Irene gasped.

I picked her up in my arms.

"We can take my car," Mr. Blalock said.

I started to carry her to the Cadillac, but she shook her head and groaned. "Take me back inside." She closed her eyes with the pain.

"You can't have it here," I said.

"Watch me!" she seethed.

I carried her back to the bedroom, helped her out of her dress and slipped a nightgown on her. Then I helped her sit back in the bed. While Mr. Blalock was out in the kitchen, calling an ambulance, Irene said she felt like she had to push. She pulled up her nightgown up and spread her legs.

"You need to wait," I said.

"Tell that to the baby!" she snapped.

Mr. Blalock came back into the bedroom. "They should be here any minute."

"No time." Irene closed her eyes with the contraction.

"What do we do?" I looked at Mr. Blalock, who took off his coat and rolled up his sleeves.

"Go out to the kitchen and crush some ice," he said, as he put a couple of more pillows behind Irene to help her sit up.

I went out to the kitchen, found a hammer, wrapped some cubes in a dish towel and crushed the ice. I was putting it in a bowl when I heard the scream. I ran back into the bedroom and found Mr. Blalock holding Irene up in bed as she pushed. Her face was as red as a cartoon thermometer.

"I can't do it, Daddy," she cried.

"Sure you can, honey," he said. "Sure you can."

"Daddy, Prate doesn't look right."

"Don't you worry about Prate."

"Here's the ice," I said, holding the bowl out to Irene, and the old man must have grabbed it before I hit the floor. When I came to, I heard a cry, but it wasn't the desperate cry of my wife in labor. More of a gasp, a little creature coming up for air. Newell.

I was looking up at my father-in-law, who was a grinning giant from where I lay, his hands covered in slickness and holding the squalling baby up for Irene to see, the throbbing bluish cord still attached. Mr. Blalock hadn't had time to move me out of the way, so he had delivered the baby on top of me. He had done it single-handed.

"Well, well," said Mr. Blalock, looking down at me. "Just in time to hold your baby boy."

"A boy?" I said, as I stood up slowly and took the baby in my arms.

"We need to cut the cord," Mr. Blalock said.

I dug in my pocket and pulled out my knife. I ran out to the kitchen and washed it.

"You do the honors," he said, when I came back. He showed me where to cut. The cord sliced easily. Mr. Blalock tied it off like he delivered babies ten times a day. He handed Newell to Irene, putting a blanket over them.

Then we heard the siren. The attendants lifted Irene and the baby onto a stretcher and whisked them out to the ambulance, like they wanted to believe there was still an emergency. I climbed into the back with them, and this time it was Mr. Blalock left standing in the road.

I have often wondered if I had been allowed to save Mr. Blalock so that he might save Newell and Irene. What I did not know at the time was that Mr. Blalock's aunt had been a midwife and that he had often gone with her out in the country to deliver babies. At one point, he had even considered medical school before, as he put it, "being distracted by the vicissitudes of law."

Anyhow, he had been there the day Newell was born and taken charge. He had talked Irene through the contractions, spooned the crushed ice into her mouth as she rested between contractions, given her hope when the head began to crown and been there to catch Newell as he squirted out into the old man's arms. And as he passed my boy into my arms, giving me something finally to hold, he knew I would never be the same. He knew that in the end the father doesn't deliver the boy, the boy delivers the father.

After a while, I closed my book, leaving Jude in Christminster, and decided to go to bed. I was letting in the cats when the phone rang. I picked up the receiver. "Newell?"

"Mr. Marshbanks?" It was a woman's voice. "This is Linda at Rolling Hills." Linda was the night nurse on Irene's unit. A Korean woman, she was one of the good nurses and had taken a real liking to Irene.

"I wanted you to know that we found Mrs. Marshbanks on the floor of her room a little while ago. She's all right."

"She didn't hurt herself?"

"She's fine."

I sat back in my chair.

"She climbed out of bed and must have fallen," Linda said. "I put her in the wheelchair and rolled her to the nurse's station so we can keep an eye on her. I'm afraid if we put her back in bed, she will crawl out and hurt herself. I was wondering if you wanted to come out?" I didn't want her sedated, but they had been calling more lately. Bill Chandler had said that the restlessness was part of Irene's illness.

"I'll come right out." I remembered the boy upstairs. "I have my grandson here."

"Maybe we should give her a sedative tonight," she said.

"I guess you'll need to," I said, hating the thought of Irene being out of it tomorrow, which usually happened when they gave her something at night.

"We'll give her a small dose," she said, reading my thoughts. She was a very good nurse, and because she was, I doubted she would last long at Rolling Hills.

"Mrs. Marshbanks has been asking for you," Linda said. "Would you like to talk to her?"

"Put her on," I said.

I heard breathing over the phone, like when a little child picks up but doesn't speak. "Irene?"

"When are you coming to . . ." She paused. "Oh pshaw," she

said. "When are you coming to the place where we lie down to-gether?" Irene asked.

"Directly," I said. "Don't you wait up."

"When?"

"Soon. You go on to bed. They are going to give you something to help you sleep."

"All right," she said. "You come soon. You have to start on the Sansburys' house tomorrow."

My lord, I thought, I must have painted that house thirty-five years ago.

Linda got back on the line, told me she would call if anything else happened and that she would keep an eye on her. I thanked her for asking me first before giving her the sedative. Sometimes when I came in the afternoon, Irene would be slumped over in her wheelchair, and if I couldn't wake her I knew the night folks had gone ahead and given Irene a sedative because they didn't want to fool with her. When I complained, they would say she had been "agitated." That was the word they trotted out, like she had pulled a gun on them.

After I hung up, I finished cutting out the lights and started to get ready for bed. I felt bad not going out to Rolling Hills, and it made me question once again if it was such a good idea taking the boy for the summer.

I was unbuttoning my shirt when I decided to go check on the boy upstairs. In my undershirt, I tiptoed upstairs and found Jackson sound asleep, *The Secret Garden* open on his chest and Rudy sitting next to him like a little stuffed watchdog. I took the book, careful to mark his place and was reminded how much he looked like Newell when he was a boy. There was a darkness beneath the eyes, little pools of worry.

It was two or three in the morning when I half woke knowing that somebody had just said something to me. "Irene?"

"A bad dream." Jackson was standing beside my bed, holding Rudy.

"Well, get in," I growled, and held the covers back for him. He hesitated for a minute, like he wasn't too sure. "You going to stand there all night?" I snapped, and he scrambled into the bed, pulling the covers up. He started out on the other side of the bed but sometime during the night he scooted up next to me. And once, his hand flopped onto my pillow. It smelled faintly of fish.

Five

Odd Man Out

The first afternoon I walked into her room with Jackson, Irene looked up from her newspaper, then looked back down. She did not read anymore but liked to go through the motions. She had always read the paper, keeping up with politics. She had been a dyed-in-the-wool Democrat. Even now she refused to read the *Greenville News,* because it was a Republican-leaning paper, so I had to go out and find a *Charlotte Observer.* She had been looking at the same paper for a month.

"Irene, it's Jackson, Newell's boy, your grandson," I said, bringing him over to her.

She looked up from her paper, frowning at him. Irene had seemed irritable lately, although nothing like she had been when she was at home.

"It's Jackson," I said, putting my arm on his shoulder. "Your grandson."

She studied the boy's face like a map she was once familiar with, then set down the paper and held out her arms.

"Here you are," she whispered, holding his head against her chest. "Here you are." Like she had misplaced him.

And I had to give it to the boy. He didn't hold back the way children often do when an old person becomes all strange and teary-eyed. He let her hold him. He seemed to want her to. I wasn't a counselor, not by a long shot, but it made me wonder if some of the boy's moodiness had been because he missed visiting his grandmother.

The boy went out to the nursing home with me every day. He didn't have much choice. He was too young to leave at home alone. Billie offered to keep him a couple of afternoons. With school out, she said she had time on her hands. Jackson didn't seem interested, and I didn't feel comfortable letting him stay with her. One more thing I would be beholden to her for. The boy was my responsibility. Although I was a lot of things, I wasn't a damned shirker.

We usually stayed at Rolling Hills a good four hours, through supper. A long time for anybody but especially long for a nine-year-old. His reading came in handy. He would sit in one of the chairs in Irene's room curled up with a book. Sometimes he would set the book down and look over at Irene, who would either be leafing through the paper or watching television or staring out at the court-yard, her face empty as a plate. He didn't seem bothered by how quiet she had become. In fact, her silence seemed to excuse his own.

Jackson's presence did seem to work on Irene. Toward the end of his first week, Irene actually walked around the building with us—something she hadn't done in a month. On Saturday, she asked if we could go to ride. Jackson sat in the backseat with her, while I chauffeured them through the countryside. I glanced back at them at one point. Irene was looking out one window and the boy was looking out the other, neither of them saying a word, both seeming content. I wondered if it wasn't me who had the problem, me who was odd man out.

One morning about a week after Jackson's arrival, Billie called to say she had to go over to school and did Jackson want to visit the library. We had already turned down her offer to watch the boy in the afternoons, so I was surprised she tried again. I handed the receiver to Jackson and went out to the den. I heard the boy say, "No thank you," then "Bye." A couple of days later, Billie appeared at our door with a book in her hand. Turned out it was the very *Redwall* book he had hoped to get his hands on. The boy brightened when he saw the book, thanked her, and didn't say much else. He read that book in two days. It must have been four hundred pages long. Then a couple of days after that, Billie came over and asked Jackson again if he wanted to go over to the library.

"I need to finish taking down my bulletin boards," I heard her say, as I came up behind the boy, who stood at the front door. "You'd have the library to yourself."

I started to tell her we appreciated the offer but that we could look after ourselves. Before I said a word, the boy had nodded that he wanted to go.

"Is it all right with you, Mr. Marshbanks?" Billie asked.

The boy looked at me hopefully. The idea of having a whole library to himself must have been too much to resist. To tell you the truth, it sounded pretty tempting to me as well. The idea of being alone with all those books. Shelves upon shelves of possibility.

I scratched my head. "If the boy wants to go, and it's not putting you out . . ."

The boy ran upstairs to get the *Redwall* book to take back.

"It's not putting me out," she said.

"Because we're doing all right on our own." It had taken me a few days to get used to having somebody else in the house, but, even with all his quiet, I didn't mind having him around as much as I thought I might.

The boy came back downstairs with the book. "You've finished it already?" she asked, as they walked back down the drive. The boy said something, but they were out of earshot by then.

A couple of mornings later, she called to see if he wanted to go swimming. He was slow to agree, but she came over again. After we had gotten a towel and his swimsuit, she led him off. The third time she called to see if he wanted to help her with making pots in her studio. Slowly she was winning him over, which shouldn't have surprised me. She was, after all, an elementary-school teacher.

Her attention to the boy unsettled me. It was one thing when she helped with Irene. Irene had been a friend to her. They had spent many hours in conversation. When Billie first moved here after her divorce, Irene consoled the girl much like a mother. I hardly talked to her for the first several years she lived here. We were friendly, but she was not my friend. She certainly didn't know Newell or the boy well at all. Every time she helped with the boy now, I felt more indebted. I had never been in debt in my life. Never had a house mortgage or a car loan, never even had a charge card.

One Saturday morning, Billie called to see if Jackson wanted to go swimming. Before I had a chance to say he ought to stay home for once, he sprinted over to her house. I decided I needed to have a talk with Billie, so I kept an eye out for her pickup. When they returned, I went over and found them in her studio—the little shed I had help hang the windows on. In a clay-splattered apron, Jackson was sitting at the kick wheel, a vase taking shape in his hands.

"Hello, Mr. Marshbanks," Billie said. "Jackson is finishing a pot."

Billie and I watched him gradually pull up the sides of the clay, wetting his hands and pulling some more so that the pot seemed to grow right out of the wheel. In a few minutes, he had fashioned a perfect little vase.

Billie took a wire and cut it off the wheel and the boy set it on a shelf with several other dried pots he had made. "We're going to have a firing soon," she said, nodding to the little yellow brick kiln beside the shed.

"I was wondering if you and I could talk?" I said to Billie.

The boy looked at me.

"Sure," she said. "We can go up to the house. Jackson, why don't you try making a bowl this time?"

The boy dug a handful of clay out of the bucket, shaped it into a ball, and threw it onto the center of the wheel, which he turned by kicking. We left him there, centering the clay.

"I've never seen anybody pick it up as quickly as he has," Billie said, as we walked back to the house. "Of course it's not surprising considering who his father is. Still, he says Newell doesn't work in clay."

We went inside and sat at her kitchen table. She offered me coffee, but I declined.

"Is everything all right with Newell?" she asked.

"As far as I know," I said.

"Mrs. Marshbanks is okay?"

"Fine," I said, finding myself unable to come to the point. I looked out the back screen toward the little shed where we could see the boy through the doorway hard at work.

"What's on your mind then?" she asked.

"I don't want you to get the wrong idea." I folded my hands on the table.

"But?" she asked.

"You're doing too much," I said.

"I am?"

"You've been taking him too much."

"Oh," she said, looking troubled. "I've been depriving you of his company. I'm sorry. I didn't think."

"That's not what I mean," I said. "I told Newell I would keep the boy. He's *my* responsibility."

"I know," she said, looking puzzled.

"You shouldn't help out so much with him." I looked at her.

I could see all kinds of feelings travel across her face, but she didn't speak.

"The boy's my job," I said, "And when I accept a job, I see it through."

She looked at me, her jaw working, like she was upset, maybe even a little angry. "Jackson's a boy, not a job," she said.

"Well . . ." I said, not sure how to reply.

"Look," she said, leaning across the table toward me. "I know you have a lot to deal with now, and I know, at times, he must feel like one more thing you have to contend with. I don't have a wife in the nursing home. I don't spend a good part of every day taking care of her. So for me Jackson is good company." Her voice eased up a bit here. "When I first started teaching, having summers off was one of the things that appealed to me about the job. Ever since the divorce, summers have seemed long, drawn-out affairs, leaving me a little on the lonely side." She shook her head at herself and smiled. "In the summer, I miss the children in my class so much I dream about them." She looked at me. "But this summer has felt . . ." She paused. ". . . a little less empty with Jackson around."

"I see," I said, and I did, at least enough to know that I had misread yet another woman's mind.

"So, to be perfectly honest," she said, "having him over has not been something I have been doing for you or for him. It isn't something I have been doing out of the goodness of my heart. When it comes right down to it, having him over has been for me. But if you think it's better that I stop, I will."

I looked at her, not knowing what to say. She was a smart woman and a generous woman. Yet by disowning her generosity, she pretty much had me. Maybe there was some truth in what she said about her long summers. Maybe the boy relieved a little of that.

"I want to show you something." She led me into her living room and stopped in front of a painting that hung over her couch. It was one of Newell's.

"That's the Middle Saluda," I said. Irene had said he had done a series of paintings along the Jones Gap Trail, but I'd never seen any of them. "And that's our fishing hole," I said. And it was, complete with the old beech tree shading Turtlehead Rock. Although nobody was in the painting, I couldn't help feeling that we were just out of the frame, eating lunch or fishing a little farther down the river.

"I haven't seen this one," I said. Newell never liked to keep his paintings long. He didn't like looking at his own work. I understood how he felt. Sometimes when I looked at houses I had finished, I always saw things I could have done better.

"I bought it years ago," Billie said, "back when his paintings were within a schoolteacher's price range."

I stood in front of the painting, taking it in. It felt like the place. That was Newell's strength as a painter. He captured a place's feel.

"I'll do whatever you think best," Billie said.

Took me a minute to realize she was talking about the boy.

"As my daddy used to say, 'If it ain't broke, don't break it.'"

"Meaning?" she asked, women always wanting things spelled out.

"Meaning that if you don't mind, and the boy doesn't mind,

why should I go to the trouble to mind?" My tone was a little on the impatient side.

She nodded to herself, fighting a smile.

"You want to give it a whirl, Granddaddy?" Jackson set a finished bowl on the shelf.

"That's all right," I said.

"Come on," Jackson said. "I tried fishing."

"As I recall, you did more releasing than fishing," I said.

"Put this on." The boy slipped the apron over my head before I had a chance to object. Billie sat me down at the wheel, showed me how to keep the wheel spinning with my foot, then showed me how to center a ball of clay, which wasn't as easy as it looked.

My lump of clay kept going all cattywampus. She stood beside me, cupped her hands over mine, and showed me how to control the clay. I could feel the calluses on her palms on top of my hands. She guided my hands, firmly moving the clay into the middle of the wheel.

"Centering the clay is key," she said. "If it isn't centered, then everything else is a waste."

"Like priming before painting," I said.

She showed me how to press down lightly with my fingertips, then how to pull up ever so gently with one hand on the inside and one on the outside to make the wall of the pot rise slowly. Either I would pull too hard or too fast or didn't keep my fingers wet enough or did something else that made the whole thing start going lopsided, and whenever that happened all was lost. I must have tried a dozen times.

"I could never do anything with people breathing down my neck," I said, throwing the crumpled clay back into the bucket.

The boy and Billie looked at each other.

I heard them walk away as I reached back into the bucket for a handful of wet clay. I don't know how long I was out there in that little shed. Long enough to try half a dozen times, until I made something that looked like a cross between a vase and a bowl. At least it stood. I cut it off the wheel with the wire and set it on the shelf with the others. Feeling sheepish for my ill temper, I went and found Billie and the boy sitting at her kitchen table, playing Parcheesi.

"Well?" Billie asked.

"I made a pot," I said, "if that's what you want to call it."

The boy ran off go see for himself.

She saw me looking at the Parcheesi board. "You want to play? We just started."

"I need to get home and fold the rest of Irene's clothes," I said. "Won't be long before we have to out to Rolling Hills. Just send the boy home when you finish your game." I stood there a minute more. "Sorry I lost my temper back there," I said. "I guess you can't show an old dog new tricks."

"You were persistent," she said.

"I was mad," I said.

"Persistence born out of anger is no less persistent."

The boy ran back in.

"It's a pot," he said sitting back down to their game. "A good pot."

"I wouldn't go that far," I said.

"I would," he said, rolling the dice.

Later that afternoon as Jackson and I drove over to Rolling Hills, I couldn't help noticing how the boy would be lively with Billie but close up around me. Like now, the way he was sitting on the seat next to me, his head buried in a book. Billie knew how to cajole the boy out of himself. Maybe going over to the nursing home was getting to be drudgery for him.

"You don't have to come every afternoon," I said.

The boy didn't look up from his book.

"Billie said you could stay with her," I said.

The boy turned the page to his book.

"Will you shut that damned book for two seconds while I talk to you?" I said louder than I meant.

The boy closed the book, looked out the window, and didn't say a word.

In a quieter voice I said, "All I'm trying to say is that you shouldn't feel like you have to come over here every day. It could be wearing on a boy, sitting around with a bunch of old people all afternoon."

The boy looked at me. "Don't you want me to come?"

I looked at the boy, then back at the road, and said, "Sure I do." I didn't sound all that convincing to myself.

We didn't say anything else the whole way there. After we pulled into the Rolling Hills parking lot, I got out, came around, and opened the door for the boy, who ran on inside. I stood there, studying the building and wondering why the boy's question had thrown me.

I was getting Irene's clothes out of the van when a familiar voice said, "Hello, Mr. Marshbanks."

The phone repairman, who had showed us the way home that day, tipped his helmet.

"What brings you out this way?" I asked, shutting the side van door.

"I had line repairs in this direction, and I dropped by to check in on Mrs. Marshbanks. She's doing well."

"That was decent of you," I said.

"I'm guessing that was your grandson who went ahead of you," he said.

"He's staying with me this summer."

"He is all your wife talks about," he said.

"You visited Irene before?"

"Last week I stopped in a couple of mornings," he said, "Hope it's all right."

"It's good for her to have visitors." I knew that Irene had morning visitors because sometimes they left candy or flowers. Old friends or former students would call and ask when they should visit, and I said mornings since I didn't want to visit with them myself, and since it kept Rolling Hills on its toes. Of course Irene hardly ever remembered who visited.

"Your wife is a charming woman," the telephone man said.

We stood there a minute more. "Irene stayed on at Greenville High after busing started," I said out of the blue. "She always liked the black kids. Some still stay in touch with her."

He smiled like what I had said amused him. Then his beeper went off, he checked it, and said, "I have to get back to the office." He looked up at me. Something about this man made me feel like he could see right through me.

"Thanks for visiting," I said. "I can't do it all."

"No, you can't," he said, and I felt he wanted to put his hand on my shoulder but thought better of it. "I realized that with my mother toward the end. It's too much for any one person." He climbed into his cherry picker and started it up. He waved as he pulled slowly out of the parking lot. It felt to me as if that fellow was a little bit like God.

I carried the clothes on inside. I found the boy already reading to Irene from one of the books he had taken from Billie's school library. It was called *A Wrinkle in Time,* and he was reading about how these children had gone to a whole other world in search of their missing father. Irene sat on the edge of her chair, leaning toward the boy, hanging on his every word. She looked more alert than she had in weeks. I was putting away Irene's underwear in a drawer when the boy's question came to me again. Did I want him to visit Irene at the nursing home? Then it hit me. As pitiful as it was to admit, I was jealous of the boy. I was jealous of how Irene came alive whenever he walked into the room. If she was coming back, she wasn't coming back because of me.

That was the hardest part about this whole business—that I mattered less and less to Irene. Sometimes I felt like I was just another aide to her, helping her dress, helping her eat, helping her into bed at night. I wasn't alone in this. I had seen the puzzled expressions on the faces of many of the wives and husbands who came each day to care for their spouses at Rolling Hills. Like me, they had learned the hard way that being loved was all about being singled out, thought about, remembered. And like me, they had learned how painful it was to not be remembered. Maybe the devil was in the details, but so was the love. And the less Irene knew me, the less I knew myself.

Six

A Change of Scenery

Over the next couple of weeks, it became the routine that the boy headed to Billie's after breakfast. They would go to the library or swim or canoe or hike. I didn't have anything to give Billie in exchange for her kindness, except the vegetables in my garden, which had started to come in. Every morning I would send the boy over with a grocery sack of tomatoes, pole beans, butter beans, cucumbers, corn, or whatever else I had picked the night before.

Billie was good for the boy. She had raised his spirits over the few weeks he had been here. Even when he was with me, he spent less time hiding behind books and more time petting the cats or helping in the garden. Not that everything was easy. I made an effort to talk to him, but he didn't say much back. I would start to lose my patience, but Irene's voice would creep up on me, *Prate, just because he doesn't talk, doesn't mean he's not listening. He takes after his granddaddy.*

All in all, the boy was better. It didn't hurt that, as far as we could tell, Newell seemed better. He called every two or three nights. With each call he sounded a little more like himself.

Whenever I asked when he might visit, he would pause and say he was in the middle of a run of new paintings and was afraid to stop. He would ask if we might come up to Penland instead. I would say I couldn't leave Irene. At this point in the conversation, Jackson, who usually sat at the kitchen table while I talked to his father, would pick up whatever book he had been reading, trying to hide his disappointment.

Billie helped make up in some ways for his father's absence. Not only did she help Jackson, but by having him in the mornings, she gave me time to get things done around the house, to run errands, to wash Irene's clothes, to pay bills. The bills were mounting. Rolling Hills was four thousand dollars a month. That didn't count the physical therapy, the speech therapy, and what all other therapies that they came up with. A hundred dollars an hour to walk her up and down the hall. A hundred and twenty dollars an hour to remind her how to swallow. *Therapy* was a mighty expensive word.

Then there were the supplies—the medical gloves, the toilet paper, the Kleenex. They nickeled-and-dimed the residents to death. Put all that together, and it came out to more than five thousand dollars a month. Thank the Lord Irene had retirement or else we wouldn't have even gotten her in Rolling Hills. They had a year waiting list for any Medicaid beds, and we wouldn't have qualified anyhow. We weren't dirt poor, at least not yet. At sixty thousand dollars a year, it wouldn't be long before Irene's retirement would be depleted, then we would need to start in on the little retirement I had set aside, then I would have to sell the house. We wouldn't qualify for Medicaid until most everything was gone. The government liked to see you on your knees.

The boy continued to go with me to the nursing home most afternoons. Irene seemed improved. She had always loved Jackson, and having him around, even though she still sometimes confused him with other boys of her past, brought the color to her cheeks.

The other thing that helped Irene was that the aides who usually tended her had been there a while and were accustomed to her ways. They made sure she was bathed, made sure she got a good breakfast and lunch, talked to her respectfully, and treated her with as much kindness as their jobs gave them time for. Irene was getting the hang of Rolling Hills, and Rolling Hills was getting the hang of her. The aides appreciated the boy, since Irene was more manageable when he was around.

The way Irene's eyes came into focus when Jackson entered the room was something to see. At night, after he said good night to her, she slept well. Since Jackson had started coming with me, the night staff called less. Even Bill Chandler, who came out to the nursing home late one day, about three weeks after the boy had first arrived, commented on Irene's improvement.

"This grandson of yours is good medicine," Chandler said to Irene, taking her pulse and winking at Jackson. He had his fingers pressed on the inside of her wrist and was looking at his watch.

"Of course he is," she said.

"Forgive me for being obvious," Chandler said.

"You can't help it," she said, "You're a . . ." She frowned at herself, like the word of what he was had escaped her. She looked at his stethoscope hanging around his neck. ". . . the profession of the heartbeat."

"Doctors say the obvious?" he asked.

"There you go again," she said.

Chandler took his eye-checking instrument out of his black bag and shined it into each of her eyes. He checked her ears and took her blood pressure. He had her breathe deep while he listened to her lungs through his stethoscope. A lot of doctors gave up their patients once they entered the nursing home, turning them over to the nursing home doctor, who, in this case, was a harried, pinch-faced woman who pushed a little cart around that amounted to her office. Chandler had insisted that he wanted to keep on as Irene's doctor. True to his word, he came every week to look in on her and a couple of other patients he followed at Rolling Hills.

After Chandler finished examining her, I told Jackson I was walking the doctor to his car, and the boy looked up from his book and nodded.

I turned on the evening news for Irene, who still liked to watch Dan Rather even though she couldn't take in much of what he said. She had always liked Dan Rather and before him, John Chancellor and before him, Walter Cronkite and all the newsmen of the past. She respected these smart, well-dressed men who showed up every night to talk us through the tragedies.

"If I were you, I would keep that grandson of yours around as much as possible," Chandler said, as we walked down the hall.

"He stays three more weeks." My worry about Jackson being trouble had been replaced by the worry of what would I do when he left.

We passed the administrator's office. Mercer had cut out the office lights and was closing his door. I hoped to slip past him, but he saw us and darted out in the hall. He fawned over the doctors, hoping they would recommend Rolling Hills to their patients.

"Well, hello, Dr. Chandler," he said, shaking the doctor's hand. Then he shook my hand. "Hope your lovely wife is well today, Mr. Marshbanks?"

"As a matter of fact, she died," I said.

"Glad to hear it," he said, hurrying toward the front door, his briefcase swinging against his leg. He hadn't heard a word I said.

Then he called back over his shoulder, "Let me know if I can do anything," and disappeared through the front door.

Chandler shook his head.

Through the big front windows, we saw Mercer out in the parking lot, as he pulled away in what looked like a brand-new BMW.

"The Zoloft might be helping Mrs. Marshbanks as well," Chandler said.

I had not been able to keep track of all the different medications Irene had been on. Soon as I got one name down, he changed her to another. Way back, he had put her on Aricept, and she was still on that. Then he put her on something for "depression"—a word I never trusted. I told Chandler that Irene and I had both lived through the Great Depression, and there weren't any pills back then.

"Doc," I said, "is there any chance Irene might have been misdiagnosed? She seems better. She's walking better, and she might even remember better."

"I've been wrong before," Chandler said, "But Alzheimer's is a disease of peaks and valleys." The automatic door swished open, and we walked into the warm, humid evening air. "Patients can be much better one day, and the next day, turn around and be worse than ever."

"Are you saying I shouldn't get my hopes up?"

"I'm saying enjoy this improvement while it lasts." He tried to stifle a yawn.

"Long day?" I could tell by his beard that he had gotten up especially early this morning. He already needed another shave. "I did rounds over at the hospital this morning," he said. He opened his car door, which creaked loudly, and pitched his black bag across the seat. He drove an old Honda Civic. One of the early models. Must have been at least fifteen years old. Another reason I liked him.

"Maybe you should get Mrs. Marshbanks out of the nursing home a little more," he said, folding his arms and leaning against the car.

"I take her for rides."

"I was thinking something more ambitious. A day at home perhaps."

"Last time I tried taking her home she became pretty upset."

Back in April, I had brought her home for a midday Mother's Day lunch. Newell and Jackson had even come down. We walked her up the front walk and onto the porch. Inside she walked around like she didn't quite know it was home, but she knew it was something. Then she picked up a tarnish-framed picture. One of our wedding pictures. Of her eating wedding cake off my fingers. She handed me the picture. "Don't bring me here again," she said, and walked on her own power out the front door, down the front walk, and got in the car by herself, and sat there, looking straight ahead till I drove her back.

"She might have forgotten enough about home by now," the doctor said, "that it wouldn't bother her. Wouldn't it be nicer for you and the boy to be with her at home?"

"Maybe," I said, sounding uncertain.

"Take her for a day-trip somewhere or go somewhere overnight, maybe even a couple of nights. You have your grandson to help you. Maybe you could go up and visit your son?"

"You were the one who said Alzheimer's patients don't like change."

"Like you said, she's better. A change of scenery might do her good." He shrugged. "Might do you good. To be with her somewhere else." He started to get in his car, the door squeaked again.

"Hold on," I said, and went over to the van and came back with a little container of 3-in-1 oil I kept in the glove compartment. I oiled the hinges on the door, worked it back and forth till the creaking was gone. I went around and oiled the other door.

The doctor opened and closed the door a couple of times, shaking his head. "It's been squeaking like that for months," he said, like I had performed some complicated surgery.

I put the 3-in-1 oil in his glove compartment. "A drop now and then is all it takes."

Chandler thanked me, said he would see me next week, then started to get in his car, but instead he turned back around. He had a funny look on his face. "Mr. Marshbanks, this might seem like a personal question."

"Yeah?"

"How long has it been since you and Mrs. Marshbanks were . . ." He paused like he was searching for the right word. ". . . intimate?"

I cocked my head at him. "Come again?"

"When was the last time you and Mrs. Marshbanks had sex?"

"None of your business, son!"

"I ask this as your physician," he said.

"You could ask it as the goddamned King of Siam, and it would still be none of your business."

Chandler raised his hand. "I understand if you would rather not discuss it. It is, after all, a very personal matter."

I pulled out my handkerchief and wiped my forehead. I had worked up a sweat all of the sudden.

"It's something I should have brought up sometime back," he said. "When we first diagnosed Mrs. Marshbanks."

"It's been about a year," I said, not able to look at him.

"That's a long time," the doctor said.

"You're telling me," I said before I thought. I felt my face go red. I looked across the parking lot at the new development of houses, where the sun was starting to set, and thought of all the young couples over there starting out, not having the least notion that forty or fifty years from now was just a block away.

"A man has needs," I heard myself say. "Even an old man like me."

"Mrs. Marshbanks has needs, too," the doctor said. "Just because she has Alzheimer's, doesn't mean she no longer has desires."

"Sometimes she hardly knows me," I said.

"I wouldn't let that stop you."

"You saying that Irene ought to have relations with a stranger?"

Mr. Greathouse's daughter, who I hadn't noticed come out the front, walked past us on her way to her car. She gave us a look, then hurried to get in her car.

"It has been my experience," Chandler began, "that couples in which one of the partners has Alzheimer's can often still enjoy each other physically."

"Is that so?"

"Pleasure doesn't require memory."

"I don't want to take advantage of her."

"I'm not saying you *have* to have sex with her or even suggesting that you should necessarily."

"What are you saying?" I asked.

"Just that, if in the course of being with her, it should ever come up."

"That's the problem," I said. "I'm not sure that after all this time, it will come up." I glanced in the direction of my lower self.

"There's medicine I can prescribe for that."

"I don't want any."

"Viagra?"

"Whatever it's called. I don't want it. It's pathetic," I said. "All these old boys popping pills, jump-starting their equipment while the wives run for the hills."

"I have prescribed it for men thirty years younger than you and for more than a few women," he said.

"No," I said.

"It's true."

"Women, too?"

"Women, too," he said.

"Lord God."

We paused and looked out across the parking lot. I was surprised to hear myself talk about any of this to the doctor. I had never been one of those who liked to talk about it. Back when I had crews work for me, and the guys would sometimes go on about doing it with their wives or their girlfriends, I never liked that talk. Made me suspicious. Made me think most of them weren't doing anything of the kind, that talking about it was about as far as they got.

"Exactly what are you driving at with all this talk about taking a trip and the other business?" I asked.

"I am not driving at anything," Chandler said, rubbing his eyes like he was tired of trying to explain things to this thickheaded old codger. "All I am saying is that your wife is better, but probably not for long. You have a window of opportunity. As someone who has spent a lot of time with Alzheimer's patients, I have a feeling—and I could easily be wrong about this—that in two or three months, maybe less, we will see that window start to close." He paused.

"I see," I said, losing my voice a little bit. I felt a kind of tremor go through me, and I had a flash of old man Gudger sitting alone in his store.

"I don't want you to have regrets," Chandler said. "I don't want you wishing you had gone somewhere or done something with her while you still had the chance."

"You're about twenty years too late, Doc."

He paused, looking at me. "Mr. Marshbanks, as clichéd as this may sound, it is never too late."

"I know you mean well," I said, feeling my face heat up and my voice tighten. "But it is all I can do to see that she gets good care. To make sure the aides look after her. To make sure she is bathed and fed and has clean clothes and that she is treated halfway like a human being. It would be good if I could do more, if I could make more of the time we have left, but to tell you the truth, I don't have energy to do one iota more than I'm doing already."

"I understand," the doctor said.

"After a lifetime together, me and Irene's little boat is sinking, and I am treading water for the both of us, and as much as I would like to get us back to shore, it's all I can do to keep our heads above water."

The doctor nodded.

I looked back at the low brick building that was Rolling Hills. When I looked at it from the outside, I could see how sealed away my wife was. No sign of her out here. No sign of any of the people inside.

"Out of sight, out of mind," he said.

"What was that?" Chandler asked.

I shook my head.

"Mr. Marshbanks, you are doing all anybody could."

He glanced at his watch. "I better hit the road." He said he would check on Irene next week. I didn't say anything as he got in his car and drove off. I was pissed, mostly at myself, for talking about things that I never talked about. By talking about Irene and me, I had made us less than what we were. And as the doctor drove off, I felt robbed.

After he was gone, I stood there on the curb. The day's heat came up off the sidewalk. There weren't many cars left in the parking lot. Most of the visitors had gone home. Daughters and sons, the ones that lived close by and visited their father or mother regularly, had dropped by after work, done their duty, then headed home to their own families. While the few husbands or wives of the patients stayed through supper, then rolled their frailer halves back to their rooms, helped them get ready for bed, said good night, and drove on home fast, hoping to get there before dark, before the house settled into its nightly emptiness.

It was about that time I saw Dot come out the front door and hurry across the parking lot, moving faster than I had seen anyone move with a walker. She was making a break for it. Now and then she would look back over her shoulder, but no one was coming after her, no one had missed her yet. I thought about telling the staff. She might wander into traffic. But then she hadn't gotten hit in all the years she had been running away from Rolling Hills. She had gained the sidewalk on the far side of the parking lot when she saw me. She stopped, seeing what I would do. I waved her on. She started back up, headed toward the new development.

A couple of the aides came running out, calling, "Mrs. Miller. Mrs. Miller, come back!" Dot picked up her pace.

I walked back to Irene's room and found the TV off and Irene already in bed asleep, and Jackson, at the foot of her bed asleep in his chair, the book open on his chest. It was a long day out here for the little fellow. It didn't seem fair to coop him up every afternoon like this. Whenever I watched him sleep, I was always reminded of Newell when he was a boy.

The first few nights Jackson had started out in the bedroom upstairs, but most nights he ended up coming down and sleeping with me. The past couple of weeks I had said why didn't we cut to the chase and start out in bed with me. That way he wouldn't wake me in the middle of the night. Sometimes I woke anyhow. Not because of the boy. His nightmares had stopped. He didn't thrash around like some children. Before the boy came, I had been waking about two o'clock, like a lot of old folks. All the day's worries gathered in that silent hour—what I thought of as my fretting hour. The worries wouldn't let me sleep until I had sat up with them a while, mulling them over, one by one.

I nudged Jackson.

He blinked and sat up like I had caught him sleeping on the job. I pulled the blanket up around Irene.

"She asked where you had gone," he said, yawning and stretching. "I told her you were working down in your shop."

"What'd she say?"

"She said to tell you not to stay up too late," he said, getting up and stretching. I opened her closet, dragged out the dirty laundry bag, and slung it over my back. I stood over Irene, thinking about what the doctor had said. How much time did we have left? How long before I didn't even remind her of her father or her brother? How long before I was anyone, or worse, no one to her?

Out in the hall there was a commotion. The two aides were walking Dot back to her room, one on either side of her. "Mrs. Miller, you know better than to run off like that," one of the aides said, between breaths. "You might get hurt." Both the aides were huffing and puffing, wiping their foreheads and trying to catch their breath. Dot wasn't the least winded.

The residents came out of their rooms in their wheelchairs or with their walkers or canes and watched her go by with more than a little interest. One of their own had escaped and not in a coffin. One of their own had made it to the outside on her own power. After Dot had passed by, the folks still stayed out in the hall, looking at each other in a little different way, talking among themselves and trying to linger in whatever it was she had brought back with her. "Hope" was too lasting a word for what they hardly had time to feel before the aides came back and shooed them into their rooms.

On the way home, we stopped at McDonald's, ordered me a Big Mac and an iced tea, and ordered the boy a large order of fries and a large chocolate milk shake. We had decided to test how long a boy could survive on fries and shakes. At home, after Jackson fed the cats, we sat down at the kitchen table, taking the food out and eating on the bags. We had started in eating, when the phone rang.

"That'll be Newell," I said, checking my watch.

Jackson answered and talked to him a good while, telling him about the bike ride he and Billie had gone on that morning over Paris Mountain. Then he handed the receiver to me. Newell said he had been painting since early in the morning.

Jackson sat across from me, dabbing his french fries in a puddle of catsup and pretending not to listen.

I told Newell that Irene seemed some better. I didn't tell him the doctor's ultimate prediction.

"Maybe I can come down in a week or so," he said. "After I finish this next group of paintings. I have never painted so much in so little time." He paused. "I suppose there is no way y'all could come up."

"We might could manage it," I said.

The boy lifted his eyes from the table, looking at me.

"Really?" Newell sounded surprised.

"When should we come up?" I asked.

Newell didn't say anything for a minute.

"We don't have to come," I said.

"No, no," he said, like he was figuring it out. "When can you come?"

"Day after tomorrow," I said.

Jackson stood.

"Saturday," Newell said, like he was thinking it through. "Saturday would be okay. In fact, it would be good."

"We would come up for the night," I said.

"What about Mama?" Newell asked. "You think she'll be all right without y'all one night?"

Jackson had frowned at me, like he knew what his father had asked and the same question had come to him.

"We'll bring her with us," I said.

"Can you manage?"

"She's better. And with Jackson's good help, we can do it," I said.

After I hung up the phone, I picked up the rest of my hamburger and commenced to eat. Jackson came around the table and hugged me.

"That's all right, son," I said, setting the burger down and patting him on the back, but he kept on hugging me. "I'm trying to eat." Jackson didn't let go, and I'll be damned if about that same time one of those cats didn't jump in my lap like it knew—with that boy hanging on to me—there wasn't a damned thing in the world I could do except pet it.

Seven

The Place Where I Live

Saturday morning I woke the boy, fed him a big breakfast of fried eggs, grits, and biscuits. He had packed his backpack the night before, and I had packed a little bag for myself. He lingered over the breakfast table, chewing his toast and glancing at the clock. He took an ice age in the bathroom, brushing his teeth so long I called to him that they must be down to nubs. He was stalling, but I couldn't figure why. He had been so eager to see his father. Maybe he was having second thoughts.

When we got out to the van, I saw him check his watch and look over at Billie's house, then he said, "We're leaving earlier than you said."

"I forgot to tell the nursing home we were coming to take her this morning," I said, "so we'll have to get her ready ourselves. I want to get an early start."

He watched Billie's house as we drove off.

At Rolling Hills, we stopped by the dining room, but Irene wasn't in her usual seat. "She never showed," said Decatur, eating a bite of scrambled eggs.

"I saw her wandering the hall pretty late," said Mr. Greathouse, who had taken off his glasses, wiping them with his handkerchief, holding them up to the light, then wiping them again. "She might be sleeping in."

Dot picked at her breakfast, eating tiny forkfuls of grits and eggs. She looked up at the boy and half smiled, then went back to eating.

"You want my orange juice?" Decatur held his glass out to the boy.

Mr. Greathouse nodded toward Decatur. "Never seen nobody hate orange juice like that one does."

"For two years they been serving it to me," Decatur said, "and for two years I hadn't been drinking it. Seems like they'd get the message."

The boy took the glass and finished it off in three gulps.

"You want my eggs?" Mr. Greathouse asked Jackson. "I hadn't touched them." The old boys were always trying to feed Jackson.

"No thanks," Jackson said. "He gives me *plenty* of eggs." He nodded toward me.

Decatur threw down his fork. "Don't ask me how you can mess up scrambled eggs." He glared back toward the kitchen with his good eye.

"They don't know how to cook," Mr. Greathouse said matter-of-factly.

"The chef must've ma-quit-ulated cooking school." Decatur grinned. I could tell they wanted us to sit with them a while. Dot wasn't exactly a conversationalist. They liked having Jackson around.

"We better find Irene," I said. "We're taking her for an overnight trip to go see our boy."

"Good for you," Mr. Greathouse said, pulling his harmonica out of his shirt pocket and giving it a couple of celebratory toots.

"We're going to see my father," Jackson said.

"Well you tell him Decatur Dixon says he's done good, raised him up a fine specimen."

We said good-bye, then Jackson and I walked on around toward Irene's unit. I felt bad leaving those fellows, who didn't really belong in this place. Their minds were as clear as mine. Maybe clearer.

Most residents were up and about, but a few were still in bed, and when we came to Irene's room, we heard what sounded like Irene yelling, "How dare you! This is the place where I live!" The door was cracked. I started to hurry in, but something held me back. I motioned for the boy to scoot up behind me, and we slowly pushed the door open.

"Rise and shine, Mrs. Marshbanks. It's time to get up," the aide said. It was one of the new temporary aides. She was from the agency, which meant she had had even less training than the regular aides. She jerked up the blinds, and Irene squinted, shading her eyes with her hand.

"Get out," Irene snarled, clutching the sheet.

The aide, a tall, light-skinned colored woman, came over and, with one hard jerk, pulled the sheet off Irene.

Irene balled herself up on the bed and moaned. "Leave me by myself!" she cried. "Will everybody please leave me absolutely by myself!" The only other time I had ever heard Irene sound like this was the night I brought her back from Mildred's.

"Listen, lady, I would love to leave you alone, but I don't get paid to leave you alone. I don't have time for this. I have a unit full of folks waiting on me." She took hold of Irene's hand.

"Get away from me, you bitch!!" Irene scratched the aide's arm with her free hand.

"Now you've done it!" the woman said, looking at her arm. The woman scowled at Irene, grabbed her by both arms, and started yanking her. "Get your butt out of bed!"

Irene bared her teeth at the woman.

That's when I walked in.

"Well, hello, Mr. Marshbanks," the aide said, gently letting Irene back down onto the bed. Her tone went sweet as molasses. "How are you doing this morning? I see you brought your precious grandson." She patted Irene's hand. "Your wife is a sleepyhead this morning."

Irene pulled away from the aide, frowning, and rubbing her wrist. She smiled uncertainly when she saw the boy. He sat down beside her on the bed. Her hair was wild, and her nightgown was off one shoulder from where the aide had been pulling on her.

"We have had a little trouble getting out of bed," the aide said, trying to sense just how much I had seen. "Your wife scratched me," she said, showing me her arm.

I came over to the aide. While I wanted to do much much worse, I grabbed her wrist.

"What are you doing, Mr. Marshbanks?"

"Sit with your grandmother till I get back," I said to Jackson. I pulled the aide out of the room and up the hall.

"Mr. Marshbanks, what do you think you're doing?" She tried to pull away, and she wasn't a weak woman. "Where do you think you're taking me? Don't hold me so tight! You are hurting my wrist, Mr. Marshbanks."

She tugged, but I held on. "Somebody help me," she pleaded. The other aides, even the fellow the size of a small truck who rolled the cart of breakfast trays down the hall, only watched. They knew. They knew how she had been treating the patients. They just hadn't had the energy to do anything about it.

I hauled her to the nurse's station, but Linda, the head nurse, wasn't around.

"You are hurting me, Mr. Marshbanks."

I dragged her in the direction of the front offices.

"Mr. Marshbanks, I can't afford to lose this job." Her voice got panicked and whiny. "I have three children."

"You should have thought about that before you began yanking on my wife like a root in the ground."

"She scratched me. That's why I was having to be a little forceful."

I led her into the main office, where the secretary was at her desk. She jumped up, standing protectively in front of Mercer's door. "Can I help you?"

I brushed past her, pulling the aide into Mercer's office. Mercer was behind his desk, drinking coffee and eating a pack of powdered doughnuts. I yanked the aide up to his desk.

"What's going on here?" Mercer demanded, standing up and brushing powered sugar off his tie.

"I tried to stop him," said the secretary, tugging on her short skirt.

"I want this woman fired," I said, nodding at the aide.

"Pardon me?"

"When I arrived here this morning, I found her wrestling my wife, telling her to get her butt out of bed."

"Is this true, Natasha?" Mr. Mercer turned to the aide.

"You know how hard it is to try to get some of these folks up," the aide said, rubbing her wrist where I had been holding her. "Sometimes you have to be firm."

"Firm, hell! She's lucky she didn't dislocate my wife's shoulders," I said.

"She scratched me, Mr. Mercer," she said, holding up her forearm.

"Irene was defending herself," I said.

"She's a dangerous patient," the aide said.

"Not half as dangerous as the aide," I said to Mercer. "Why do you hire such sorry people?"

"I share your concern," said Mr. Mercer, tapping his fingers together and frowning at the aide, who was in tears. I felt a tad sorry for her, because it was Mercer and his ilk who had not trained her, who had paid her dirt, who had put her in a situation that brought out the worst in her.

"I will fully investigate the matter," said Mercer. He turned to Natasha. "You may return to your duties."

"Thank you, sir. Thank you so much!" she said. For a minute I thought she was going to kneel down and kiss his pinky ring. She ran out of the room.

"How can you let her go back to work after what she's done?!" I asked.

"We are short-staffed," he said. "If I send her home, then residents don't get fed, they don't get the attention they need."

"They can do without her kind of attention."

"If I find the allegations to be true, I will take appropriate action."

"All I know is that you better keep that woman the hell away from my wife," I said.

"I can request that she be transferred to another unit."

"You do that," I said.

"Mr. Marshbanks," he said very calmly, "it may be that your wife is becoming too aggressive for this facility. It may be she will require a lockdown Alzheimer's unit."

"All she requires is to be treated like a human being," I said, and walked out.

When I came out of the office, the secretary was pretending to do paperwork, but I knew she had been listening in.

"You better get on in there, honey," I said, nodding toward Mercer's office. "He's waiting on his *dic*-tation." As I walked away, I thought what a stupid thing for me to do. Another nail in Irene's coffin. He had pissed me off, saying Irene needed a lockdown unit. A goddamned prison!

On the way back to Irene's room, I couldn't shake the image of Irene baring her teeth at the aide. The doctor had been right. She was already worse again. She had been up late last night. She hadn't done that in a while. This morning she had looked downright vicious. The aide had been a bitch, but part of the reason she had been a bitch was because Irene was being difficult. For all I knew, maybe she did need a lockdown unit. I didn't see how I would manage an overnight trip with her. I'd have to call Newell and tell him we weren't coming.

When I walked into the room, there was Irene, dressed and sitting up in her chair, eating breakfast, composed and calm, like her old civilized self. Jackson stood beside her, buttering a piece of toast for her.

"Good morning," Irene said.

"Who dressed you?" I asked.

That's when I saw Billie. She had Irene's overnight bag open on the bed and was setting one of Irene's flannel nightgowns in it. "I hope you don't mind, but I packed for her," she said. "Jackson told me what happened with the aide. That's awful." She opened a drawer. "Does Irene have a sweater? It will be chilly up there at night."

I must have had a surprised look on my face as I went over to the closet, took down a blue cardigan, and handed it to Billie.

"I'm sorry," Billie said, folding the sweater and setting it in the suitcase. "Did you want to pack for her?"

I shook my head, looking at Irene, who didn't seem to have a trace of the anger she had been burning with a few minutes earlier.

"Sorry I missed you this morning," she said. "Jackson and I miscommunicated. He had thought we weren't leaving until eight."

I looked at the boy, who kept his eyes on the toast he was still buttering.

"You did invite me, didn't you?" Billie asked.

If I had been a bit quicker, I might have pulled it off, but I couldn't think of anything to say.

Billie's face turned red.

"Oh, I'm sorry," Billie said. "When Jackson came over yesterday he said you were going up to Penland to see Newell and that you had invited me to come along. When I saw you had gone this morning, I thought I had gotten the time wrong. I drove over here hoping to catch you."

I was looking at Irene. "Who dressed her?"

"I helped her get cleaned up," Billie said, "then we found one of the dresses, and she let me comb her hair back. Jackson tracked down a breakfast tray for her."

Irene smiled at Billie.

"I should have checked with you," Billie said to me. "I didn't dream Jackson wouldn't consult you." We both looked at Jackson.

"You've about buttered that toast to death," I said to the boy.

He blushed and set it down on Irene's plate.

I could tell by the way her jaw was working that Billie was put out with the boy, and I knew that the boy would feel bad about what he had done. I also saw, from what she'd done already, that Billie would be a lot of help with Irene, that Billie might make this little trip work.

"Well, now that you're here," I said, "why don't you come along?"

Jackson looked up at me.

"I don't want to barge my way into anything," she said.

"You aren't," I said. "You were invited."

Billie and I looked at the boy, whose face was still a bit red.

"To be frank," I said to Billie, lowering my voice, "I'm thinking you might be a big help with . . ." I nodded toward Irene.

"I don't know," Billie said.

"Jackson and I want you to come," I said.

"Yes," Irene said, taking a sip of coffee. "Wherever it is . . . we are destined." She smiled one of her hopeless little smiles.

"To see Newell," I said to Irene.

"Oh, good," Irene said. "I like him."

"I hope so," I said, "he's your son."

"He is, isn't he?"

"Newell doesn't know I'm coming," Billie said, closing up the little suitcase and setting it on the floor. "I don't want to get in the way of Jackson seeing his father."

"Newell won't mind," I said, hoping that to be true. I knew he wouldn't mind once he saw how much help she was with Irene.

Irene had stopped eating when she saw Billie set down her little suitcase. She frowned. "Prate," Irene said, catching me off guard. It had gotten to where I was surprised whenever she knew my name.

"Yes?" I sat down on the bed beside her chair.

"Am I going somewhere else?" She kept her eye on the suitcase like it was a dog that might bite.

"We all are," I said, putting my arm around her. "We're all going on a little trip. You, me, and Jackson." And I looked up at Billie. "And Billie. We're going together."

She sat back in her chair, looking relieved.

"We're going to see Newell at this confounded artists' commune."

"Colony," Irene said, correcting me. "Artists' colony."

"It isn't easy having an English teacher for a wife," I said.

Irene took another sip of coffee, then said to me, with mild surprise, "You're married?"

"To you," I said.

"Is that so?" she said, looking me up and down.

"What do you think?" I asked.

She dabbed her mouth with her napkin, refolded it, set it carefully on the tray, and said matter-of-factly, "I could have done worse."

Eight

Thinking of Something

It was a clear morning, a good day for driving, as I headed up U.S. 25 in the general direction of Jones Gap. Instead of taking a left through Traveler's Rest, we bore right, staying on 25. We passed a produce stand where a young boy, about Jackson's age, was lifting its big side doors. Beside it was a boiled-peanut stand tended by a man in overalls, maybe the boy's father. He had had his fire going for some time, the woodsmoke settling across the little valley like morning fog. Just down the road a woman hung quilts on a line in the front of a log cabin crafts shop. Around the curve was a shabby motel with a single pickup parked out front. A big fancy cursive sign that had seen better days said, *Pleasant View Motor Court*—the view being a field full of used school buses across the road.

We were in the upper reaches of Greenville County, where folks eked out a living the best way they could. Developers had not sunk their claws in here yet, but the bulldozers weren't far down the road.

The ride into the mountains was going better than I had led myself to expect. Irene, who sat next to me in the passenger's seat, seemed content, the way she studied everything we passed. Billie sat in the back with Jackson. She had thrown her sleeping bag and knapsack into the back of the van, leaving her pickup in the nursing home parking lot.

"I'm glad to get off that cruise ship," Irene said after a while.

I glanced at Billie in the rearview.

Linda, the charge nurse, a short dark Asian woman with smart brown eyes, had come into Irene's room as we were leaving. She had heard about the aide's behavior and apologized. "Natasha's a loose cannon," she said. "We've had several complaints. She won't be around much longer if I have anything to do with it." Then she reminded us about Irene's medications, gave us what she would need, and said, "I'm also including a sedative so she'll sleep through the night. We don't want her wandering off into the woods up there."

We had driven a little way up the mountain when Irene looked around. "It has been a long time since I have been on this road."

The last time had been for Sandy's funeral, but there was no need to remind her. It was the last time either of us had been up this way. I had never had the inclination to visit Newell on my own. Even now, some of my uneasiness about driving this highway was the fear that it might deliver us to the mortuary in Asheville where they had Sandy laid out, looking so young and with child.

Irene would turn around in the car seat to watch Jackson and Billie, who were in the back playing "I'm Thinking of Something." A guessing game where you tried to guess what the other person was thinking. I wouldn't play.

"He never liked car games," Irene said.

Billie knew how to play with the boy. She thought of things that weren't too easy or too hard like Thomas Jefferson or London, England, or a baseball mitt, which the boy would figure out in six or seven yes-or-no questions. Jackson went out of his way to stump her.

"I'm thinking of something," the boy said. I watched him in my rearview. He held Rudy in his lap. Rudy was keeping an eye on me.

"This isn't one of your weird impossible ones, is it?" Billie asked.

The boy shook his head.

"Is it a person?" Billie asked.

"No."

"Place?"

"Sort of."

"Jackson, are you sure this isn't a really weird impossible one?"

The boy scratched his nose.

"It's a thing?" she asked.

"Well, yes."

"What do you mean 'Well, yes'? Either it is a thing or it isn't."

"It's kind of all three," he said.

After Billie had used up her twenty questions, she threw up her hands. "I give."

"The inside of an eyeball," he said.

"The inside of an eyeball?" Billie put her hand to her forehead. "But of course! Why didn't I think of that? I'm just glad it wasn't one of your weird impossible ones."

"The inside of an eyeball," Irene repeated to herself, like it made perfect sense.

We were well up the steep eight-mile incline that wound through the mountains and eventually delivered travelers into North Carolina. A featureless four-lane that followed the ridges, it had replaced the original two-lane about twenty years ago. The old U.S. 25 was off to the right, hidden among the trees and the coves. It was a slow, meandering road that with all its curves and switchbacks ended up being twice as long a drive and twice as interesting. It passed by folks' houses and their little businesses—

apple houses, craft stores, and neat motels. We used to come up U.S. 25 when Newell was a boy. It cut right through the Greenville watershed, passing a pristine lake with miniature uninhabited islands all over it. Above the watershed, it followed the Green River into North Carolina. The old way gave you a real feel of going up into the mountains. The four-lane was nothing but a way to get there.

We had gone about halfway up the four-lane. The old van was starting to complain, so I slipped into low gear. I noticed a new gold-letter-engraved sign framed by rhododendron, which said, "Glassy Mountain Acres." Beyond the sign where I was used to looking out over a set of little mountains circling a quiet wooded valley, I saw in its place a golf course with a big pond in the middle and monster houses set out all around it. Beyond the golf course were red scars running through the valley, zigzagging up the mountainsides and cutting along the tops of the ridges—new-cut roads where new houses were being framed in.

I was wrong. The bulldozers had beaten us.

"Since when did that happen?" I said.

Irene looked down at the new golf course, and said, "Since Sandy died." She had known exactly where we were all along. That was the thing about Irene. I couldn't be sure at any given moment what she knew and what she didn't. Her mind was an unreliable compass that pointed true north every now and then.

"That was a sad day," she said.

"Can't believe they built all that in such a short time," I said, looking down at the golf course and hoping to steer the subject away from Sandy, especially with the boy sitting in the backseat.

"Sandy was a good wife," she said, "and a doting mother."

I glanced in the rearview. The boy didn't seem to have heard.

He was in the middle of trying to guess what Billie was thinking. "Would it squeal if I poked it with a sharp stick?" he asked.

"I loved Sandy as if she were my own," Irene said.

"Wonder what plans Newell has for us up at Penland?" I said.

"Newell will never get over Sandy's death," she said. It was something she used to say.

"Irene," I said under my breath. "The boy."

"He won't get over her either," she said.

Everything got quiet in the backseat, and I didn't look in the rearview.

"Irene," I whispered. "Think of the boy."

She turned around and looked at Jackson. "Death isn't something to get over, is it?"

I glanced in the rearview and saw Billie put her hand on the boy's shoulder. He hugged his dog and looked at Irene.

"Death is to be lived with," Irene said, looking kindly at the boy.

I might have turned the van around if there had been a place to turn around. I wanted to take Irene back to the nursing home, then call Newell and tell him to come get his boy.

Irene sat back in her seat and looked out over the mountains. A haze had gathered, as the sun rose higher, making the mountains gray and distant. We rode in silence for the rest of the way up the mountain.

We had reached the top, crossed over into North Carolina where the road flattened out, when Irene says, "I'm thinking of something."

The boy sat up in his seat, leaning toward her, and said quietly. "Is it a person, Grandma?"

She paused, then shook her head.

"Is it a place, Mrs. Marshbanks?" Billie asked.

Irene thought a minute. "I don't believe so."

"Well, then it's gotta be a thing," I couldn't help saying.

Irene turned to me, started to speak, hesitated, started to speak again, smiled her little hopeless smile, touched my hand on the steering wheel, and said, "It is whatever it was I was thinking."

The boy looked out the window and seemed somehow reassured by her lack of an answer. As the road leveled out, I could feel the engine stop straining.

An hour later we skirted Asheville, then headed north on Highway 19-23, stopping for lunch at the Stony Knob Restaurant, a diner, where we all got vegetable plates except the boy, who ordered a grilled cheese.

"You know what I've figured out?" I said to Jackson after the waitress, who looked a little familiar, set down the boy's plate.

"You're a vegetarian who doesn't eat vegetables," I said. I studied the waitress's face as she set the plates down.

The boy ate a potato chip and pointed to the big pile of them on his plate. "Technically, those are vegetables."

"What self-respecting boy is actually going to like vegetables?" Irene said to me, as the waitress set her plate down.

"He's the one claiming vegetarianship," I said.

Irene turned to Jackson and smiled, then she smiled at Billie the same way. "We're all here, together again." She gave Billie a puzzled look. "But where's . . . Where's the father?"

Billie looked at me, understanding and not knowing what to say.

"Newell?" I asked.

"Yes," Irene said.

"That's who we're on our way to see," I said, cutting a biscuit in two for Irene and starting to butter it for her.

"Then we'll all really be together," she said. "I have always wanted us to be in one place." She smiled kindly at Billie.

"Can I get y'all anything else?" the waitress asked in a thick mountain accent.

"Jones Gap," I said, pointing at her. "Down by the river that morning."

"I wondered if you'd remember." She smiled. "You changed my life by stopping and talking to us that morning."

"I did?"

"Right after that," she said, "my boyfriend and I had the biggest argument we ever had and broke up a week later."

"I'm sorry," I said.

"Best thing that ever happened to me," she said. She put her hand on my shoulder. She looked at Jackson. "I remember seeing your grandson that morning, too. He came up with your son." Then she looked at Billie. "You weren't with them."

"Oh," said Billie, swallowing a bite of mashed potatoes and waving her fork in the air, "I'm not with them. I mean, I'm not the mother."

Irene frowned at this.

"Y'all holler if you need anything," the waitress said, hurrying over to take another table's order. I watched her, remembering, with a pang of guilt, her boyfriend inviting me to have breakfast with them.

Irene leaned over to me, and while keeping an eye on Billie, whispered, "She says she's not the mother."

"She's not," I whispered back.

"Who is she?" Irene asked.

"Our next-door neighbor."

"I see," Irene said, biting into a biscuit and watching Billie.

Billie and the boy had heard everything but kept their eyes on their plates.

Irene, who must have been famished or maybe was just happy to be eating something other than Rolling Hills fare, fed herself, finishing before the rest of us. As the waitress cleared her plate, Irene asked where the lady's room was.

"There in the back." The waitress pointed to a latticework screen, which hid the doors to the bathrooms.

I started to help Irene, but Billie pushed her chair back. "I need to go, too," she said. She helped Irene stand and led her to the bathroom.

The boy and I ate in silence.

"That was conniving," I finally said, reaching over and eating one of his potato chips.

"I know they don't really count as vegetables," the boy said.

"I'm talking about you inviting Billie along on our trip behind my back."

The boy picked up his glass, took a big swallow of milk, then set it down and, wiping his mouth with the back of his hand, met my eyes. "I thought you wouldn't want her to come," he said.

"You thought right," I said.

The boy looked down.

"But," I sighed, "I have to admit, having Billie come along was a pretty good idea. She's already been a big help. And I have a feeling she's going to be a bigger help before it's all over."

The boy looked up.

"Just don't do it again," I said.

"Yes, sir."

About that time, the waitress brought out a tray full of four dishes of ice cream with chocolate sauce and whipped cream. She cleared the boy's plate and mine, then set the sundaes down in front of us.

"We didn't order dessert," I said.

"It's on the house," she said. "My way of saying thanks." She set the first one down in front of the boy.

"You didn't have to do that," I said to the waitress.

"You didn't have to speak your mind, but you did." She leaned over, kissed my cheek, then headed off to the kitchen.

"Your face has turned all red," the boy said.

"Eat your sundae," I said, taking a bite of mine.

After a good while had passed, Billie and Irene hadn't come back from the bathroom. "What do you think is taking them so long?" the boy asked.

"They're women," I said.

He looked at me as if he didn't understand.

"When women go into a bathroom, the actual going to the bathroom part is only one of a hundred tasks they perform in there."

"Is that right?" the boy said, looking off toward the bathroom like he was seeing it in a whole different light. "What do they do?"

"Nobody can say for sure," I said.

When they finally did come out, Billie was smiling uncertainly, and Irene seemed flustered as I pulled the seat out for her. She didn't let go of Billie's hand at first. "This girl," she said, shaking Billie's hand. "She . . . she threw me a lifesaver."

"She locked herself in the stall," Billie said, "and couldn't open it."

"What did you do?" I asked.

"I had to climb over the stall," Billie said, patting Irene on the shoulder and sitting down.

"Granddaddy said you were taking so long because you were women," the boy said, looking at me.

"He did, did he?" Billie raised an eyebrow at me.

"Thanks a lot," I said to the boy.

"Did you order the sundaes?" Billie asked me, taking up her spoon.

"They were on the house," the waitress said as she passed by with a tray of food for the table next to us. "For what he said to us that day."

"What did you say?" Billie asked me.

The waitress, who had had her back to us, turned around to Billie. "He said, 'This is the best time of your life.' " The waitress hurried back to the kitchen.

"What a good thing to say to somebody," Billie said.

"Unless it turns out to be a terrible time in their life," I said, "and they figure if this really is the best time of my life, I might as well end it all."

"Well, there's that," Billie said, taking another bite of sundae.

"I have considered ending it all," Irene said quietly. She licked whipped cream from her lips.

We all looked at her.

"Sometimes late at night in . . . in that place where I am kept, I consider putting an end to all these little forgettings with the one big forget." She glanced at me. "But then I remember you're out there remembering for the both of us."

I reached across the table and took her hand.

With her free hand, she shakily spooned up a bite of ice cream, but instead of putting it into her own mouth, she detoured it into mine.

Nine

Penland

Back in the van, we headed up Highway 19-23, a four-lane they were in the middle of building all the way up through the mountains to Johnson City, Tennessee, where it would meet with Interstate 26. They were blasting away mountaintops, raising valley floors, changing the course of more than one river.

We drove through the construction with the bulldozers and graders and dump trucks weaving in and out of each other, raising a mile-long cloud of red dust. The whole operation was organized bedlam, like ants running around, each knowing how to do his little part. I never had any interest in being an ant, which is why I never lasted on construction jobs or factory work. Took me half a dozen jobs to realize I was the only boss I could tolerate.

In a little while the highway forked. Highway 23 and its four-lane construction continued off to the left. We veered to the right on the Highway 19 part, a quiet two-lane which took us away from all the hubbub and threaded us deeper into the mountains of western North Carolina. It was a much gentler road than Highway 23, winding easily between tobacco allotments, corn fields, cow pastures, produce stands, neat brick houses tucked up against hillsides, and a trout pond with sprung couches set all around. Two-lanes were better for my blood pressure.

Irene, who napped more lately, had leaned her head back and fallen asleep. In the rearview I saw the boy had fallen asleep, too, slumped against Billie.

"Is that uncomfortable?" I asked her.

"Not at all," Billie said.

We passed a white church, which the sign out front said was the Forks of Ivy Baptist Church—the Ivy being the river the road had been built along.

"I hope Newell won't mind me showing up unannounced," Billie said.

"If he's in the middle of one of his painting series," I said, "he might not even notice."

She looked out the window.

I moved my eyes back to the road. "I mean he won't notice any of us," I said. I looked at her in the rearview mirror. "I mean, not that you care whether he notices you."

"What do you mean, Mr. Marshbanks?"

"I am a babbling idiot."

"Far from it," she said. "You are one of the smartest men I have ever met."

"That doesn't say much for the men you've met."

"Mrs. Marshbanks was right about you."

I glanced over at Irene still sound asleep. "What'd she say about me?"

"She said that you could be a self-deprecating son of a gun."

It sounded like Irene, yet it surprised me that she had talked about me to this girl. It made me wonder if I didn't know Irene as well as I thought. I could have written it off to the Alzheimer's.

Bill Chandler said it changed people. On the other hand, maybe it just meant that even if you were married to someone for fifty years, you had no business thinking you knew them.

I had my window rolled down. The air became dank and cool. The road curved more, and mountains rose around us, closing in. As the road climbed the mountains, it lifted us above the river. It was more remote up this way. Fewer houses, more woods. As the crow flies, we were only twenty miles from Asheville, but we had to thread our way through big mountains. Penland was a good hour's drive.

Newell had given me directions over the phone last night when he called to double-check that we were still coming. He had sounded more excited about our visit than the night I sprang the idea on him.

We turned north on a road that was even more closed in, with houses and pastures pressed up against the road by the steep hillsides. With a single shove, the whole landscape might have toppled over.

Irene sat up, yawned, and looked around.

"Almost there," I said.

"Almost where?"

"Penland."

She folded her hands into her lap. "We're going to see . . . my son."

"*Our* son," I said.

She looked at me dubiously. She turned around in her seat and saw Billie and the boy, who was awake, too.

For three weeks he had done his best to keep under wraps how much he missed Newell, but the way he leaned forward and gripped the back of my seat told me he couldn't contain it much longer. "How far now?"

"A couple of miles," I said.

Finally, the road leveled out, and there was a small sign, WEL-
COME TO PENLAND SCHOOL. I had never been to an art school, unless you counted the drives Irene and I made to the University of
South Carolina to visit Newell. I had pictured Penland with low,
flat buildings like Frank Lloyd Wright might have designed. I had
actually painted a house next door to a house in Greenville that had
been designed by Wright. I never saw what all the fuss was about.
Looked to me like he had taken a regular house and stretched it out.

We drove down the road to a settlement of cabins, houses, and
other buildings that looked like a neighborhood, not much different than what we had been driving past the last thirty miles.

"This is it?" I asked. "Looks like everywhere else we have passed."

"I think that's the point," Billie said.

I parked by a big rambling building, which stood central
among the smaller cabins and buildings. Turned out to be the dining hall. I opened the van door for Irene and tried to take her
hand. She waved it away.

"I can manage," she said impatiently. Although I stood close by
in case she should slip, she had no trouble walking. She was very
alert. The more distance we had put between Rolling Hills and
Irene, the better she seemed.

"What an inspiring setting," Irene said, looking at the fields and
trees and the cabins set out all around. A big pasture fell away from
cluster of buildings, giving a good view of the mountains in the distance. "So bucolic." She was even pulling out some of her English
teacher words. Vocabulary was a gauge with Irene—the bigger the
word, the better she felt.

What I had mistaken for cows in the pasture, weren't cows at
all. "What're those?" I asked.

"Alpacas," Jackson said.

I looked at the boy, surprised at his knowledge.

"I imagine they collect their wool and weave with it," Billie said.

"Ugly critters," I said, as one of the alpacas loped over to the fence where we stood and pursed his big lips at us. We didn't see anyone among the buildings. "Where is everybody?"

"Working," Billie said. "Either they are in studio or class. People pay a lot to come here and take courses and workshops, unless you're invited like Newell."

"Speaking of Newell. Where the hell is he?" I asked.

"When did you say we would be here?" Billie asked.

"Around three," I said.

"It's not even two," Billie said, checking her watch.

The four of us walked up the dining hall stairs. I held Irene's elbow, but she didn't need me to. She was steady on her feet. The dining hall looked like it had been added on to half a dozen times, tacking on rooms whenever needed. We found a big, bearded fellow in the kitchen, wearing an apron and cutting up onions on a chopping block. He looked up at us, tears in his eyes and a fierce expression on his face.

"Mr. Marshbanks." He set the knife down on the chopping block, dabbed his eyes with his apron, and shook my hand with a grip like a vise.

"I'm Paul," he said. "Paul Schulman."

Paul Bunyan was what I was thinking, as I flexed my fingers. The way he studied me made me uncomfortable. "The resemblance is uncanny." Then he took Irene's hand gently. "And you're Mrs. Marshbanks."

"Hello," Irene said.

Paul smiled at the boy. "And the infamous Jackson." The man's voice was so deep the dishes rattled in the dish drain. Then the big fellow noticed Billie, who had been standing back a little. "Welcome."

"I'm Billie," she said. "A family friend."

"We're early," I said.

"Newell said you're always early, Mr. Marshbanks," he said. "He asked me to keep an eye out. He's down in Squire's Orchard, where he's been every day since he got here."

"Could you point us in the right direction?" I asked.

"I'll take you to him," Paul said, untying his apron and draping it neatly over a chair.

"That's not necessary," I said.

"I need a break from the onions." He wiped his eyes with the back of his hands. So we followed big old lumbering Paul out of the dining hall and down a dirt road. I remembered how the BellSouth man had led us back to Rolling Hills that afternoon when Irene and I had gotten lost. Had I reached the point in life when I needed to be led everywhere?

We passed cabins and buildings that were thrown together, or at least they were built to look thrown together. When I got closer I saw they had been built to look old. One log cabin we passed must have just been finished. The place didn't resemble any school I had ever seen. More like a shantytown for artists. The disgraceful thing, the thing I couldn't get over, was that here was a school for painters and such, and more than half the buildings were in sore need of a paint job.

The boy ran ahead. Irene and Paul walked in front and Billie and me walked behind.

"So you're the chef?" Billie asked him.

"I'm a woodworker," Paul said. "I make bowls out of tree trunks. But all the artists take turns preparing meals. It just happens I'm cooking this week. I hope you all like tempeh."

"We're having watercolors for supper?" I asked.

Paul smiled. "Newell said you had a great sense of humor."

I looked at Billie, who leaned over and whispered, "Not tempera. Tempeh. It's made out of soy beans."

"Soy beans?"

"Many here are vegans," Paul said.

"Sounds like a cult," I said.

"Means no dairy products," Billie said. "No milk, no cheese. No animal products of any kind."

"No eggs?" I asked.

Paul shook his head.

"Then that lets Granddaddy out," Jackson said from up ahead.

Paul pointed out a hidden gravel drive. "Our cabins are up there," he said. "You want to wait here, and I can bring him back?"

"Good idea," I said, "We don't want Irene to overdo it."

"Nonsense," Irene said, having taken a liking to Paul. "Lead on." So we followed him farther down the road, and I couldn't get over how easily Irene was walking. We passed another cluster of buildings, which Paul said were the residential artists' studios. We passed a large yellow brick oven—a much bigger version of Billie's kiln.

"You could fire a thousand pots in there," the boy said, poking his head in the open front of it.

We walked on a little farther, and I happened to look down in a wooded hollow where a whitewashed church stood in the middle of a clearing. It had no sign, identifying it with one denomination or another. From where we stood it looked like somebody maintained it.

Paul led us down a grass path that veered off before we actually reached the church.

"What's the story with that place?" I asked.

"I'm not sure," Paul said. "It's not part of the school. It's not on Penland property, and as far as I know, nobody uses it. I've never seen anybody come or go."

"But it looks kept up. Have you been in it?"

"I've been down in those woods looking for fallen trees," Paul said, "but I never went inside."

I looked back at the church once more, then followed Paul and the rest of them down the grass path. The path followed a rushing creek full of tiny waterfalls the boy couldn't resist hopping in.

"I'm glad you've come," Paul said. "Newell needs a break. He's up at the crack of dawn, and he's out there sometimes till last light. If I didn't come get him, I think he might paint all night."

"How do you know my son so well?" I asked.

"We're the only fellows up here this summer."

"Is that a fact?" I asked. No wonder Newell was all fired eager to get up here, although he hadn't seemed to take much interest in the opposite sex since Sandy died.

Billie read my mind. "He means they were chosen to come here for free and work on their art," she said. "That's what a fellow is. Can be a man or woman."

The terrain began to open up, and the creek widened into a stream. The rhododendron and laurel gave way to a meadow of ferns, May apple, and trillium. Their leaves trembled in the breeze. A little farther, the meadow opened onto a long-neglected apple orchard on the side of a hill, with a valley below and the mountains beyond. The air felt so much lighter and cooler. It didn't weigh you down like it did in the summer in Greenville. We walked along the rows till we spotted Newell at the far end with his back to us, painting. Among the gnarled apple trees with their unpruned limbs, he looked like a boy standing in the shade of shaggy old men.

As we approached I saw he had on shorts, sandals, and a straw hat a little like the hat van Gogh used to wear to keep the sun from driving him mad, according to the movie *Lust for Life* Irene and I went to almost forty years ago.

Newell didn't seem to hear us. The wind singing in the trees might have been at least part of why he didn't hear us. Still, you would have thought with us talking and tromping our way through the grass he might have heard something.

Paul motioned for us to stop, like a guide on safari who has spotted a lion. "See you all tonight," he said in a low voice like he didn't want to be the one to interrupt Newell. Then he lumbered back up the path.

We walked down the row toward Newell. The grass was a foot high. I took Irene's elbow, afraid she might fall on this uneven ground. We were fifteen feet away, and he still hadn't turned. Any other time Jackson would have bolted the rest of the way, but he was held in check, as were we all, by his father painting—if that's what you wanted to call it. Looked more like he was punishing the canvas, the way he jabbed and swiped and smacked it with his brush. As we neared we saw he was painting a quiet, calm scene of afternoon light streaking across the valley. It was hard to believe that such a still and tranquil picture could come from such fierce brushstrokes.

We watched him storm around in front of the canvas until the boy couldn't stand it any longer, ran up to Newell, and hugged him around the waist. Newell turned around with that same empty expression he always had whenever he was painting. I could see him come back into himself, like some hypnotist offstage had snapped his fingers. He gave the boy a big hug, then kissed Irene's cheek. "You made it, Mama!" Then he turned to me. "She walked all the way down here?"

"She was determined," I said.

Newell frowned when he noticed Billie standing off to the side. For a minute I thought we had made a mistake.

"You remember our neighbor, Billie Athens?" I said.

"I apologize for showing up unannounced like this," Billie said. "Your father was kind enough to let me tag along."

Newell studied her, as the boy leaned against him, then seemed to come to some conclusion in his head. "Jackson has spent a lot of time with you," he said. "You've been very kind." I had worried that Billie showing up might irritate Newell, even set him off. After all, it had only been a few weeks ago that he had turned on the boy on our fishing expedition.

"I love your work," Billie said, stepping up to the easel.

"Thanks," Newell said, frowning again, but this time at the painting.

Irene came over, looked at the painting with Billie and, after studying it a while, said, "The mountains remind me of . . . the Frenchman, the man who painted the mountains over and over."

"Cezanne," I said.

Everybody turned to me, like all of the sudden they didn't know me.

"Can't a man know a thing or two?" I asked.

Irene began to look tired, and Newell helped her onto a canvas foldout stool. He squatted beside her and held her hand. "How have you been?" he asked.

Irene turned to me. "How have I been?"

"Better," I said.

"Really?" she asked.

"Good enough to make a fool of me two or three times today," I said.

"Oh," she said, waving her hand. "That's no test."

Jackson had wandered to the edge of an old barbed-wire fence that must have once marked a farmer's pasture. He was picking blackberries and eating them.

Billie still stood in front of the half-finished painting. I stepped up beside her and examined the picture again. I liked it, but even if I hadn't, I wouldn't have said word one. When I was a boy, my father was hard on me when I worked with him in his butcher shop. Either I left too much fat on the meat or I wrapped it sloppily or he couldn't read the price I'd printed on the package. That's why I went into an altogether different line of work. When Newell was born, I swore I would not do him the way my father had done me. That's not to say I didn't slip up almost always. I took it as a sign that I had not altogether failed in the end, when my boy wound up with a paintbrush in his hand, even if it wasn't for painting houses.

Jackson put a fistful of blackberries into my hand. I popped a couple into my mouth. "Man, those are sweet," I said.

Newell packed his paints and folded his easel, then we headed back up the path. Irene and I brought up the rear, following Newell carrying the unfinished painting and Billie with the easel. They walked ahead of us, caught up in conversation. The boy trudged behind them, struggling with Newell's case of oil paints. The look on Jackson's face reminded me of the look he had worn three weeks ago at Jones Gap when he had watched his father drive off without him. As I was thinking, *What kind of son have I raised?,* Newell stopped in midsentence and, looking back, waited for Jackson.

Ten

Storm Walking

Newell's cabin was tucked so deep among the hemlocks that even though Paul pointed it out to us earlier, I might have walked right by it if Newell had not been with us. We turned in at the gravel drive and found ourselves in front of two log cabins about thirty feet apart. Newell's Subaru was parked in front of one and Paul's old pickup was in front of the other. There were a couple of big sections of tree stumps lying in the front of Paul's cabin, along with a carpet of shavings, which Jackson ran over to inspect.

"Is this where he makes his bowls?" he asked, letting some shavings fall through his fingers.

"He cuts them out of the stumps out here," Newell said, "and does the finish work up on his porch or in the studio."

Both cabins had tin roofs and long front porches. I helped Irene onto Newell's porch, which seemed as big as the rest of the house, with an old green glider and several rockers painted white. Inside, there was a small den with a smaller kitchen, a bathroom, and a tiny bedroom. Tight quarters made even tighter by all the paintings we had to wade through. Canvases were propped everywhere—

against walls, on the mantel, against the fireplace, against the re-frigerator, even on the back of the toilet.

It took a minute to absorb that all these paintings were Newell's. All involved that orchard in one way or another. Some were of the valley as seen through the orchard, some of the mountains as seen through the orchard. Some of the orchard as seen from the meadow. Some of the meadow as seen from the orchard. Some of the sun ris-ing on the orchard and some of the sun setting on the orchard. There must have been at least fifty or sixty orchard paintings set out all over Newell's cabin.

"Have you painted all these since you have been up here?" Billie asked.

Newell nodded.

"Is this a gallery?" Irene asked seriously.

Now I could see why Newell hadn't wanted to come down to Greenville. He had painted more in three weeks than he had in three years.

With stacks of dirty dishes in the sink, clothes tossed over the furniture, empty Diet Coke cans and Almond Joy wrappers on about every level surface and a too-ripe odor coming from somewhere, the cabin was home to a man possessed. The mess was a welcomed sight. Standing at the center of this explosion of paintings, I saw that my unshaven, disheveled boy was climbing out of his grief. So I did what fathers down through the ages have managed to do—held my tongue.

Billie walked around the cabin with her hands behind her back like she was in a museum. She paused in front of one canvas after another. "They're different," she said.

"You think?" Newell asked, coming up beside her and looking at the painting with her.

"From your other work," she said, stopping in front of another one. "They're richer."

"Happy," Irene said, looking at one.

"Really?" Newell frowned.

"That's exactly what they are," Billie said.

"Not Norman Rockwell happy I hope," he said.

"More like Chagall," Billie said.

Newell stopped looking at the painting and was now looking at Billie.

She blushed. "I'm sorry. I got caught up in them. I've never been around a real artist in the middle of producing his paintings."

"I didn't mean to make you self-conscious," Newell said. "It's just that everything you say is . . . well, remarkable."

"It's your paintings that are remarkable," she said. There was an awkward pause.

"Something stinks," the boy said, wrinkling his nose.

"I smell it, too," I said.

Newell looked around at the cabin and gave us a sheepish shrug. "I'm sorry about the mess," he said. He started picking up his clothes off the floor. "I sleep out here," he said, pulling a couple of T-shirts from under the couch. "That way I don't have to bother with making a bed. I've been doing like you used to, Daddy. I wake at five, eat a bowl of Shredded Wheat, and head down to the orchard in time for the sunrise."

"I never ate Shredded Wheat," I said.

"When I was a kid, you did," he said.

"Never," I said.

"I remember you tearing open the little paper wrappings they come in," he said.

"I guess I know what I ate," I said.

"You used to cut up bananas on it," Irene said. "Sprinkled brown sugar over it."

I looked at Irene. My wife couldn't hardly remember my name, but she remembered what I had for breakfast forty years ago.

Newell got a garbage bag out of the kitchen and gathered drink cans, candy bar wrappers, and other trash strewn about. Then he headed to the bathroom, armed with a sponge and a bottle of Lysol.

Deciding to help, I led Irene to a rocker on the front porch. Thunder rumbled in the distance, several mountains away. She sat back in the chair and breathed deep.

"Call me if you need anything," I said.

She looked out at the sun-dappled woods.

"I'll see if I can help Newell straighten up the place."

"You do housework?" She laid her head back in the chair and closed her eyes. Something told me not to leave her alone out there on the porch, but if I paid attention to every premonition that came along, I wouldn't get out of bed in the morning.

I went in the kitchen, figuring I would tackle the mountain of dishes. Jackson was already at the sink, up to his elbows in soapsuds. At home he had taken to washing the dishes after supper without my asking.

"What is that foul smell?" I said.

Jackson nodded disgustedly to the trash can in the corner, over-flowing with melon rinds, apple cores, pork and beans cans, chicken bones, and other less identifiable remnants.

"You figured you'd rather wash the dishes than deal with this," I said, standing over the garbage.

The boy grinned down at the soapy water. Ever since we had gotten up here, I felt more comfortable with the boy, and unless I was off the mark, he felt more comfortable with me.

"Your daddy has been too busy painting to take out the garbage."

I toted the whole stinking business outside and emptied it into a big covered trash can. I found a broom and a dustpan on the little back porch and started on the cabin floors, which, judging from the dust balls, had not felt the brush of a broom since Newell had arrived.

While Jackson tackled the dishes, Billie had come in, found a clean dish towel, and started drying and putting them away. I swept my way through the kitchen and out into the hallway. Newell had started in on his bedroom, straightening and changing the sheets. I went in to see if the room needed sweeping.

"Let me help with the sheets," I said, leaning the broom against the wall.

"Thanks," Newell said, handing me one end of the fitted sheet, which I tucked in.

"Mama looks good," Newell said, tucking in his end of the sheet. "Rolling Hills agrees with her."

I had already decided not to mention the ugly scene with the aide.

"Jackson looks good, too," he said, handing me one end of the top sheet, which I tucked in. "He doesn't seem as moody."

"He's a good boy," I said.

"He is," he said, folding the bedspread back over the pillows. "Especially considering all he's been through. There's nothing much worse than losing your mother when you're five years old."

"You've done your best by him, Newell."

"He's had a good time with you," he said. "I could tell the moment I saw him down in the orchard."

"He's done wonders for Irene," I said. "I'm a little worried about what'll happen when he leaves."

"We'll visit more."

"It would mean a lot to Irene," I said.

"And, Daddy, I want to help pay for the nursing home," he said. "I got a substantial raise at the college, and my paintings are selling well."

"That won't be necessary," I said, picking up the broom and sweeping. "We're getting by."

"I know you are," he said. "That's not the point . . ."

"I don't want to talk about it," I said, still sweeping.

He paused. I guess he decided he better change the subject. "You and Mama will sleep in here tonight," he said.

I stopped sweeping. "What about Billie?"

"She can have the couch," he said.

"Where will you and Jackson sleep?"

"In sleeping bags on the front porch," Newell said. "Jackson is excited about it."

"Why don't we let Billie sleep with Irene?" I said. "The bed is more comfortable. I'll take the couch."

"I won't hear of it," Billie said, sticking her head in the bedroom. "You sleep with your wife."

"Talk some sense into this girl, Newell," I said.

"She just said she wouldn't hear of it," Newell said. "You and Mama sleep in here."

"Suit yourself," I said, but what I didn't say was that Irene and I hadn't slept together since she had gone into Rolling Hills. Would she want me to sleep with her? Would sleeping with me be like sleeping with a stranger? If worse came to worst, I could always sleep on the floor.

"Some host," Newell said, after we were done cleaning the house and all sitting out on the porch with Irene. "Y'all didn't even have a chance to sit down before I put you to work."

It thundered again. It had been thundering louder, and, as we cleaned the house, the woods had darkened gradually, like a premature night. The breeze had picked up.

"I smell rain," Irene said, raising her head.

"It storms up here almost every afternoon," Newell said.

It thundered again, a little closer.

I went off to the bathroom to piss and found myself staring at a painting of a mother bear and two cubs in the orchard. I carried the painting out to him and asked if he had seen bears.

"They're eating blackberries right where I was picking them," Jackson said.

"That's right," Newell said. "Some evenings, about nine o'clock, as the sun sets, this mother bear shows up with her two cubs to eat the blackberries in that same patch. At first they would run away when they saw me, but they've gotten used to me."

"Can we go see them?" Jackson said.

"After supper, we'll walk down."

Newell took Irene's hand. "Would you like some tea, Mama?"

She looked up at him.

"Hot tea?" Newell asked. "Would you like a cup?"

"Indeed," she said.

"Let me make it." Billie headed off to the kitchen without giving Newell a chance to object.

"Daddy, if you give me your keys, I'll drive the van down from the dining hall," Newell said, "and we can unload your things."

"I don't mind doing it," I said.

"You sit here and relax with Mama," Newell said. "Jackson can come with me." Jackson brightened at this. He would finally be alone with his father. And my ankle had started aching. So I gave Newell the keys. About ten minutes after Newell and Jackson left, the breeze picked up, there was a flash of lightning, and it thundered close by.

"You want to move inside?" I asked Irene.

"No," she said, her face turned in the direction of the oncoming storm.

There was another flash of lightning and a crack of thunder right after it, then we heard a hard rain approach through the trees, until it was drumming loud on the tin roof.

"Hope they didn't get drenched," I said, having to talk loud.

Irene became very still, as the rain drummed louder. The trees tossed all around us, the leaves making big sweeping noises. A good-sized limb dropped off one of the hemlocks and thudded down beside Newell's Subaru. The air cooled down considerably, and little clouds of spray blew across the porch. Irene shivered, her hair blown back by the wind. I went inside to get her the jacket I'd seen hanging on the nail inside the door. When I came back she was gone.

"Irene?"

I saw her standing out in the rain, holding her hands up to the sky as it lightninged and thundered.

"Irene!" I ran down the steps and grabbed her.

"Let go!" she screamed. She slapped me hard and pulled away, but I grabbed her again. "Let go!" She tried to hit me with her fist, but I grabbed both arms and dragged her back toward the porch.

"Let's go back," I said.

"No, no, no," she said, trying to pull away. I lifted her off the ground and carried her, like an angry child, back to the porch with her kicking at the air. As we reached the porch, another hemlock limb crashed down close to where she had been standing.

I forced her into the glider, but kept hold of her arms. My cheek still stung from where she had slapped me. She stopped struggling and went limp. She sat back in her seat and frowned, sticking out her lower lip. Her hair was wet and pasted to her face.

"Are you trying to get yourself killed?" I shouted, pointing at the hemlock limb that would've done both of us in.

She looked at me, then out at the rain. "I like it out there," she said, sounding very sad. Then she looked up at me. "I've always liked it out there." And the regret in her voice came from the part of her that I had heard from less, the part that watched what was happening to her. "I always liked it out there," she said, her face about to crumple.

"Don't cry," I said. I sat beside her and put my arm around her. "It's going to be all right." As I dabbed the tears from her cheeks with my handkerchief, she started shivering.

"You're sopping wet," I said. "I'll go get a towel if you promise to stay put. We need to get you out of these clothes."

"Stay," she said, grabbing my arm in a desperate way. Since I couldn't be sure she wouldn't run right back out there, I sat with her until the rain began to slacken, leaving only the sound of water rushing down the gutter pipes. The dripping woods began to lighten, the wet leaves shiny and deep green in the reemerging dappled light. Out of nowhere, a tiny dust-colored bird appeared on the limb of a sapling off the porch and began to sing his heart out, like he was trying to tell us something. There was a rush of cool air that felt like a lid had been lifted on the atmosphere.

I looked at the hemlock limb where Irene had been standing, then, as if she could read my mind, she took my hand, and I could tell by the easy way she held it, that, for the moment at least, she was with me.

"Remember that time up at Jones Gap?" I said.

"Yes," she said. I had no idea if she did or not.

"That was back in your storm-walking days," I said.

She nodded, but who knew?

It was after we had been married, and we had been camping at

Jones Gap. A thunderstorm had come up, and we were in our tent. Lightning struck all around. We had the tent flap pulled back and were watching the storm, when a bolt struck a tree thirty feet right in front of us. There was a pop, followed by a sizzle, and a huge limb splintered off.

"Let's go look at it," Irene had said. With lightning still striking all around, Irene strolled out of the tent. It was like watching somebody calmly cross a battlefield with artillery going off all around. What I hadn't altogether known at that early point in our marriage was, if Irene wanted to do something, there wasn't a thing in the world I, or anybody, could do to stop her.

I hollered after her, but she didn't turn around. I went after her, my heart pounding, as another bolt struck nearby. When I reached her, she was soaked but didn't care. She was interested in the scorch mark up the trunk. You could smell the burnt wood.

"Isn't it astonishing?" she said, her hair plastered to her face.

"Now let's get back to the tent before we end up like this tree," I said.

"Lightning never strikes twice in the same place," she said.

"That's not a fact," I said.

Then she kissed me.

"What are you doing?" Another bolt of lightning struck somewhere behind us. "We're going to die."

"Sooner or later," she said, and kissed me again.

"I'd rather it be later," I said, pulling away. "Besides, you're soaked. And now I'm soaked."

"You're right," she said, and began to unbutton her blouse.

"What are you doing?" Lightning crackled somewhere off to the right.

"Getting out of these wet things," she said, taking off her blouse, then stepping out of her pants so that she was standing there in the hard rain with not a stitch on.

"What if someone comes by?"

"In the middle of a thunderstorm?"

Then she started unbuttoning my shirt, but I stopped her.

"At least let's go back to the tent."

She kept unbuttoning and unzipping my clothes until she had me standing there beside her in the middle of this storm stark naked.

There was a huge clap of thunder that was so close I felt the displaced air at my back. Unfazed, she placed my hands on her breasts slick with rain. Before I knew what had happened, she had pulled me down right beside that smoldering tree and, with the air reeking of ozone, she made love to me on a bed of wet leaves. She sat on top of me, guided me into her, then leaned over me, her wet hair grazing my cheeks and at one point when I looked up at her, the lightning seemed to radiate from her head, like a jagged crown.

Later she said she believed Newell was conceived then. Given our boy's temperament, she might have been right.

It took Newell, Jackson, and me to drag that hemlock limb off to the side of the house. Earlier, Billie had brought out the tea and been surprised to find me sitting with a soaked Irene. She had led her into the bedroom to help her change out of her clothes.

"This thing is heavy," Newell said, grunting with effort, as we slid it into the woods behind the cabin. When we got it there, we stood around tugging on the branches, stroking the bark, crumpling the needles in our hands, and smelling them.

"There's an aphid that's killing hemlocks," Newell said, nodding back to the tree looming over the cabin. "It decimated them in the Northeast, and now it has started down here. They've found them in the Smokies. Came over from Japan or China."

"That's a shame," I said. Hemlocks were among my favorite trees. Hemlocks cleared out the woods beneath them, making a kind of shaded meadow.

"Seems like just about everything is endangered in one way or another," Newell said.

"A tiger swallowtail," the boy said, spotting a butterfly on the edge of the woods and sprinting off after it with the butterfly net Billie had given him last week. She'd also given him an identification book.

Newell and I walked back around to the front porch. Irene was sitting in the glider, wearing a dry blouse and dry slacks. Her hair was wet but combed. She looked peaceful, content. There wasn't a trace of the ornery child I had had to carry, kicking, out of the rain. Her fit had passed like the storm. Billie hung Irene's dress on a little clothesline on the other side of the cabin.

Newell sat down beside Irene in the glider as an amused expression came over his face. "Not everybody sees storms the way we do," Newell said, taking Irene's hand. When he was in college, he often headed to the coast when tropical storms were about to hit. This wasn't something he told us about at the time. It came out when he had a whole show of hurricane paintings, where the grass, the trees, the rain all seemed to blow off the paintings, like the center of gravity was to the side.

The boy ran up on the porch, holding the butterfly in his cupped hands. "It's a tiger swallowtail," he said. "Swallowtails get their names because of their swallowlike wings."

"So you collect them?" Newell asked.

"I look at them and let them go."

"Sort of like he fishes," I said, clearing my throat.

"Butterflies only live a few weeks," Jackson said to Newell. He showed the butterfly to all of us, then he walked back outside and opened up the net. He watched the butterfly zigzag its way toward the woods.

"He's keeping a list of each kind and how many he catches," Billie said to Newell.

"What a great idea," Newell said. "It gets him outside and interested in nature."

"Oh, she's gotten him interested in nature all right," I said, "Instead of helping me pull weeds, he spends most of his time trampling my beans and my okra, chasing down butterflies." I took off my glasses and wiped them on my shirt. We sat there on the porch, listening to the rain drip from the trees. A cicada landed on the power line and started singing.

"I am glad to be away from . . ." Irene began to say but paused. ". . . that place I am kept." She had not taken her eye off the boy, who stood in a shadowy place on the edge of woods where the butterfly had disappeared.

Newell and Billie and I looked at each other.

Irene kept her eye on the boy, who had raised his net and stood very very still, facing the woods.

Eleven

Irene Holds Court

We ate supper at the dining hall with all the other artists. Newell introduced us around as we stood in a serving line with painters, sculptors, printmakers, and potters. Paul and a couple of other artists were behind the line, piling plates with undercooked vegetables, dirty-looking rice, and rubbery strips of something that, if you asked me, looked more suited for insulation.

"That's the tempeh," Billie said, seeing me stare at the steaming plate one of the fellows had handed me.

"Looks like something I might winterize my house with," I said.

I sat Irene at one of the big long tables so she wouldn't have to stand in line, brought her plate, and went back for mine. I sat on one side of Irene, and Newell sat on the other with Billie beside him. Jackson sat beside me. I started cutting up Irene's food, but she shooed me away and cut it herself. Irene was in the best form I had seen her in since her pre-nursing-home days. The Rolling Hills dining room ladies wouldn't have given us any lip this evening.

After we had been eating a while, Paul, who had sat down across from us along with other artists, asked Irene, "What was your greatest challenge as an English teacher, Mrs. Marshbanks?"

Irene thought about it a minute. "Getting to school on time," she said. Everybody laughed, although I knew she hadn't been joking. She was the only teacher I ever knew who was regularly tardy, but it's a testament to what a highly regarded teacher she was that the principal never dared say a word to her.

"What makes a good English teacher?" a young woman sitting next to Paul asked Irene.

Again Irene thought about it. I was about to say that these questions might be a little tricky for her. Hadn't Newell explained Irene's condition to his friends?

"Getting students to see the connection between life and literature," Irene said.

"And how did you do that?" another fellow asked.

I was about to step in when Irene said, "Taught them to read with their hearts."

I couldn't believe my ears. It was something she used to say, but I hadn't heard her say it in ages.

So the artists asked Irene other questions. Some she answered. Some they helped her answer. The conversation took on a momentum of its own. Although Irene didn't say much more, she was at the center of it and clearly enjoyed it.

I had worried that coming up here and being around all these people would tire and confuse her. It had focused her. If I thought about it, it made sense. Irene had always been a people person, having friends and family over, making plans for get-togethers and family vacations. That's what she always looked forward to—doing things with people, often a lot of people. Even her job as a school-teacher had been very social, being with children all day long, meeting with parents in the afternoons, talking with other teachers.

I had seen to her physical needs at the nursing home, but I had overlooked her social side. Sure, friends and old students would drop by Rolling Hills now and then, but it wasn't the same as getting Irene out to see people. I had failed in that department. I could see the wisdom in Chandler's suggestion to get her away from Rolling Hills, even for a night. It wasn't a change of scenery she had needed as much as a change of society.

With Irene occupied with the artists, and Newell and Billie deep in conversation, the boy and I were left to ourselves.

"Granddaddy, would you like me to make you a peanut butter sandwich?" Jackson was looking at my untouched food. He was halfway through a peanut butter sandwich of his own.

"A man has to do what a man has to do," I said, looking at my plate.

"I'm glad I'm not a man," he said, frowning at my food. He took another bite of his sandwich, chewed thoughtfully, then nodded in the direction of Newell and Billie.

"Daddy likes her," he said. He said it as if he wasn't sure what to think of this development. I had thought that he had invited her along because he wanted Newell to like her.

His eyes wandered back to my plate. "Are you really going to eat that?"

"My mama taught me to eat what was put in front of me." I carved up the tempeh and put a bite in my mouth, chewed and swallowed, the boy watching me.

"PBJ?" he asked.

I nodded.

"I'll be right back," he said, hurrying off toward the kitchen, happy to have something to do.

The tables had filled up around us with men and women, most I guessed to be in their thirties or forties, some in their fifties, even a few in their sixties. Most had on jeans and T-shirts speckled with paint or clay or whatever they had spent the day working with. Crowds make me lonely. I can paint a house by myself from sunup to sundown and never feel lonesome. I can work in the garden or down in the shop for hours and never have the slightest twinge of melancholy. But put me in a roomful of people, a roomful of artists for instance, and I want to sit down and cry.

"Are you going to the dance tonight, Mr. Marshbanks?" asked a woman who had been sitting next to Jackson. We had been introduced to her when we first came in. Her name was Jane. She was a small, wiry woman in tight jeans and a faded short-sleeved blouse. She had big biceps. Turned out she was a blacksmith. Her long blond hair, pulled back in a ponytail, was streaked with gray. I guessed her to be about forty.

"What dance?" I asked.

"Every Friday evening they have a big square dance down in the barn. Local musicians come from Burnsville, and other folks come in from town, too. Your son is a good dancer," she said like she had danced with him. "And he told me you were a legendary clogger."

"I used to clog a little, but my knees have been shot for about thirty years, and I have a bad ankle," I said. "Besides, my wife tires easy. We'll probably turn in early."

There was a burst of laughter from the little knot of folks around Irene. They were laughing at something she had said.

"Doesn't look tired to me," the woman said. And it was true— Irene looked totally caught up in these people around her, her eyes shone, and she sat on the edge of her seat, like she didn't want to miss a word of what was said. The young people seemed to enjoy her and waited patiently for any little tidbit she might offer, like she was holding court.

"Your wife might enjoy the music," Jane said to me.

"Maybe," I said, knowing we wouldn't go.

"If you do come, save a dance for me," she said, getting up with her tray.

I had never known Newell square-danced. In fact, I was surprised that was something he would enjoy. When he was in high school all he ever listened to was rock and roll. Whenever I'd put one of my old-timey records on, he'd plug his ears.

"Here you go." The boy set a mammoth peanut butter and jelly sandwich in front of me, along with a big glass of milk, and sat down beside me.

"Food at last!" I said, biting into the sandwich. I took a big swallow of milk and patted the boy's back.

"Is the sandwich good?" he asked.

With my mouth full of peanut butter, I made a thumbs-up sign, and the boy sat there and watched like it pleased him to watch me eat something he had made.

Newell, Jackson, and I walked off the main road onto the dark trail through the woods that led down to Squire's Orchard. There was the rush of the stream still full from the afternoon rains and the sweet, close smell of wet ferns and rotting leaves among the rhododendron. The deeper we walked into the woods, the louder the crickets sang, rocking the mountainside with their chorus.

"Will they be there?" Jackson asked.

"Have been every night this week," Newell said.

I had offered to stay with Irene so Billie could go. I had seen plenty of black bears in my time, but Billie insisted that I go along with the boys, saying she would help Irene get ready for bed. In spite of her liveliness at supper, on the way back to the cabin, Irene had yawned and said she was ready to retire. After all, they put the residents to bed early at Rolling Hills.

We gave Irene her various pills, except the sedative. I decided she was too tired from the long day to get up and wander during the night. I left Billie to help Irene into her nightgown. The longer Irene was at Rolling Hills, the less I had to do with dressing her, especially dressing her for bed. Lately, I had been leaving the room when the aide dressed her, because Irene had started waiting for me to leave. I was relieved that Billie handled it. My bigger worry was sleeping in the same bed with Irene.

Night came early to the trail, ceilinged as it was by hemlocks and tulip poplars, then understoried with rhododendron the size of small trees. It made a dark tunnel with a light at the far end, which were the meadow and the orchard beyond. Newell had brought along a flashlight but didn't want to use it because it might frighten the bears.

"Step quietly," Newell whispered, as we came out into the soft light of the grassy meadow. We were about to the orchard's edge when he held up his hand for us to stop. "They're here," he whispered. He waved us forward slowly.

On the far side of the orchard along the broken-down fence where the boy had been picking blackberries was a mama black bear, who must have weighed four hundred pounds, with her two cubs. They snuffled and grunted as they ate. The cubs didn't notice anything except the berries in front of them, but the mama kept sitting back on her haunches and looking around, keeping watch. She looked right at us. We kept still, and after a while she went back to eating. We stood like that till the sun was almost down and the bears, full of blackberries, lumbered off.

"Wow," Jackson said, as we turned around and headed back up through the meadow.

"They say there have been a lot of bears around this summer," Newell said. "More than usual."

"The acorn mast was up last fall," Jackson said. "More acorns in the fall, more cubs in the spring."

Newell gave me a look, like how did his son know that.

When we left the meadow behind and entered the trail, it was cool and black as a cave.

"I'm putting you in charge of lighting." Newell turned on his flashlight and handed it to the boy. Jackson shined it on the path for a while, but he became more interested in the light itself than where it was shining and began flicking it through the woods and up into the trees—everywhere but in front of us. It wasn't long before I caught my foot on a root. The actual fall seemed to take forever, like everything slowed way down. Part of it might have been that it was so dark I could not see what I was falling toward. As I fell, I thought, *Please don't let me break my ankle again.* I would be laid up for weeks, maybe months and would be no use to Irene or the boy or anybody for that matter. The house would go uncleaned, the garden untended, and Irene's clothes unironed. Hell, the ankle might not heal this time and I would end up in the nursing home myself and there would be no one to care for either of us. In the millisecond it took for me to fall, I went from healthy old goat to bedridden invalid.

"Daddy?" Newell said, as the boy shined the flashlight on me. "Did you hurt anything?"

"Nothing but my pride," I said. I had landed in a big bed of ferns, which was like falling onto a feather mattress. The boy and Newell helped me up and brushed me off. Newell turned toward the boy, about to grab the flashlight and tear into him. But he did neither. Instead, we all stood there for a minute, with the crickets singing even louder, an audible pulse, a million tiny hearts beating in rhythm.

The boy felt bad. "I'm sorry, Granddaddy," he said, and without a word from either of us, Jackson dutifully shined the flashlight on the ground right in front of me the whole rest of the way up the trail.

"Did you injure your ankle?" Newell asked.

"It's fine," I said. It ached, but I didn't want the boy to feel any worse.

After we had walked a little farther, Newell said to me, "I sure am glad you came."

"A boy shouldn't go too long without seeing his father," I said.

"You said it," Newell said, taking hold of my arm.

"That's not necessary," I said, starting to pull away. "I won't fall again."

"But I might," Newell said, keeping a firm grip on my arm all the way back up the trail.

When we came out on the dirt road that wound through the campus, there was a faint ghost of daylight left. We walked a little farther and found the boy watching a potter, who was stoking the big yellow brick kiln we had seen earlier. He was stoking it with firewood. We stopped and watched. The potter didn't say a word, just went about his work. When he opened the door to the kiln, the inside glowed dull orange, like hell itself. For the first time, we could see his face—a young fellow, clean-shaven, maybe in his midtwenties, intent on his work.

We started back up the road. The boy turned on the flashlight again and shined it straight up into the sky.

"You think they could see the flashlight on Mars?" he asked.

"I wouldn't be surprised," Newell said.

"That is if there's anybody there to see it," the boy added. Then he turned to me, shining the light in my eyes. "Do you believe there's life on other planets?"

"I have enough trouble believing in life on this one," I said, shading my eyes from the flashlight.

Just before we turned into Newell's drive, we noticed the dining hall all lit up at the top of the hill. Strains of fiddle and banjo echoed down to us.

"The band's tuning up," Newell said.

"That's 'Old Joe Clark,'" I said. It was a tune the old-timers down at the River Falls Lodge used to play in Jones Gap back in my dancing days. "I didn't know you square-danced," I said.

"Like father, like son," Newell said.

"You hated those old-timey records I used to play."

"That's true," he said.

"What changed?"

"Me, I guess."

Then we turned up the drive and walked into the darkness of the trees; the yellow bug lights of the cabin porches were up ahead. The boy fell back with us, shining the flashlight in front of me, anticipating my every step.

"Would you like to go to the dance?" Newell asked me.

"I better keep an eye on your mother."

"I can stay with her," Newell said.

"My dancing days are long gone, son," I said.

When we got to the house, Billie was cleaning up the kitchen. She had already gotten Irene in bed. When I went in to check on her, she was sound asleep. Billie had let Irene's hair down, and she looked as peaceful as a sleeping child. I started to touch her cheek but decided against it for fear of waking her. At my bedtime, I would ease onto my side of the bed. Then in the morning, I would wake before she did, and she would never know I was in the same bed with her.

When I went back out, everybody was sitting on the porch,

listening to the music echo down from the dining hall. Whoever was playing was playing as strong and quick as the old men who used to play at the River Falls Lodge.

"Now they're playing 'Elzik's Farewell,'" I said. One of my favorite songs, it was a dark but lively tune that a fiddler had written at his dying mother's request. "They're good. Real good."

"Daddy, why don't you and Billie and Jackson go up to the dance?" Newell asked. "I'll watch Mama."

"I'll stay," Jackson said.

"Why don't you let me stay? I have two left feet," Billie said.

The boy looked down at Billie's feet.

"I don't want to hear another word," I said, feeling my face flush. "Y'all get your tails on up there. I'm a tired old man with a bad ankle and an attitude to match, and I'll be damned if I'm going to drag this old carcass back up that hill and make a fool of myself on the damned dance floor."

Twelve

Elzik's Farewell

I swung Jane, holding her hand in mine and my other hand planted firm in the upper middle of her back. Hold a girl too low, and her back aches after you have danced a while.

"You're a smooth dancer," she said, the color having come into her cheeks a couple of dances back. This was our third dance. She was so strong that at first I wasn't sure who was swinging who. After a while she began to trust me. She eased up, and the more she relaxed the faster we swung.

The caller, a balding fellow about Newell's age with a handlebar mustache and wire-rimmed glasses, spoke into the microphone, "Move on to the next." Jane and I circled up with the potter we had watched earlier that evening and a pretty, serious-looking girl in a tie-dye skirt, who, from the way she kept her eyes on the potter, must have been his girlfriend.

"Dig for the oyster," the caller said. Jane and I raised our hands, forming an arch, and the other couple ducked underneath, then pulled back out.

"Dive for the clam." The other couple raised their arms, and Jane and I ducked under.

"Shoot for the hole in the old tin can." We raised our arms, the other couple ducked under and kept on going, but we all kept holding hands so that the other couple turned around and pulled us under their arms, and we all popped out into a circle again.

"Swing your opposite," the caller said, and I swung the young girl, her skirt swishing against my legs, and Jane swung the potter. The more we swung, the more she looked at me, till a smile flickered across her face, and for a minute she might have seen past the old man in me. You can tell more about a person in two minutes of dancing, than you can in a lifetime of conversation.

"Now swing your partner." The potter and the girl swung and Jane and I swung again. Every time we came back to each other, our swing was stronger. My wind wasn't bad, and my ankle only ached when I thought about it.

"Move on to the next," the caller said, and Jane and I moved on to the next waiting couple. We went on like that, making our way around the big circle in the dining hall—the tables and chairs pushed against the walls. I spotted Jackson, sitting on the tables where I had left him, patting his thighs in time to the music. Earlier, Billie had tried dragging him out on the floor, but he had darted away.

The band played at the front of the dining hall. Instead of old men in bib overalls, they were young women in bib overalls. One of the women, wearing a feed cap, stood toward the front playing the fiddle. Another woman in a feed cap played piano. Off to the side a slight woman manhandled a standup bass that was twice her size, and another sat beside her, playing claw hammer banjo. They were tight and fast, watching each other for cues when to start, when to stop, when to play it through one more time. It had been decades since I had heard some of the songs they played.

It had been the music that had finally lured me to come up and dance in the first place, that and the fact that while we had all been sitting on Newell's porch debating about who would stay with Irene, a voice like the voice of God had boomed out from the dark, saying, "I will keep an eye on Mrs. Marshbanks." Then Paul stepped out of the dark and into the circle of yellow bug light, walked up onto the porch carrying a half-finished bowl in one hand and some woodworking tools in the other. He had said he had no interest in dancing and would work on his bowl on the porch and listen out for Irene. He pulled up a chair and got right to work, digging away at his bowl with his steel gouge. And it was about that time, too, that the band up at the dining hall started playing "Elzik's Farewell"—a tune that I had never been able to stand still to.

"On to the next," said the caller. The next was Billie and Newell. When we swung opposites, I swung Billie and Newell swung Jane. Billie danced vertically, hopping up and down.

"Take it easy," I said, "This isn't a race."

"I told you I had two left feet," she said.

"Well keep them on the floor," I said. "*Walk* in time to the music. Now lean back a little and give weight. Let your partner know you're there," I said, showing her how to bend her arms. "That's it." And in no time she had the hang of it, and we were swinging fine.

"Swing your partner," the caller said.

Billie went back to dance with Newell, and Jane slipped into my arms and we spun faster. Then the music shifted and without either of us saying a word, Jane and I broke off and started clogging. Whoops and hollers went up all around the dining hall, and I could feel folks watch us. I saw Jackson slide off the table and stare, his mouth open. Then the music shifted again.

"Everybody join hands," the caller said, riding the wave of good spirits that ran through the hall, and the couples backed into a big circle that reached all the way around the dining hall. The caller stepped into the circle, took a girl's hand and led the line into a circle inside the circle, going around till we were a tight knot in the center of the dining hall. Then the caller wound the line out again until we were a big circle again. Then we promenaded until the caller said, "Lead that lady right off the floor, that's all there is, they ain't no more."

I led Jane off the floor, bowing to her. I pulled out my handkerchief and wiped my forehead. "Thanks for the dances," I said, after I had caught my breath.

"The pleasure was mine," Jane said.

"I didn't know you could dance like that," the boy said, running up to me.

Newell patted my back. "I didn't know you still had it in you."

"Not sure I do." I sat down in a chair against the wall as the band eased into a waltz, signaling that it was nearly intermission. Couples paired up around the dining hall, and Newell was turning to Billie, when Jane asked him if he would like to waltz.

Newell looked at Billie.

"That's all right," Billie said. "Go ahead."

"You sure?" Newell asked.

"Please," Billie said.

Newell and Jane glided across the dance floor, obviously having waltzed together before.

Billie turned to me. "Would you do me the honor?"

"My ankle has had about enough for one night," I said.

"I'm not as bad a waltzer," she said.

"Dance with Jackson," I said.

Billie held her arms out to the boy.

Jackson crossed his arms. "I don't know how."

"It's easy," I said, getting up and taking his hand. "All you do is take three steps and then take three more, then three more." I waltzed him in a little circle, but when we finished the boy just scratched his head. "I don't get it."

"You don't want to get it," I said.

He grinned and sat back down on the table.

"Let's show Jackson how," Billie said, taking my hand and leading me out onto the dance floor. Unlike the stiff steps she used for the square dance, she moved easily across the floor. It was like dancing with a different woman. She moved in any direction with only the slightest pressure.

"My father used to waltz me around the living room after supper," she said.

As we danced, I remembered my first waltz with Irene. It had been down at Jones Gap at the River Falls Lodge, that very same night we had steamed up the car windows. Afterwards, we had gotten out. And with the band playing a sad sweet waltz called "The Lover's Lament" inside the old lodge, we had danced outside by moonlight on the edge of a plowed field. A low fog rolled in from the river, like we were dancing on top of the clouds, and, because we couldn't see, every now and then we'd misstep. Once she fell, dirtying her skirt.

"What will your father say?" I said, trying to dust off some of the dirt.

"Nothing if he knows what's good for him," Irene said, as we began waltzing again.

"This all makes me a little nervous," I said.

"What's that?"

"Courting a lawyer's daughter," I said.

"I don't know why you're so afraid of my father," she said. "He doesn't bite."

"Does he sue?"

"Never," she said.

"Oh," I said, feeling better.

"He only prosecutes."

"Oh," I said, feeling worse.

"But not boys I go out with," she said. Then she added, "Providing they don't break my heart."

"Have any broken your heart?" I asked, my throat tightening. "Not that it's my business."

"No one has had my heart to break," she said. "Until now."

I could not speak.

"Oh, don't stop dancing, Prate," she said, as she leaned into me and we started back into our ragged waltz on the edge of the field.

At intermission, Billie, Jackson, and I had had enough and headed back down to the cabin, all of us whipped from starting out so early that morning. Newell, who was clearly enjoying himself, offered to go back with us, but we insisted he stay as long as he wanted.

"I'll just stay a couple more dances," Newell had said. And as we left, I saw him work his way back over to talk to Jane and a couple of other women.

Billie, Jackson, and I wound through the milling crowd of dancers who had stepped outside to cool off in the night air. We walked down the road, the night air chilly. A nighthawk shrieked from high in a big oak and followed us as we walked down the hill. Maybe it was the dancing or maybe it was the change of scenery or maybe it was both, but I felt lighter, aired out, like a shirt that's been in the closet all winter.

The boy dutifully shined the flashlight on the road and stifled his yawns.

"Tired?" Billie asked, her arm around Jackson's shoulder.

"A little."

Halfway down the hill, we heard the band crank back up. They started in on "Old Sally Goodin," another one of the songs they used to play at River Falls Lodge, and as the music and the nighthawk followed us down the hill, a lonely feeling crept up on me. My ankle really began to ache about that time, pain shooting up my calf. I had overdone it, old fool that I was, dancing like a man of twenty, to impress Newell's crowd, to hold the waists of young women, to dance my way back to the way things used to be.

When we reached the cabin, Paul was sitting where we left him, still working on that bowl, a pile of shavings on the floor. The bowl looked about finished, but when I got a good look at it I was embarrassed for him. It was crooked and misshapen.

"You're limping, Mr. Marshbanks," he said, when we came up on the porch.

"I overdid it," I said, easing down in the rocking chair next to him.

Paul stood, gathering up his bowl and his tools. "I guess Newell is still up there."

"He wanted to dance a couple more," I said, as Billie took the boy into the kitchen for a plate of Oreos and a glass of milk. The boy sat down to the kitchen table and ate without a word. He was hungry and tired.

"Irene been okay?" I asked Paul, looking off toward the closed door of the bedroom.

"I haven't heard a peep out of her," he said.

I was glad to hear that. At the nursing home, if she didn't get back up the first hour or two, she didn't usually wake the whole night.

"I appreciate you watching her," I said to Paul, who was gathering his tools.

Billie came back out of the kitchen, eating a cookie. "Are you leaving so soon?" she said to Paul.

"I have to help with breakfast," Paul said, making his way toward the door.

"Beautiful bowl," Billie said, nodding at the bowl tucked under his arm. I had to look at her to see if she was serious. "I've never seen anything like it."

I had to agree with her on that one.

"See you at breakfast," Paul called as he walked down the stairs, the cabin shaking with his steps, then lumbered off in the direction of his cabin. Without another word, Billie went inside and started making up the couch. She had to move a few of Newell's paintings, which she did very carefully.

"You sure you don't want to sleep with Irene?" I said, following her inside. My ankle started throbbing again as soon as I stood on it. I leaned against a chair. "I could sleep out here on the couch."

"You should sleep with your wife," Billie said almost curtly. She unfolded a sheet and tucked it in under the cushions. I looked around the room at all the paintings, which in the dim light looked like dozens of little windows onto a lighter world. The boy came in from the kitchen, wiping cookie crumbs from his lips. He was holding his stuffed dog, Rudy—a sure sign he was ready for bed.

"You want to sleep in the bedroom with your grandmother?" I asked. "The bed looks mighty comfortable."

"Daddy and I are sleeping on the porch," he said. "Can I roll the sleeping bags out so they'll be ready when he gets back?"

"I'll help," Billie said, handing him one of the bags from behind the couch and carrying the other out herself.

So the boy and Billie went out on the porch, and I limped into the kitchen, boiled some water, and fixed me a cup of instant coffee, thinking I would stay up all night, playing solitaire. The window was open, and I could hear the band play a fast reel up at the dining hall.

I was sipping my coffee when Billie came back in. She said the boy had already curled up in his bag and gone to sleep. She didn't say anything else for a minute. She was preoccupied with something. Then she looked up at me.

"You're drinking coffee at this hour?" she asked. "Won't it keep you up?"

"That's the idea," I said.

She paused. "Why don't you want to sleep with Mrs. Marshbanks?"

I sighed. "It's not that I don't want to sleep with her. I don't know if she wants to sleep with me. After all, it has been six months, and I am not the man I once was—to her."

She leaned back in her chair. "If you would rather me sleep with her . . ."

"Naw," I said, knowing as soon as she offered that I wouldn't take her up on it. "She's my wife. I better stay with her."

"In that case you should stop drinking that coffee," she said. Ever since we had gotten back from the dance, her voice had had more of an edge to it than I was used to.

I set down the mug.

She seemed restless. She started looking around in the cupboard. "I thought I saw some chamomile in here." She pulled out a box of tea bags. "This will help us sleep. I'll make a pot." She poured water from the kettle into a teapot, put in a couple of bags, and brought the pot and three mugs to the table.

"Aren't you sleepy either?" I asked, as she sat back down.

"It's strange," she said. "I'm tired, but I'm not sleepy. The air around this place is . . . charged." She looked up at me. "I hope I'm not in anybody's way."

"You were invited."

"Not really."

"I couldn't have made the trip without you," I blurted. There was an awkward silence. "Hell, if it weren't for you, she'd still be locked in that bathroom back in Weaverville."

"You would have managed," she said.

We heard the creak of the porch screen and heavy footsteps, thinking Paul had forgotten something. Newell walked into the kitchen. I had been certain when he'd said he would only stay a couple more dances that he would stay till the end. In the old days, that was what I would have done.

"Jackson's already asleep?" he asked.

"He wanted to put the sleeping bags out so they would be ready for you," Billie said, "and when I turned around, he had already crawled in his and fallen asleep."

"I've missed him," Newell said.

"Who wouldn't?" she said.

He looked at me. "Are you drinking coffee? Haven't you been having trouble sleeping?"

I was afraid I might have to go into not wanting to sleep with Irene. For some reason, it seemed harder to tell my son I didn't want to sleep with his mother than to tell Billie.

"He's not drinking it anymore," Billie said, moving the conversation past where I would need to tell him. "I made some chamomile tea," she said. She put the coffee mug in the sink and filled the three mugs with tea.

I held the mug to my nose. "Smells like boiled grass," I said.

"You never had chamomile tea, Daddy?" Newell said, sipping his. "I drink it every night before I go to bed. Helps me unwind."

"Me too," Billie said, sounding a little more like her old upbeat self.

I took a sip. "*Tastes* like boiled grass." I set the mug back down. "You say it helps you sleep?"

"It relaxes you," Billie said.

"Next time I have trouble sleeping, I'll go out in the yard, rake up some grass clippings, and boil them up." I took another sip of the awful stuff and felt Billie and Newell smile at each other over their mugs. I was reminded yet again what an old codger I must have become that I could evoke tolerant smiles from the young people. My throbbing ankle and the settling in of just how ancient I had become tired me.

"I think I'll turn in," I said, pushing myself up.

"The tea works fast," Newell said.

"Sleep well," Billie said with a knowing look.

I went to check on the boy first. I had gotten so used to sleeping with Jackson that it felt strange to go to bed without at least seeing him. I found him curled up in his sleeping bag. He had his arm around Rudy, who kept one eye on me. Rudy was the only stuffed dog I had ever come across who looked, under the right circumstances, like he might bite.

I turned out the yellow porch light and stood over the boy. I thought about having told Billie that I couldn't have managed without her. I felt a tinge of embarrassment, but embarrassment was more of a young person's emotion. Nothing embarrassed me too much anymore—not even my own embarrassment.

Newell and Billie came out of the kitchen, but stopped talking when they saw me standing there like maybe they had been talking about me. They joined me on the porch, and we all stood in the dark for a moment, looking at the boy. No one said a word. We just stood over the boy. And for the strangest split second, it felt like we were a sort of an impromptu family.

"They're playing the last waltz," Newell said, nodding in the direction of the dining hall.

"But do you hear what it is?" Billie asked us.

Newell put his arm on my shoulder in a way that told me he understood my reservations about sleeping with his mother and that whatever I decided was all right with him. Or maybe that's what I wanted to read in my son's touch. No matter. It was, I still believe, a gesture of forgiveness.

"I made a request," my son said.

When I turned my attention to the high, lonely fiddle notes filtering down to us through the hemlocks, I heard they were playing a slow, easy, unforgettable rendition of "Good Night, Irene."

Thirteen

Owls

I was careful to shut the door quietly behind me. The light was off, but moonlight through a window whitewashed the room. Irene slept on her side, her knees pulled halfway up to her chest and her hands tucked under her head. I could hear Newell and Billie through the wall. I couldn't make out what they were saying, but they sounded different, quiet. Whatever they were talking about, it wasn't art.

My ankle ached, and I eased myself down on the end of the bed. I had sat in Irene's room at Rolling Hills dozens of times while she slept, but that wasn't the same. At the nursing home, I never knew when a nurse or an aide might check on her. We had no privacy, and therefore no possibilities. Hell, I felt self-conscious kissing her good night. Now I was alone with her in a room full of possibility.

Except that, of course, it wasn't. Nothing would happen here. I had known that ever since Chandler had brought up the idea of a trip for us. I remembered thinking at the time that I would do like he said and take her somewhere. I also remembered thinking that nothing would happen. I had to wonder if I had arranged this whole visit with Newell just to prove Chandler wrong? Or it might have been a little more complicated than that. Maybe it wasn't that I wanted to prove the doctor wrong, but that I wanted to eliminate any irritating hope. Coming up here had improved Irene's mood, maybe even cleared her mind some, but the idea of us ever sleeping together again remained about as hopeless as rekindling a fire from rain-soaked wood.

I walked over to the open window, tempted to raise the screen and slip out for a long walk, but I didn't. The air had turned even cooler, smelling dank and clean, a sweet mix of rotting leaves and evergreen. The last drawn out phrases of "Good Night, Irene" rode the breeze. It had been thoughtful of Newell to ask the band to play that. Before Sandy died, thoughtful was not a word I would have used to describe my son. Tragedy had made a man out of Newell, like the War had for the young fellows of my generation. Nowadays men grew up late, in the trenches of home.

I closed the window, which had no curtain. Guess there wasn't anybody around to see in, except maybe the owls, raccoons, skunks, and other nocturnal creatures. I pulled the blanket up on Irene, my hand getting away from me, stroking the back of her neck. It was a smooth, shapely neck. The same smooth white neck I had known for fifty years. I stroked her neck for a long time. Wispy strands of hair curled up from it. Finally, I bent over and buried my nose in her hair, smelling her dark, sweaty scent. Something stirred in me that hadn't stirred in a long time. My blood was pumping, making me feel on fire from the tips of my fingers to the tips of my toes. Before I knew it, I was crawling into her bed and spooning up behind her like I used to. And in her sleep, she moved back against me, giving a little sigh, and my hand followed the sweet curve of her hip, but then I stopped.

She wasn't even awake for Lord's sake.

I heard Billie's laugh through the wall, followed by Newell's deeper laugh.

"Such a desperate old fool," I said out loud to myself, my heart still racing.

I slipped out of bed and stood over Irene, waiting for my pulse to slow. What had come over me? Had I gotten so bad off I was going to take advantage of a woman who wasn't even conscious? And if she was my wife, she didn't know it a good portion of the time, and who knew who I would be when she came to?

I rummaged around in a chest of drawers and found a couple of musty old quilts and an army blanket in the bottom drawer. I folded them in half and made a pallet in the tight space between the bed and the wall. I took one of the pillows off the bed and set it at the top. I stood back and admired my work. Reminded me of an army cot without the legs.

I grabbed my travel kit, eased open the door and headed toward the bathroom to brush my teeth. I heard them laugh again. I stopped and listened. I peeked around the corner. They were playing cards, studying their hands. Billie laid all her cards on the table, looked up at Newell and said, "Gin."

"Already?" Newell shook his head. "I can't believe your luck," he said, tossing his cards on the table.

She gathered the cards and started shuffling. "Play again?" she asked.

Newell sighed and nodded. "I'm a glutton for punishment."

My shaving cream dropped out of my travel kit and rolled noisily into the kitchen. I followed the rattling can, which had rolled to Billie's feet. She picked it up and handed it to me.

"Are we keeping you up?" she asked.

I put the can back in my travel kit. "Need to brush my choppers." I dug my toothbrush out of the kit and held it up.

"We'll try to keep it down," Billie said.

"You're not bothering me," I said.

"I put clean towels in the bathroom," Newell said. "Mama sleeping all right?"

"The sleep of the dead," I said. "The long day tired her out."

"I'm glad you all came," Newell said. "I know it wasn't easy."

There was an awkward pause. Then as if something about what Newell and I had just said somehow embarrassed or irritated Billie, she got up abruptly, took the teacups to the sink, and started washing them.

I went out to the bathroom and brushed my teeth. I would pause now and then, lean my head out the door, but I didn't hear a thing except dishes being put away.

When I finished in the bathroom, I tiptoed past the kitchen and glanced in long enough to see that Billie was back at the kitchen table and Newell was shuffling the cards. All I could see was the girl looking down in her lap. I wasn't sure what had thrown her. She was always the cheery one, always making conversation, always lifting people's spirits. Maybe she was tired from all that lifting.

In the bedroom, I slipped out of my clothes and into a T-shirt. I checked on Irene. My hand wanted to stroke her forehead, but I held back. Who knew where that might lead? I hunkered down on my pallet. Although it wasn't as comfortable as a bed, after such a long day, I probably could have slept on concrete slab. As I was drifting off I heard voices. I put my ear to the wall, and even though I could not make out what Newell and Billie said, at least they were talking.

I woke late in the night, having to piss. The older I got, the weaker my bladder had become. Sometimes I had to get up two or three times in the night. The house was still and dark, the moonlight having waned. I checked my watch, reading the fluorescent hands. It was nearly three o'clock. I pulled on my pants. "Ow!" My ankle throbbed when I put weight on it.

I looked to see if I had waked Irene. Sometime during the night, she had turned over, facing away from me. Her breathing was regular and easy. She seemed to be in a good deep sleep. It would make tomorrow easier. She was more manageable when she was rested.

I found the bottle of ibuprofen in my travel kit, then hobbled as quiet as I could out to the bathroom. Then I went out to the kitchen. Newell had left a light on over the sink. I drew a glass of water, took three tablets, and sat down at the kitchen table and waited for the pain to back off. This is what you get. This is what you get for not acting your age, my ankle reminded me with every twinge it sent up my leg.

I knew that once I was up I wouldn't be able to go back to sleep till I had stayed up for a while. As usual, my bladder had delivered me to my worry hour. When the pain in my ankle eased a bit, I put the kettle on real quiet, found the box of chamomile, and made me some tea. Then I sat back down, sipped the vile-tasting stuff, and listened to the night sounds.

The cabin was cradled in a deep quiet, much deeper than that of home, where a car might whiz by any hour of the night. Here we were in the woods, and the sounds I heard through the open kitchen window were cushioned in loamy silence—the wind in the trees, the scratchy song of the crickets, and the far-off call of an owl. I listened as close as I could. It was the strong deep call of a barred owl, as alone as it could be. Then deeper in the woods, another barred owl answered. Maybe its mate. They went back and forth like that for half an hour. I sat and listened to the owls' conversation. Each pause between calls was full of dread. Are you still there? Are you still there? And every answering call reassured, I am, it said. But then came the wait again, and what I noticed was that the dread only stayed away for the duration of the call. It started again with the silence and grew and grew. They went back and forth like that, and each time that I thought there would be no more calls, that the end had finally come, a call would travel across the air and change everything. They were both moving away from the cabin, and after a while, even though I listened hard, I couldn't hear them anymore, and I couldn't help worrying after them. Had they moved off together or had they finally lost track of each other in these complicated woods?

After I finished my tea, I rinsed out my cup and quietly set it in the dish drain. My ankle was better. I tiptoed through the living room, where Billie was asleep on the couch, and out to the front porch, where Newell and Jackson were both curled up in their sleeping bags. As I situated Rudy in the boy's sleeping bag, it seemed the stuffed dog gave me a kinder eye. I stood on the porch and looked around. Everyone present and accounted for. I listened for the owls again, but they were out of range. There was a flicker of thunderless heat lightning.

I tiptoed back to the bedroom, slipped out of my pants and was about to lie down on my pallet when I looked over and saw Irene sitting up in bed.

"Hello," she said.

"Damn!" I said, my hand to my chest.

"Did I startle you?"

I waited for my heart to settle down.

"Why pull your pants back up?" she asked. She sounded as lucid as her old self. "When are you coming to bed?"

I nodded to my pallet. "I'm sleeping on the floor."

"Do you walk on hot coals as well?"

"I didn't want to bother you," I said.

"Since when did you sleep on the floor?"

"We haven't slept together in quite a while," I said.

"Since when?"

I hesitated. "Since Rolling Hills."

She frowned as if she didn't understand.

"Since the nursing home," I said.

"The what?" she asked, pulling back the bedspread for me.

"Are you sure?" I felt the blood start to pulse through me as it had before.

"Where else should you be?"

"And you know you're Irene Marshbanks?"

She raised her eyebrows.

"And who I am?" I asked. "You know I am your husband, Prate Marshbanks, the father of your child, Newell Marshbanks, who is the father of Jackson Marshbanks, your grandson."

"Are you a family tree?"

"I want to be sure you know who I am and who you are," I said.

She frowned to herself, then smiled a smile that seemed to come from decades back. "I know you're a rascal," she said in a voice full of her old girlish self.

"I'm serious about this, Irene," I said.

She rolled her eyes and sighed. "All right," she said. "I know I'm . . ." She looked a little uncertain. ". . . who I am. And I know you're . . . who you are. And I know . . ." She paused and her face had been clouding with confusion but she kept her eyes on me, seeming to will herself to stay in this room with me.

She held out her arms, and I slid into the bed next to her and held her for the longest time, thinking that might be all, and it would have been more than enough. After a little while, when I thought she might have fallen asleep, she sat up, looked at me, and said, "Can you help?"

"I wish I knew how," I said, sitting up.

"No," she said, a little impatient, "Help."

"I am doing all I know to do. Maybe we could ask Chandler if there are any other medications . . ."

She tugged at her sleeves and said, "Just help me get this goddamned . . . garment off!"

"Oh," I said, and with her holding her arms in the air, I lifted her nightgown ever so slowly over her head. I felt as dry-mouthed as I had on our wedding night, when she came out of the bathroom and stood at the foot of the hotel bed wearing nothing but a grin.

"Your turn," she said, trying to help me off with my T-shirt. "This nuisance, too," she said, fingering my underwear, which I slipped out of. "Hurry," she said, "before my father catches us."

"You know who I am, right?" I said, pulling away from her.

Irene put her finger over my lips, then leaned me back and lay down on me, kissing me. And I couldn't remember when the last time was that I felt the weight of her. My heart began beating like crazy. And as I ran my hands down the ribs of her back and along her flanks, I had to wonder if I might be taking advantage of her. But then I stopped thinking and forgot everything except that she had somehow slipped herself onto a hardness I did not believe I had left in me. And for at least the length of an owl's lonely exchange in deepest woods, Irene and I knew each other.

Fourteen

The Woods

My eyes opened at five-thirty, like they had for most of my adult life, without aid of rooster or alarm clock. I was turned toward the window, which looked out onto a slate gray predawn sky. The cabin was full of early-morning quiet. No sounds of anyone stirring yet. I felt a kind of peacefulness I had not felt in a long time.

Outside the window a gray catbird began singing in the loud show-off way they do. Even through the closed window he was loud. Afraid he might wake Irene, I opened the window, which was enough to send him flying off up the drive, where he perched in one of the hemlocks and started up again.

The chilly morning breeze felt good on my face, but the sky was overcast, and a fine mist was falling. It had all the signs of a raw day ahead, which surprised me. Yesterday afternoon the big thunderstorm had come through ahead of a cold front. I would have expected the morning sky to be clear and crisp. Instead, the sky was gauzy and gray, and the mist had a settled-in feel. This was autumn weather in the middle of summer. Even the smell was fallish, a hint of the end of things.

The wind shifted, and I smelled biscuits. Somebody was already up at the dining hall preparing breakfast. I watched the trees take shape in the early light. I had sorely missed sleeping with my wife, and I did mean just sleeping with her. I wasn't complaining about last night's bounty, but I would have forfeited all other pleasures for the simple warmth of my wife's back pressed against mine.

Bill Chandler had said she needed Rolling Hills because she needed twenty-four-hour care. What kind of care was it to have a resentful angry dimwit jerk her out of bed in the mornings?

I remembered a voice of nearly half a century ago saying, *She's all yours.* And there I was standing with the priest and my brother, the best man, at the altar of Christ Church. Mr. Blalock looked frail yet pleased as he walked Irene up the aisle toward us in front of a packed and mostly disbelieving church—Irene Blalock, valedictorian at Agnes Scott and apple of her father's eye, marrying a house-painter? Mr. Blalock kissed her cheek and, as he stepped back, leaned over and, somewhere between blessing and threat, whispered into my ear, "She's all yours." And then I was vowing before God and Mr. Blalock and a churchful of whispering naysayers that I would provide for her as long as we both shall live.

"And we are both still here," I said to myself, looking out the open bedroom window toward the woods, feeling the mist on my face. Maybe I could bring her back home. It would be hard work, but I had never shied from hard work. The boy could help. Even if he would be gone in three weeks, maybe Newell could come down with him more on the weekends now. I could hire an aide to sit with her. They charged an arm and a leg, but maybe it was time to take Newell up on his offer to help financially. Couldn't I sacrifice a little pride for Irene's sake?

I slapped the windowsill. "What do we have to lose, Irene?" I asked aloud as I turned around. I think I even laughed. "What do we have to lose?"

That's when I saw the empty bed.

A screen door slammed, and the sound made my stomach lurch. Through the window I saw Paul hurry up the drive, headed toward the dining hall on his way to help with breakfast. The sound of his door reminded me of another screen slam I had heard sometime in the small hours of the morning.

My eyes kept going back to the woods. That must have been two hours ago. I remembered the sedative I had decided not to give her last night. I remembered the nurse's words, *We don't want her wandering off into the woods up there.*

I pulled on my pants and went out to the bathroom, but she wasn't there. She wasn't in the kitchen either. I went out to the front room where Billie was asleep on the couch. I went out to the porch, hoping Irene might have settled into a rocking chair. Newell and the boy were asleep in their sleeping bags.

Looking back on it, I should have woken everybody, but at that point, I still didn't believe she could be gone. I still believed she had wandered someplace close by and that I could find her on my own. Maybe part of it was that I was embarrassed. I had lost my wife or, even worse, had upset her by making love to her. I had run her off.

I went back to the bedroom, pulled on the sweater I had brought, then picked up my shoes and tiptoed out, careful not to let the screen slam, and put my socks and shoes on outside. I noticed my ankle was swollen and discolored. It hurt like hell to put weight on it. I had started toward the dining hall as fast as I could manage, hoping she had wandered up there. The fine rain made the road slick so I had to slow down. I was halfway up the drive when Jackson ran up behind me.

"I thought you were asleep," I said.

"Where are you going?" he asked, falling in beside me.

"Did you see your grandma go out this morning?"

He shook his head.

"I'm hoping she wandered up to the dining hall," I said.

We found Paul and several others in the dining hall kitchen, bustling around, making breakfast for the school. One tall, pinch-faced woman with her hair tied back in a scarf was pouring a big bag of grits into a giant pot of boiling water on the big stove. Another fellow with his hair hanging down around his face in matted bunches was cracking eggs, two at a time, into a huge bowl. A heavy older woman who must have been in her mid-fifties was cutting up fruit into a big bowl. And Paul was pulling a giant tray of biscuits out of the big oven with his mittened hand. He set the tray on a table, pulled out another tray, then slid two more trays of uncooked biscuits into the oven and shut the door.

"Have y'all seen Irene?" I asked.

Paul set his big mittens down. "No."

"I was hoping she had wandered up here," I said, my ankle hurting so bad I pulled out a chair and sat. "I can't find her."

"She isn't in the cabin?" Paul asked.

"When I got up this morning she wasn't in bed."

"When did you see her last?"

"I don't know," I said, not wanting to say the last time I had seen her was after we had made love. "I remember hearing the screen slam sometime early this morning. Must've been around three."

Paul turned to the kitchen, asking in a big old rumbling voice. "Has anybody seen Mrs. Marshbanks this morning?"

The tall girl looked up from pouring salt into the boiling pot of grits. "I haven't seen her," she said.

The fellow with the matted hair stopped cracking eggs and said, "I haven't seen her since supper."

The older heavy woman put down her knife and came over to us. "Is she missing?" My chest tightened at the mention of that word. *Missing.*

Paul turned to me. "So you last saw her at three this morning?"

"I didn't even really see her. I just heard the screen slam. I guess it was her."

He looked at the clock on the wall. "So she's been missing for nearly three hours." There was that word again, and all of the sudden everybody was looking at me.

"Is Newell out looking for her?" Paul asked.

"I didn't wake him," I said feeling suddenly foolish. "I hoped she was up here."

"Somebody needs to go wake Newell," Paul said.

Jackson raced right out of there, back toward the cabin.

Paul untied his apron and so did the others.

"I don't want to bother y'all," I said. "I'm sure I can find her on my own. She has wandered off before. You go on and make breakfast. I'm sure Newell, the boy, and I will find her."

"Mr. Marshbanks, I don't want to alarm you, but if your wife walked off three hours ago, there is no telling how far she has gone by now. And in this weather . . . well . . ." He glanced out the big glass windows that looked out onto the pasture and the mountains beyond. Gray as far as you could see.

"What was she wearing?" he asked.

I saw what he was getting at. It had been a chilly night. Hypothermia. It didn't take freezing temperatures for a person to die of exposure, especially an elderly woman. "Just her nightgown as far as I know. But long-sleeved and flannel," I added, thanking the

Lord that Billie had foreseen it might be chilly and had packed Irene's warmest nightgown. Still, if she had been wandering around out there for three hours in the mist, a wet flannel nightgown wouldn't be much use.

"Debbie," Paul said to the tall girl, "go ring the bell and don't stop ringing until everybody is up and looking for Mrs. Marshbanks."

The girl shot out the door, and immediately we heard the bell clanging away.

"Walter," Paul said, turning to the fellow with the matted hair, "bang on cabin doors, see if anybody has seen Mrs. Marshbanks."

"Sure thing," the fellow said, and hurried out of the kitchen.

"Beverly," he said to the older heavy woman, "check the studios. She could have wandered into one of them."

I tried to stand, thinking I would look for Irene, too, but my ankle hurt too bad, and I was forced to sit down.

"You take it easy, Mr. Marshbanks," Paul said, checking the biscuits in the oven and sliding out the pan. "Mrs. Marshbanks will turn up."

The girl rang the dinner bell fast and furious. Sounded more like a fire alarm. They must have heard it all the way to Burnsville. It wasn't long after that that Newell and Billie came hurrying into the dining hall followed by Jackson.

"Why didn't you wake us?" Newell said, unshaven and his hair going every which way.

"I thought she had wandered up here," I said.

"I'm worried that she's wandered into the forest," Paul said, "and with it being an especially chilly night and with the weather not supposed to get much better . . ."

"I doubt that she went into the woods," I said. "Whenever she wanders, she goes looking for company." The few times she had wandered out of the house, she had always ended up knocking on a neighbor's door. Even at the nursing home, she never tried to escape the building like Dot but always went to another room or the nurse's station in search of somebody to talk to.

"She must have stepped right over me," Newell said. "How in the hell couldn't I have heard her? I should have latched the screen."

"I didn't hear her either," Billie said, putting her hand on his shoulder. He pulled away and headed for the door.

"Maybe we should come up with a plan," Paul called to Newell.

"I'm not going to sit here while my mother is out there freezing to death!" Newell said, and started out again.

"You want me to come with you?" Billie called after him.

"No," Newell snapped. Then his shoulders fell, and he spoke a little more softly. "Stay here and help Paul coordinate things, if it comes to that." Then he saw Jackson standing there looking down at the floor. "Come on, son. Let's go find your grandmother."

The boy ran off with his father out into the morning rain.

Billie came up behind me and rested her hands on my shoulders. Outside, the girl rang the bell like mad. If that didn't rouse Penland, nothing would.

"They'll find her," Billie said.

"I hate to think of Irene wandering around out there," I said. What I didn't say was that I was responsible. I had taken advantage of my wife last night, and this was the result.

Billie brought me a cup of coffee.

"The one time Irene needs me," I said, "I have to sit here like a cripple."

Paul unfolded a map he had found rummaging in a desk in the back office. He spread it out on the table in front of me. It was of the school and the surrounding area.

"We'll organize them into groups and comb the area till we find her," Paul said. I thought getting the whole camp to come look for Irene was an overreaction.

About half an hour later, Walter and Beverly returned. No one had seen Irene. The artists trickled into the dining hall all wearing long pants and either sweatshirts or parkas. They gathered around the big coffee urns with their mugs, irritated to be rung out of their beds so early. As the word spread that Newell Marshbanks's mother was missing, frowns gave way to looks of concern.

Newell and the boy were still out searching.

"Can I have everybody's attention," Paul said, banging a big spoon on a pot. "As you know by now, Newell's mother wandered off early this morning." They all looked toward me. "She was only wearing a long-sleeved flannel nightgown so . . ." He paused to let the weight of that settle on everybody. ". . . the sooner we find her the better."

"I saw her this morning," someone said. The crowd parted and the young potter we'd watched at his kiln walked up to the front.

"When?" I asked.

"She came by my kiln about three or three-thirty this morning." He was bleary-eyed, looking exhausted. "Maybe she saw the fire and walked up. She didn't say much. She seemed to want company, so I found a chair and she sat and watched the kiln. We sat together till about four-thirty or five, when I unloaded my pots."

"Did she seem upset?" Paul asked.

I held my breath, afraid that Irene might have said something to the boy about what had happened.

The boy shook his head. "She seemed peaceful, real settled. I'm sorry," he said to me. "I had no idea she had wandered away."

"It's all right," I said. The fact that she wasn't upset was a little solace. Maybe she hadn't been running away from me after all. On the other hand, maybe by the time she had gotten to the kiln, she had simply forgotten.

"She's a nice lady," the boy said to me. "Has a real presence about her."

"Was she wearing her nightgown?" Paul asked.

"And bedroom slippers," the potter said.

I hadn't given any thought to her feet. If she had gone out in the woods barefoot, her feet would have been shredded by now. How much protection did slippers give her?

"She started shivering," the potter said, "so I gave her a blanket Grace had made for me." He looked back at his girlfriend, who had followed him in. "She wrapped up in that. After I had unloaded the pots, she got up to leave. She tried to give me the blanket back, but I told her to give it to me later."

"Did she say where she was going?"

He shook his head. "I assumed back to bed. I offered to walk her to the cabin, but she walked off before I could."

"Did she head back to the cabin?" Newell asked.

"I didn't notice. I was too busy with my pots."

"But you think it was around five?"

"I did notice that, because that's when I finally turned in myself," he said, yawning. The boy had stayed up all night to unload his pots.

"So she's only actually been missing an hour and a half," Paul said to me. "Which is better news."

"And at least she has that blanket," Billie said.

"It's made out of alpaca wool," the potter's girlfriend said in a quiet voice. "It should keep her warm, even if it gets wet."

If she hasn't lost it, I thought.

Paul and Billie divided the artists into groups, then assigned them sections of the campus, using Paul's map. By eight o'clock shouts of "Irene" could be heard from one end of the school to the other. By midmorning the artists had gone through every cabin, every studio, every bathroom, every closet, every attic, and every crawl space.

I sat at the table, crossing off sections of the campus whenever a group reported back that they hadn't found her. Billie then would assign them another section. As groups came back with nothing to report, my Xs began to cover the campus. My eyes wandered to the edge of the map, where the woods backed up to national forest. That's what Paul had been worried about, I knew. Maybe I had been wrong. Maybe she had headed into the woods, determined not to go back to Rolling Hills or to escape me.

By midmorning, Penland Road was lined with pickups, jeeps, and other four-wheel-drive vehicles. Penland's director had called the Yancey County Rescue Squad—polite, kind-faced men in feed caps who got all the facts, then quietly went about their work. The artists kept on searching, too. Paul joined Newell and Jackson, searching out toward the orchard. Billie stayed in the dining hall with Beverly and Debbie, making coffee and cooking biscuits and making sandwiches for the searchers who would come in soaked, dirty, and tired.

Billie had found some ibuprofen and after taking a few, I could get around the kitchen and help. I poured coffee for the searchers, who would come in long enough for a bite to eat and a swig of coffee. The sky had remained overcast, the fine rain had slackened, but the temperature hovered in the upper forties. This was December weather in July. The searchers would come in with their cheeks and noses red. Paul even started a fire in the fireplace so they could warm their hands.

The rescue squad asked for an article of Irene's clothing for the search dogs. I gave them the blouse she had been wearing yesterday.

As the fellows let the wrinkled-faced hound dogs sniff Irene's blouse, I knew the sweet, dark scent those dogs smelled, and I prayed they would lead us to her. I followed along with the searchers through the campus, keeping up as best I could, but my blood ran cold when the dogs turned and headed up into the woods, in the direction of national forest. Those woods didn't let up for thirty miles.

During emergencies, time is a runaway train, hurtling toward bad news. It seemed only minutes had passed from the time I'd discovered Irene gone to when I looked up at the dining hall clock and saw it was nearly six o'clock. Dark was already creeping into the cove where the dogs had led the searchers. There was a chill in the air that promised a cold night. By this time, a whole company of park rangers had joined the hunt, along with a search helicopter, which beat the air with its great wings way up the cove. We could faintly hear the dogs barking.

Billie and Debbie and Beverly had stayed at the dining hall all day, fixing food for the searchers. Newell and Paul had joined the searchers who had gone into the woods. They had left Jackson with me, who looked sad and exhausted. We sat in the dining hall and watched out the huge windows as the gray sky, which had not changed all day, began to fade, and the pasture and the mountains beyond looked like dreamy suggestions of themselves. I was sitting there, staring at the map as I had stared at it most of the day. Every square of it crossed off.

I turned to the boy. "Something tells me she's not in the woods," I said to him. "But every inch of this place has been checked and rechecked."

Jackson got up, studying the map, and his finger lighted on a tiny little space in the very bottom corner between a couple of the X's. "What does that little cross stand for?" he asked.

I looked to where he pointed. "Means it's a church," I said without thinking. I looked closer, and it said in tiny print underneath the cross, Beacon Chapel.

"Oh," he said, his finger still lingering on the spot.

"A chapel," I said to myself, then looked again at the place he had pointed to, then I smacked the table. "That chapel!"

The boy looked puzzled.

"What did you say?" asked Billie, coming out from the kitchen.

I put my finger to my lips indicating for Jackson to keep quiet. I had made a fool of myself enough today. This was something we could check on our own.

"Nothing," I said, getting to my feet. "Come on, Jackson!"

"Where are you two headed?" Billie asked.

"Jackson has an idea," I said, pushing him ahead of me.

"Do you want me to come with you?" Billie asked.

Several artists came in, looking exhausted. They had been searching for Irene since first thing that morning. They plopped down at one of the tables, their faces smudged, their arms and legs scratched from bushwhacking through the woods.

"See to them," I said to Billie. "The boy and I will be back directly."

"At least take these," Billie said, giving us each a flashlight.

Jackson and I headed down the dirt road away from the hubbub. The squad cars and rescue vehicles with their radios screeching, the searchlights moving across the woods, the thwack of the helicopter, and the occasional eerie bay of the dogs. They sounded far away, as if they had gone into some other world.

I didn't realize how close dark was till we were out in the twilight. No doubt about it, it was much colder than last night. Once darkness fell, Irene would be lost forever. We didn't need the flashlights yet, but it wouldn't be long. The boy and I didn't talk the whole way. When we reached the leveled-out place above the chapel, I pointed down to it. "That's the cross on the map."

The boy nodded, but then he looked at me like he knew something he didn't want to tell me.

"What is it?"

"Daddy and I checked there already this morning."

I looked down through the dark woods at the white chapel, which looked whiter in the oncoming dark, downright luminescent. It was all over. My last hope gone.

"You went inside?" I asked.

He nodded.

The flame of hope that had flickered in my chest since I followed the boy's finger to the little cross on the map was blown right out. Still, we had come this far. It felt better to be doing something, even if it was futile. The path was overgrown with blackberry bushes, and I went first so I could stamp down the briars with my boots. I was amazed how much darker everything became under trees. Night had already come to the woods. Irene was wandering in the dark somewhere. We walked up onto the little porch, and I opened the front door, which was unlocked.

What we felt first was the surprising warmth of the place. The tin roof had collected the day's heat. Dust filtered through a ray of sunlight that had managed to cut through the gathering dark. My heart fell as we looked around and saw the empty pews. There was a little podium for the pulpit. On the front wall above the podium was a framed picture of Jesus, with his crown of thorns. Blood on the tips of the thorns. It was a stark little church and quiet. The place swallowed outside sounds. We couldn't hear the helicopter or the radios or anything other than our own breathing. I shined my flashlight around. The floors looked swept. No cobwebs had gathered in the corners. Somebody kept this place up.

I tried the light switches, but the power was off. I sat in the back pew and turned my flashlight off. My ankle ached worse than ever.

"The dogs were right," I said. "And I was wrong. She's gone up into those woods."

The boy sat down beside me and stared at the pulpit. I don't know how long we sat there. Long enough for the last light to begin to soften and fade, leaving only shadows. The boy reached for his flashlight. "I'm going around outside. Look for tracks," he said, not sounding hopeful. I stared at the framed picture of Jesus over the pulpit, which was getting harder to make out.

Irene had gone on to another world, and I had sent her, having no regard for anything but my own selfish needs. I tried to remind myself that she had been the one who made the advances, but she had been my responsibility. I should have put a stop to things. Then I wondered if Irene had made love to me, knowing all along that she was leaving. Even with her mind mutinying on her, Irene had given me one last gift. I felt the foundations of the house that was our life give way.

I leaned my head onto the pew in front of me, feeling the hard wood against my forehead, then I looked up at the picture of Jesus, and said, "Lord, I know you and me aren't on close terms, but I'm not praying for me. I'm praying for Irene." My voice echoed, sounding strange and nothing like me. "If you're listening, I hope you will see fit to protect Irene tonight and watch over her. And if she's cold and suffering, please . . ." My voice broke at this and for a minute I could not go on. "If she's suffering, Lord, please let her go on to sleep . . . for all time." Looking up at the picture of Jesus, I said, "She's all yours."

The silence was like nothing I had ever heard. It was cottony and stifling, like the inside of a tomb. You could almost touch the rich emptiness of it. Was I wishing Irene dead? I didn't want her suffering out there, that was certain, but was there something self-ish in my prayer? A kind of release I yearned for?

I slowly leaned back into my seat. Every now and then I could see the boy's flashlight flit around outside through the old wavy glass. Time passed, and the night deepened around that little chapel. I couldn't say how long I sat there, time becoming beside the point. My heart felt as hollow and scraped out as a gourd.

Then, what seemed years later, I heard something. The boy outside. No, a rustling in the walls, maybe a lone field mouse we had disturbed. I heard a yawn, but it wasn't outside. It was in the church with me. A yawn from God, I thought, bored with my tribulations. I had come to him, not in faith, but out of despera-tion. A foul-weather worshipper.

I heard the yawn again, and it was about that time that a shadow lifted above a pew down in front. My heart beat in my throat, and the hair raised on the back of my neck. A ghost. Maybe I was al-ready dead myself, crossed on over. The ghost sat up and stretched. I reached for my flashlight but knocked it onto the floor. I was down on my knees feeling for it when the door behind me banged open and the boy came back in the chapel. Seeing what I saw, he shined the flashlight on it.

Still wrapped in the potter's blanket, Irene shielded her wild eyes from the light. Her face was smudged, her hair matted and full of leaves. Burrs and pine needles clung to the blanket. She looked like some aged wood nymph disturbed from her nap.

Fifteen

Too Much for Me

I could see the beam of Jackson's flashlight as he tore through the woods, running back to the dining hall for help. I examined Irene by the light of my own flashlight. The blanket, smelling of wet wool, had kept her warm and dry. Somehow her bedroom slippers had stayed on, and even though they were shredded, had protected her feet. Irene's hair was full of twigs and leaves, and her face was scraped and dirty, and the blanket was sticky with pine resin. It seemed she had wandered the woods for some time before she finally found her way here.

"How long have you been here?" I asked, picking burrs from the damp hem of her nightgown.

She didn't say anything.

"Do you remember when you came here? Was it this morning or this afternoon?"

She smiled her hopeless little smile.

"Was it dark or light?"

"Is this for a grade?" she asked.

"No," I said, unable to keep from smiling, "it's not for a grade."

She relaxed against the pew. "I am not prepared."

After I saw she was physically all right, there was nothing else to do but wait until help arrived. I sat with my arm around her, trying to keep her warm, although the blanket was already doing a good job of that. The wind had picked up outside and roared through the woods. A cold draft came in from somewhere. Occasionally small limbs would clatter onto the tin roof and slide slowly off.

"I couldn't find the kitchen," she said, looking around the chapel.

"You're hungry," I said, realizing she hadn't eaten since last night. "Someone should be coming soon."

She nodded toward the picture of Jesus above the podium, and her eyes widened.

"I don't think He's coming," she said.

A little more time passed, and she turned and looked at me.

"Someone getting . . . hitched?" she asked.

"No."

She frowned. "Then did someone . . ."

"No," I said. "This isn't a funeral. We're just waiting."

She was quiet for a little while, then turned to me and whispered, "For whom?"

"For help."

"Oh," she said, nodding. More time passed. As the wind continued to roar outside, I realized that it had been irresponsible to send Jackson into the woods on a night like this. He might lose his way, and we would have to start this search business all over again.

"I know you." Irene studied my face.

"I'm your husband."

"Ah," she said, as if that explained it. She folded her hands in her lap and looked straight ahead. We sat there in the little chapel like lone travelers in a way station.

"Irene?" I asked taking her hand.

She turned to me.

"Were you running away from me?" I asked.

"From you?"

"Were you running away because of what happened last night? Because of what I did to you?"

She squinted as if concentrating hard to remember.

"Last night you and me . . ." I cleared my throat. "Last night, well, we slept together."

She studied me hard.

"In the Biblical sense," I added.

She was almost scowling, but then a smile slowly spread across her face. She remembered . . . something. I read it as a smile of exoneration, that she hadn't been fleeing from me or from what happened. That is not to say that in letting happen what happened, I had not stirred her up in a way that sent her wandering. So, in that way, I was just as responsible.

In a while, we saw through the window a twinkle or two of what I guessed to be flashlights. Then a whole parade of them came down the path I had seen the boy disappear up earlier. We couldn't see the people, just the lights bounce down toward the chapel through the dark. Must have been thirty or forty of them, streaming toward the chapel. A few people carried lanterns, which punctuated the strand with brightness—a necklace of light weaving through the woods.

"The souls of the dead," Irene whispered in awe, her eyes shining.

We could hear excited voices outside above the wind, then feet on the porch. I opened the church door. There was a cold blast, and the searchers streamed in, artists as well as the men from town filling the church with their lights.

Newell ran up to Irene. His face was streaked with dirt, his shirt and pants were nearly as full of burrs as Irene's blanket. He sank down on his knees before his mother and buried his head in her lap. Irene put her hand on his head and stroked it, but looked at me as if to ask, What is all the fuss about?

After Newell had regained himself he turned to me, "Jackson and I checked here this morning."

"Maybe she was wandering the woods, then ended up here later," I said.

"When did you come here, Mama?" Newell asked her.

Irene looked at me, like she wanted me to explain it.

"She doesn't remember," I said.

"We didn't check the pews," Jackson said, who had been standing off to the side.

"What's that?" Newell turned to Jackson.

"When we checked the chapel this morning we didn't walk to the front and check all the pews," Jackson said. "We couldn't have seen her from where we were standing."

"He's right," I said. "I didn't see Irene till she sat up and stretched."

Newell looked at Jackson and me. "So she could have been here this morning when Jackson and I checked the church. And while we were scouring every inch of this mountainside, she could have been sleeping peacefully right here all the time?"

We turned to Irene, who smiled uncomfortably, like we were speaking a language she didn't understand.

A couple of the Burnsville volunteer firemen checked Irene over, taking her pulse, her temperature, her blood pressure. When they found that she was in good shape, they held up a blanket, making a screen to allow Billie to help Irene out of her damp nightgown and into a change of clothes Billie had brought from the cabin. She had even brought along Irene's shoes and socks.

Irene was too worn-out to walk. The firemen had brought

along a stretcher, but it was going to be hard carrying her back up the overgrown trail through the woods. So Newell took her in his arms and carried her all the way back to the dining hall.

Anticipating that the search might go all night, the kitchen crew had already made two giant pots of stew—one with beef and one without—and a dozen pans of corn bread. Newell set Irene down at one of the tables. I sat beside her and fed her beef stew and bites of buttered corn bread. She was so famished she grabbed the spoon out of my hand and ate the rest herself.

Meanwhile, the hungry searchers, their ears and faces red from the night cold, filed in to eat, but not before coming by our table and paying their respects to Irene. The men from town were especially cheery, patting me on the back, taking their hats off to Irene. They knew how lucky we were. They had been on too many searches that hadn't ended this way.

As the men from town and the artists settled down side by side to eat their stew and corn bread, there was an air of goodwill. Potters sat next to volunteer firemen, glassblowers next to members of the rescue squad, weavers next to EMTs. Everybody talking loud as if all the pent-up tension of the day was being let loose. Every now and then a strong gust of wind would shake the dining hall, rattling the big windowpanes and whistling under the eaves. Conversation quieted and eyes wandered to the dark window.

After a while, Newell, looking like the Wild Man of Borneo with his day-old beard, his uncombed hair, and his tired, dazed eyes, stood up and thanked the searchers. In a trembling voice he said that he and his family would always be indebted to the Penland community for returning his mother to us. I looked away while he talked, feeling embarrassed and responsible.

I realized that we would need to stay another night since it was too late to return to Rolling Hills. I asked Newell if it was all right.

"I assumed you would," Newell said.

"I'll need to call the nursing home," I said.

Newell showed me the phone in the back office. It was the only phone in the place, and it was where Newell sat and talked to Jackson when he called him in the evenings. I sat at the desk and called Rolling Hills. It rang for a long time. Finally, Linda, the charge nurse, picked up. I told her we wouldn't be back until tomorrow.

"That's fine, Mr. Marshbanks," she said, sounding out of breath. She had obviously run up to the nurses' station from someone's room. "Oh, and for your information Natasha has been terminated."

"Mercer fired her?" I asked, astonished.

"We had another complaint later in the day," she said. "And I told Mr. Mercer that it was either that aide or me."

"Thank you," I said.

"I did it as much for me," she said. "She was making my life miserable."

After I hung up, I sat in the office a minute thinking about Rolling Hills and about Linda. It was a brave thing she had done, forcing Mercer to fire the aide. Not everyone out at Rolling Hills was a bad person. In fact the good probably outnumbered the bad. There were plenty of aides who were gentle and kind with Irene, treating her respectfully. I thought about my vow first thing this morning, before I knew Irene had disappeared, that I would try her at home again. But thinking how in a single twenty-four-hour period she had locked herself in a bathroom stall, nearly been killed by walking out into a thunderstorm, and could have easily been lost forever by wandering into the woods, I knew she would be too much for me at home.

After supper, Irene was strong enough to walk back to the cabin under her own steam. Newell held one arm, Paul held the other, and Jackson shined the flashlight in front of us. The wind was still blowing hard. The boy ran ahead and kicked fallen limbs and sticks out of Irene's way. It was unbelievably cold for a July night. One of the men gave Irene his jacket, which had YANCEY COUNTY RESCUE SQUAD written in big letters across the back. When I said I would bring it back, he told us to keep it.

The wind whipped through the trees as we walked down to the cabin. We were all tired, and even if we could have been heard over the wind, we would have been too tired to say much. Irene had the most energy of any of us, which, when I thought about it, made sense. She had probably slept in that chapel undisturbed a good portion of the day.

I gave Irene her sedative the minute we set foot in the cabin, and Newell locked the back door and the front door. The weather had turned so cold he and Jackson moved their sleeping bags off the front porch and slept on the floor in the main room. They spread their sleeping bags in front of the doorway, so Irene would have to climb over them to get out.

Billie helped Irene take a warm shower, then we got her ready for bed. The rest of us took showers and sat by the fire Newell had started in the fireplace, it being such a chilly night.

By nine o'clock, Newell and Jackson were asleep in their sleeping bags in the main room. They had been on the run most of the day, searching. Irene was in the bedroom asleep from the sedative. Billie and I were both exhausted but weren't quite ready for bed. Billie fixed tea, and we sat at the kitchen table. We could hear the wind outside, which, just when it seemed to die down, would pick up again. I thought about those barred owls holed up in some hollow tree.

I don't know how long Billie and I had been sitting there in the quiet kitchen. She was studying one of Newell's paintings propped against a cupboard, when she finally looked at me, and with her sad eyes said, "I wish I could have more time with him."

"That could probably be arranged," I said.

"He's leaving at the end of the summer," she said.

"Oh, you're talking about Jackson."

She looked back toward the living room, then lowered her voice. "Now, Mr. Marshbanks, you have to understand I have no designs on Newell." She traced her finger along the rim of her teacup. "Besides, if there's one thing I have learned, he's not really like you."

"That's got to be a plus."

"Not in my book," Billie said.

"He has my ears, poor boy."

"I do like his ears."

"And he's got my temper," I said.

"Your passion," she said, looking at me. "I can see that in his best paintings."

I paused. "You remind me of Irene in some ways," I said.

An awkwardness settled between us. A little more time passed as we sipped on our tea and listened to the fire pop in the other room. She looked at me, then back toward the bedroom where Irene was asleep. "You're stalling again, aren't you?"

"I think I disturbed her sleep last night," I said.

"It's not always a bad thing for a husband to disturb his wife's sleep," she said.

"It is if his wife walks off into the woods and causes half the county to turn out searching for her."

She nodded like she understood. "I'll sleep with her," she said.

"Thanks," I said, unable to look at her.

I went back to get a couple of things out of the bedroom. Irene was sound asleep. I then went on out to the main room, where Billie was getting her pack.

"Good night," she whispered.

"Good night," I said.

She headed back to the bedroom and closed the door.

The fire in the fireplace was getting low, so I went out to the woodpile beside the cabin. It was bitter cold now. I could see my breath. If I hadn't known better, I would have thought it was November or even December. The night sky was a sea of stars. The more I looked at it, the more I felt like I was falling into it. Hard little pinpoints, giving way to more pinpoints. Now that Irene was safe inside, there was something about this cold snap that heartened me. Winter had always been the season I was most at home in, when the bleak weather met my state of mind. I had always felt at odds with spring and summer.

I carried the split logs inside, put a couple of more on the fire, then sat down on the couch to unlace my shoes. That was when I noticed Newell staring at the fire, his eyes wide-open.

"Did I wake you?" I said low not to wake the boy.

He shook his head, propping his head on his elbow and still looking at the fire. "Billie sure is a nice girl," Newell said quietly.

I had to wonder if he had overheard us in the kitchen. "She is," I said, pulling my boots off with a groan.

"Jackson is smitten with her," Newell said. "And I know you like her." He looked back at me.

"She's been a good neighbor." I leaned my head back on my pillow. I hadn't slept worth a tinker's damn last night.

A little while went by, and I was indeed falling asleep, when Newell said, "I know Jackson must miss having a mother."

"What boy wouldn't?" I said.

Newell turned and looked at me, then looked back at the fire.

"Now that I'm finally feeling better," Newell said. "I guess I'm hesitant to enter into anything. Besides . . ." He lowered his voice and looked off in the direction of the bedroom. "She probably wants a family of her own. Children of her own."

"Maybe," I said.

A log shifted in the fireplace, sending up sparks.

"What if I asked her if she would like to . . . see me, and she turned me down?" he asked.

"You wouldn't be the first," I said.

"Or even if she was willing to go out, what would I do? My dating skills have atrophied."

"You've got nothing to lose, Newell."

"What about my self-respect?" he said, sitting up.

"Like I said."

He smiled. In the firelight his face looked softer somehow, broken in, like he had reached that point in midlife when he was too tired to be anything other than comfortable with himself.

"What if she isn't interested in me?"

"Then it's her loss," I said.

He looked up at me like he was surprised I had said that. I had surprised myself. And the thought flitted through my head that Irene's gradual mental departure from us might allow Newell and me to grow a little closer. And the next thought, a terrible one, was that in a way, by being the best mother a mother could be to her son and the best wife a wife could be to her husband, Irene had inadvertently kept Newell and me at a distance from one another. She had done all our work for us.

Newell slid the sleeping boy gently next to him, held his head in his lap and said quietly more to himself than to me, "*He* is what I have to lose." I saw that Newell had with his son something I had not had with mine, but then it had been a trade-off for Newell, a nightmarish car wreck of a trade-off.

"Nothing's going to happen to Jackson," I said.

"Being away from him," Newell said, holding the sleeping boy's head in his lap, "has reminded me how much he means to me."

"It's funny," I said, "But these days it's when I am with your mother that I miss her most."

We didn't talk anymore. Just looked at the fire. After a little while Newell laid the boy back down, said good night, and scooted into his sleeping bag. Wasn't long before the fire died, and I was just this side of sleep when a hand took hold of my own in the dark. At first I thought it was Jackson's. But the size and strength of it told me it was Newell's.

We left after breakfast. Everyone was quiet as we drove down the winding road away from Penland, and then turned onto 19-23, which would take us past Asheville and down the mountain to Greenville. Jackson sat next to me in the passenger seat, clutching Rudy and looking straight ahead. Billie sat with Irene in the back, who, from her resigned expression, seemed to know she was headed back.

Billie had a distant look as I braked the van down the mountain. I guessed that she was confused about Newell since, from what he had said last night, he had been confused about her. As she was leaving this morning, Newell and she had started to hug, but both seemed to think better of it and awkwardly shook hands.

When we pulled into the Rolling Hills parking lot, my heart sank at the sight of the place. Irene sat in her seat, staring and I thought, *Oh, Lord.* I went around and took her hand, but she shook her head.

"Now, Irene, you have to go back," I said.

"The chair on wheels," she said. She had been waiting for me to unfold the wheelchair, which we hadn't used the whole time up at Penland. She was probably tired from the trip, or maybe seeing the place took something out of her.

Billie rolled the wheelchair around. Irene climbed in, and Billie pushed her inside. The boy walked beside Irene, and I brought up the rear with her overnight bag. My heart was heavy as the big glass doors whooshed open, then whooshed closed behind us. We all breathed a bit easier with the cool air-conditioning. But the smell of the place, while not sour, was a little sharp, a little antiseptic—a smell hiding other smells.

Several folks in wheelchairs had looked up hopefully when we walked in, and although they greeted us, happy to have anyone break up the monotony, we weren't who they had been expecting.

We passed the administrator's office, and Mercer was talking to his secretary very quietly. Mercer looked up at us, and I thought to myself, he says one cheery thing I am going to punch his lights out. But he didn't. In fact, he looked at us and didn't say a word, didn't even smile. He just looked at us, and, for the first time in all the months I had been coming here, I felt like he had actually seen us.

We passed the dining hall, where the dining room ladies were setting out the silverware for supper. One of them waved at Irene and Irene half waved back. Then we went on down the long hallway and turned onto Irene's unit. Linda was at the nurses' station and as soon as she saw Irene, she came around and hugged her. "Welcome back, Mrs. Marshbanks. Did you have a good time?"

"As far as I can remember," she said, looking at me.

"You have color in your cheeks," Linda said to Irene, then looked at me. "Looks like she got outside."

"She got outside all right," I said, and while I was debating whether to go into it, Irene had pushed herself out of her wheelchair and, holding the boy's hand, walked herself down the hall toward her room.

"Everything go all right?" Linda asked me.

"Fine," I said.

"She looks better, and so do you." Linda patted my arm.

I started to follow Irene, but Linda held my arm.

"Mr. Marshbanks," she said, lowering her voice, "I thought you should know that the board of trustees asked for Mr. Mercer's resignation this morning."

"So that explains it," I said. Now I understood why the old boy had looked different this morning.

"Apparently, Mr. Swanson, one of the trustees whose mother is a resident here, came in last night and found Natasha wrestling her out of a chair and cursing her."

"I thought Mercer had fired her."

"He hired her back," Linda said. "Anyway, when Mr. Swanson learned that Natasha had been fired because of previous abuses to patients, he called a meeting of the board. By ten o'clock this morning they had asked for Mr. Mercer's letter of resignation."

"I noticed everybody seemed to be in a better mood," I said, thinking back on the waving dining room lady and the aides and nurses who had greeted Irene on our way back to the unit.

"Who knows who they'll get to replace him," Linda said, then lowered her voice. "But it would be hard to find anyone as inept."

The phone rang, and Linda answered it as I walked on down to Irene's room. I found her sitting back in her easy chair and smiling at Jackson, who sat holding her hand while Billie unpacked Irene's bag. Irene beamed at me when I came into the room. "Long time no see," she said, grinning. She was making fun of herself. I think.

"Long time no see," I said.

Decatur Dixon, who had been rolling past in his wheelchair on his daily rounds, stopped and pivoted his chair and rolled in Irene's room. He squinted at us with his good eye, the other covered with his patch. A brainy pirate.

"Welcome home, Miss Irene."

"Thank you," she said, frowning a bit as if she wasn't sure she had been away.

"How'd the mountains treat you?"

"Very well," she said. "Very well indeed."

He looked at me. "Did you hear about The Mercenary?"

"Linda told me," I said.

"It's been like Armistice Day around here," Decatur said. "'Course tomorrow they will bring some other administrator they fished out of the shallow end of the gene pool." He looked at Irene, then said, "She got some color, she looks better."

I told him it had been a hell of a lot cooler up there.

"I tried to go out this morning," Decatur said, "but I couldn't take the heat."

We all looked out the window at the barren little halfhearted attempt of a courtyard that the inside rooms faced at Rolling Hills. In the spring, I had often rolled Irene out there, or on her good days she walked out there and we sat on one of the wooden benches and admired the jonquils and the tulips and other miracle flowers that bloomed in spite of total neglect.

"See you at supper." Decatur deftly backed his wheelchair out of the room and started to roll away, but before he did, he stuck his head back in the room and said, "Glad you're back."

"Me too," Irene said, saying it like she meant it. Or maybe that was how I wanted to hear it.

Sixteen

Newell Comes

Although Irene was never quite as aware as she had been that weekend up at Penland, she became more adjusted to Rolling Hills during the last weeks of Jackson's stay. She played bingo, attended sing-alongs, went to birthday parties. As often as not, when Jackson and I arrived in the afternoons, she wouldn't be in her room, and we would have to track her down in the crafts room or the game room.

Jackson and I were on our way home from our last day together at Rolling Hills. Irene had gone to bed early. She had attended an exercise class in the morning, a paper-folding class after lunch, and gone to Dot's birthday party that evening. Irene had become so active that she often tired herself out and went to bed early.

It was almost dark as we drove home—the evenings came earlier now that we were into August. It had rained and cooled things off. A line of thunderstorms had passed through, leaving a clear sky and a pinkish gold light that varnished the streets and the buildings and the trees. We rode with our windows down, the tires hissed along the steaming pavement. Even though some days had been hotter than July, the evenings brought a lighter air. At night, after the boy had fallen asleep, I would pause on the back steps and smell the faint dry scent of fall, even if it was still a good month away. This was how I had marked the last couple of weeks with the boy. He would leave before fall arrived, but I could smell his absence on the night air. Newell was coming tomorrow.

"What is it tonight? McDonald's? Burger King?" I asked.

"I'm in the mood for the Colonel tonight," he said.

That was my line. He preferred a big order of fries and a chocolate milk shake from McDonald's or Burger King.

"What will you eat there?" I asked. "We could go by McDonald's first."

The boy crossed his arms. "You said I could choose."

"Suit yourself," I said. I turned in at Kentucky Fried Chicken. The only people there were a family in a booth—a mother and father with a young son and daughter.

Jackson stared up at the menu on the wall behind the server, like he was trying to figure out what a vegetarian could eat in a place like this.

"You could have a couple of biscuits, an order of mashed potatoes, and an order of cole slaw," I said.

"I want a two-piece meal with dark meat," he said to the server, sounding like he had been rehearsing his order. "Extra crispy."

"You sure about this?" I asked.

The boy nodded to the server, a white, pimply-faced teenager who entered Jackson's order on the register. "A two-piece, extra crispy," the teenage boy said back to Jackson.

"With a large iced tea," Jackson said.

Then the teenager looked at me.

"I'll have the same."

"That'll be seven dollars and eighty-five cents," the fellow said.

I was pulling out my wallet, when Jackson handed the cashier a little wad of bills out of his pants pocket. "It's on me."

"Don't be silly," I said.

The server had already unfolded the bills and counted out what the meal cost and handed the change back to the boy.

"I forgot Daddy gave me a little spending money at the beginning of the summer," Jackson said. "I found it in my backpack last night. I thought I would take you out for once."

I felt a lump rise in my throat at the image of him getting out his backpack last night.

Jackson carried the tray with the food back to the table, while I filled our drink glasses with iced tea. On my way to the table, I passed by the family, who looked like they were finishing up. I had nodded to them without thinking, when the father said, "How's Mrs. Marshbanks?"

I stopped and looked at the fellow, who was familiar, but I couldn't place him.

"Nate Baker, the phone repairman," he said. "Showed you the way back to Rolling Hills that rainy afternoon a couple of months ago."

"Sure, sure," I said, indicating I couldn't shake his hands because I was carrying the drinks. "I'm sorry I didn't recognize you, but these days I'm about as good with faces as I am directions."

"He looks different without his helmet," said the wife in a kind voice. She spoke like her husband did, in a crisp Yankee accent. She was a pretty woman with smooth, coffee-colored skin and high cheekbones. A dead ringer for Lena Horne. "You're the man whose wife has Alzheimer's," she said.

"How is Mrs. Marshbanks?" Nate asked. "Ma Bell has me working in the southern part of the county. I haven't been by Rolling Hills in a while."

"Holding her own," I said. "At least in some ways."

"It's a strange disease," the phone repairman's wife said. "Nate's mother had been a bitter old woman until the Alzheimer's."

"Then she forgot what she had been bitter about," Nate said to me. "Your wife is lucky to have a devoted husband to take care of her."

"She doesn't need much tending these days," I said. I couldn't hardly stand any of the nursing home activities. Sometimes I would drop Irene off at a sing-along or to play bingo or to attend a little play some schoolkids put on, then go back to her room and read the paper or watch baseball. Sometimes it felt like I spent more time in her room than she did.

"I'll stop by and see her soon," the man said.

"She'd like that," I said. "Nice meeting you," I said to the wife, then carried the iced teas to the table, where the boy was patiently waiting. He had set out napkins and plastic knives and forks. When I sat down with the drinks, he took a drumstick out of his box and bit into it with a vengeance.

Except for a bowl of stew up at Penland, the boy had stayed true to his vegetarian diet the whole summer. I had noticed him eye my hamburgers at supper lately, and the other morning I saw him finger a piece of bacon, but then put it back.

"I had forgotten how good fried chicken is," the boy said as he finished the drumstick, then washed it down with some sweet tea. He took a big bite of mashed potatoes, then pulled the thigh out and commenced to eat. He had ordered exactly what I always ordered.

"You aren't doing this on my account, are you?"

The boy licked the chicken grease off his fingers. "I'm tired of being a herbivore," he said.

"Who's been calling you names?" I said.

"It means plant eater," he said, not sure if I was kidding.

"Oh, well then," I said. "I bet you are tired of that."

I started in on my chicken, too, and though I enjoyed it, I took even greater pleasure in watching Jackson finish off the thigh and then go back to the counter and order himself a whole other two-piece.

"Your grandson has quite an appetite," Nate Baker said as he and his family passed our table on their way out.

"He's a recovering vegetarian," I said.

Jackson set down the chicken breast he had been working on, wiping his hands on his napkin, then picked it back up and tore into it again. Nate's handsome boy, who must have been around Jackson's age, watched him like he had never seen anybody eat so hungrily. The little girl, who was much smaller, and you could tell would grow up to be as pretty as her mother, stared at Jackson, too, like she was watching some wild animal tear into its prey.

"So long," Nate said to me, shepherding his children out the door. I watched as Nate and his family climbed in a new van, the kind whose back doors open on both sides. I watched them drive off. They were a solid family. You could tell by the way that they had sat together in the booth. They had a closeness they carried with them, like pegs holding down four corners of a roomy tent.

After the boy had finally had his fill of chicken, we headed home. I was a little sorry to leave the Kentucky Fried. More people had come in and sat down around us, eating and talking. There was a brightness, a liveliness to the greasy old place that I didn't want to leave. I could have sat there and watched that boy eat chicken all night.

When we got back in the van and I turned down Jones Avenue, I felt a kind of closing in. Our world, or mine anyway, was about to narrow again. Even when I pulled into the drive, I was thinking, this is the last time I pull into the drive with the boy. Everything we did the rest of the night, watching a nature show on TV, him feeding the cats, me reading to him out of an old copy of *Robin Hood* I used to read to Newell, him going into the bathroom and noisily brushing his teeth, every little thing that was said or done had a taste of the end about it.

That night he slept in my bed as he had most of the summer. I had said good night to him and went out to the den to read my book. About half an hour later, long after he had usually gone to sleep, I heard him pad up the hall and he came into the den.

"What time did Daddy say he was coming tomorrow?"

"About one o'clock," I said. "Can't sleep?"

He shook his head.

"Maybe it's all that iced tea you drank," I said.

He nodded slightly.

"You go on back to bed. I'll heat some milk and bring it up to you."

He stood there, looking at me, like he was about to say something, but then turned and went back to my bedroom. I went into the kitchen and heated up a pan of milk, but as I was pouring it in the glass I noticed a fly in it. I didn't have any more milk, so I called Billie and asked if I could borrow a glass of milk. I had started out the front door, when Billie appeared on my front porch with a glass of milk.

"You didn't have to bring it over," I said.

"No trouble," she said.

"You want to come in?"

"I've got something in the oven," she said. "Newell's arriving around one tomorrow." She wasn't asking, she was telling. "And y'all are having supper with me tomorrow night." Again, she wasn't asking but telling. She and Newell talked on the phone almost every night now. Weekend before last, she had driven up to Penland by herself. When Billie returned from that first weekend alone with Newell, she didn't say much. It was easy to tell by the distracted look in her eye and the color in her cheeks that her time had not been disagreeable. Still, I was surprised when she went back last weekend, too. Neither Billie nor Newell said much about these weekend visits, which made me think things were getting a bit more than friendly.

By the time I took the warm milk to the boy, he was sound asleep, his arm around Rudy. So I pulled up a chair beside him and drank the milk myself. I hadn't had warm milk since I was a child when my daddy used to bring it to me when I couldn't sleep.

After a while, I brushed my teeth, turned out all the lights and climbed in bed beside the boy. I leaned over and buried my nose in his hair, which smelled of dust and sweat. I sat there on my side, propped on my elbow, studying the boy. My summer with him was over. I remembered when Newell had called back in May, and I had dreaded having to care for him.

I smelled his hair one more time, then turned and pulled the covers over us. And as I was about to fall asleep, the boy sidled up against me.

Newell arrived the next afternoon, pulling into the drive with a car full of paintings. Jackson had been sitting on the front porch, his eyes trained up the street in the direction Newell would come. When Newell's Subaru finally did turn in our drive, he gave a whoop and ran down, hugging his father as soon as he stepped out of the car.

Newell had filled out a little, his eyes weren't hollow anymore. The dark circles were all but gone. And smiles seemed to come easy to him. He got his bag out of the car, but the boy took it from him and carried it on into the house, with us following.

I made us a late lunch of BLTs, and we were halfway through

the meal before Newell noticed that Jackson hadn't taken the bacon out of his sandwich like he used to at restaurants.

"You're eating meat," Newell said, sounding shocked.

The boy took another bite of sandwich.

"How long has this been going on?" Newell looked at me.

"Since yesterday," I said.

Newell frowned like he was trying to restrain himself. After the boy had finished and taken Newell's night bag upstairs, Newell turned to me, and I figured he was going to let me have it.

"I never forced him . . ." I began.

"What a relief," he said, keeping his voice down, looking in the direction of the staircase up to his old room. "You don't know what it's been like trying to cook for a vegetarian boy and make sure he got enough protein."

"You *want* him to eat meat?" I asked. "But I thought . . ."

"When he started eating vegetarian," he said, "the therapist said it might be Jackson's way of keeping a connection to his mother. The therapist said it was a probably a healthy response, an active way of honoring Sandy's memory. And that made sense. Of course, the therapist didn't have to cook for him."

"I see," I said.

"One other thing the therapist said was that Jackson would probably give up the vegetarian diet when he had recovered enough." Newell looked at me. "So this might be a sign that he's better."

"I'll be damned," I said, having not given any thought to the deeper meaning of the boy's tearing into Kentucky Fried Chicken.

"Daddy," called Jackson from upstairs, "come on up."

"In a minute," Newell called, and he started to help me clear the dishes.

"You go on up," I said.

Newell started out of the room, then stopped and looked at me. "We will visit a lot more."

"Irene will like that," I said.

"Maybe Jackson can come down for weekends by himself every now and then," Newell said.

I didn't look at him. "If it would help you out," I said.

"Daddy!" the boy called again, and Newell disappeared upstairs.

I had stacked the dishes in the sink and was running hot water over them when I heard Newell cry out. "Lord, God!" I dried my hands on a dishrag and headed upstairs. I found him in the middle of his old room, looking around, dumbstruck.

"I had no idea you had done this." He looked at me.

"I decided to spruce it up a little," I said.

"A little?" He walked over to his mural and ran his hand over it. "And this, this looks as if I painted it yesterday."

"You'd be surprised what a little 409 will do."

Newell laughed, and I had to give it to him, he didn't take his paintings nearly as seriously as the collectors. That's not to say he didn't take *painting* seriously. He was dead serious about the act but not so much about the results.

One time I had heard Irene go on and on about one of his paintings, and Newell had said, "You should have seen it before I painted it." I knew what he meant. In my own work, I had always pictured a house painted before I painted it, and try as I might, I could never make the finished job live up to the paint job in my head.

After Newell settled in, he and Jackson went to Rolling Hills to stay with Irene for the afternoon. Billie came over almost as soon after they drove off. She must have been watching from her house.

"How does he seem?" she asked. She was a little flushed.

"More like himself," I said.

"His time up there has done him good," Billie said.

"To tell you the truth," I said, "I didn't believe this Penland business would make a damned bit of difference."

"We all need a break every now and then," she said, raising her eyebrows at me.

"I am getting a break," I said. "Newell went over there today. You went over the other day."

"I'm talking about a real break," she said. "Like a week or two." For a while she had been suggesting I not go over to Rolling Hills every afternoon, that she wouldn't mind going over more often. One afternoon last week, when I wanted to take the boy fishing, she had gone over to Rolling Hills, and the boy and I had had a whole day of fishing up at Jones Gap.

"Mrs. Marshbanks has settled in over there now," Billie said.

"That's a nice way of saying she doesn't need me anymore."

"Most of your married life you were both pretty independent," Billie said. "You both went to work, you both did different things when you got home, you both had different friends."

"*She* had friends."

"In other words, you two didn't spend every waking minute together."

"But most of the sleeping ones," I said.

"My point is that y'all's independence was part of why you had such a good marriage. I think Mrs. Marshbanks has finally gotten into the routine of Rolling Hills, and in a way, things have gotten back to normal."

"Normal?" I asked, raising my voice. "My wife lives in a nursing home, and half the time doesn't know me from Adam. You call that normal?"

"This is a new normal," she said.

"This is hell!"

"If you make it hell," she said unflustered.

"Easy for you to say," I said.

"You're right," Billie said. "It is easy for me to say, and I didn't mean to upset you."

"You didn't upset me. You just pissed me off a little," I said. "When you take care of somebody for as long as I've taken care of Irene, you think you're the only person who can take care of her. When she stops needing you, you find yourself wondering what exactly is your purpose in life."

"Your purpose in life, Mr. Marshbanks," Billie said, her voice going flinty, "is to be a husband to your wife, a father to your son, a grandfather to your grandson." She counted on her fingers. "And a friend to me."

"Well . . ." I said.

"Sounds to me like you have your hands full."

"If you put it that way," I said.

"We won't all need you all the time," she said, "but we'll need to know that when we do need you, you'll be available. I guess it's sort of like being on call."

"There's a lot of that in old age," I said.

"The truth is," she said, "now that Mrs. Marshbanks has settled in over there, you have a little more freedom."

"Or boredom," I said, "depending on how you look at it."

"Depending on what you do with it," she said, nailing me with her gaze. "I think a week-long trip up to Asheville to visit Newell and Jackson might be in order soon."

"They don't want an old buzzard like me circling around up there," I said.

"That's not what I hear," she said.

"Y'all been talking about me?" I said.

"Of course," she said. "What kind of friend would I be, what

kind of son would he be, if we weren't talking about you?" Before
I could decide if I was irritated, she turned and walked across the
yard toward her house. "Supper will be ready whenever they get
back from Rolling Hills," she called.

That evening, when Newell and Jackson came home, we walked
over together to Billie's. When she met us at the door, she was
wearing a short, low-cut black dress, sparkling earrings, and a pearl
necklace. She had pulled her hair back, showing the elegant curve
of her neck and the sweet soft line of her jaw. It has always mysti-
fied me how women could look so many completely different
ways, as if they kept a closetful of selves.

I had thought of Billie as pretty, even very pretty. The woman
who showed us into her living room and asked what we would like
to drink was in a whole other league. And I couldn't really say that
the impression relied upon any one thing. It was as if what she had
chosen to wear and the excitement of Newell's return and the sad-
ness of the boy's departure had all somehow convened in her that
evening.

Billie cocked her head at Newell. "Mrs. Marshbanks all right
today?"

I could see the effort Newell had to make to pry his mind from
the woman standing before him to answer her question. "Mama
seems more at home out there," he said, looking at me. We hadn't
had a chance to talk since he'd gotten back from Rolling Hills.
"She stays so busy I don't see how you keep up with her."

"I don't," I said.

"She wore Jackson and me out." Then he added a little sadly,
"I'm not sure she knew who we were."

Billie smiled, but the smile was more than sympathetic. "You
seem like you're somewhere else," she said to Newell.

"It's because you're dressed up," Jackson said. "He used to get the same way when Mama would dress up to go out with him."

"Jackson . . ." Newell said again, but he didn't say it angrily.

"And I bet your mother looked beautiful," Billie said.

The boy nodded.

"Well, tonight's a special night," Billie said, putting her arm around Jackson. "So I thought I would dress up a little. Do you mind?"

Jackson shook his head.

"Want to help me get the food on the table?" she asked.

Jackson followed her out to the kitchen.

Newell watched her leave the room, then for the first time, noticed his painting over the couch.

"How did she get this?" Newell asked.

"She bought it," I said. "Back when your paintings didn't cost an arm and a leg." Then I added, half-kidding and half-not, "You should have given it to me, since it is my fishing hole."

Newell looked at me.

"I guess you didn't think about giving it to your old man?" I asked.

"I didn't think you would want it," he said.

"Why would you go and think a thing like that?"

"Because I've never been real sure you liked my paintings." He didn't sound mad or even hurt.

" 'Course, I liked 'em," I said, looking up at the painting.

"You never said much," he said.

"Irene was always making such a big fuss, I couldn't get a word in edgewise."

"But you're the painter in the family," he said.

"Housepainter," I said.

"That's another thing. You and I both know that painting is

painting, whether it's a twelve-inch canvas or a two-story clap-board." He looked back at his painting. "I thought you didn't like my work."

"I thought you didn't care what I thought," I said.

"Well," he said, "that's what we get for thinking." He nodded at the painting, and said, "How 'bout I paint you another one. I'll paint you a whole series of that fishing hole."

"One would be plenty," I said, as we both studied the painting. After a little while, Billie called from the other room, "Dinner's on!"

"Oh," Newell said as if he had just remembered something. Looking off toward the kitchen, he pulled a little felt-covered box out of his pocket. "I meant to show you this," he said in a low voice. "It's for Billie."

"A ring?" I asked.

He started to open it, but Billie came in, and he slid it back into his pocket.

"We're ready," she said, and led us into the dining room.

Billie walked over and stood with the boy behind the candlelit table, where they had set out a feast. Bowls heaped with rice, fruit, and about every vegetable from my garden, all surrounded a beau-tiful half-carved browned hen. She had broken out her best china and her silverware. She had set out nice wineglasses and crystal goblets filled with water. The candlelight shimmered and reflected off so many surfaces, the effect was like looking through a prism.

"Jesus," was all Newell said.

Billie motioned to me. "Why don't you sit at the head of the table, Mr. Marshbanks?"

I moved toward the chair, wondering what in world Newell was going to do with that ring.

"And, Newell, you sit across from him," she said, "and Jackson and I will sit on the sides."

"Would you like some wine?" Billie asked, standing beside me with a bottle of red wine.

"No thanks," I said. I had never been big on drinking, since I didn't want people saying about me what they said about a lot of housepainters.

"I'll give you just a little," Billie said, filling my wineglass anyway. She filled Newell's and her own, then sat down.

Newell held his wineglass out to Billie.

"I would like to propose," Newell said, pausing, ". . . a toast. To Billie, who has done so much for my family this summer."

I raised my wineglass, and the boy raised his wineglass, which held 7-up, and we clinked our glasses. Whatever crazy scheme Newell might have, it looked like he wasn't going to spring it on her before supper.

As we passed around the food, I know I filled my plate. I saw myself do it. I remember that much, but then I became so preoccupied with the box bulging in Newell's pocket that I didn't notice what I ate or drank. All I know is that I kept sipping the wine, and Billie kept filling my glass.

Was Newell planning to do with that ring what I thought he might be? Bigger questions started to assert themselves. What about the boy? Had he told the boy his plans? Sure, the boy liked Billie. That was clear. But making her his new mother was an altogether different prospect. Something to be discussed. Hell, even the boy's counselor would have agreed with me on that. Jackson served his plate with sliced tomatoes from the garden. He hadn't said a whole lot, not that that was unusual, but he looked like he knew something, like he had shared a secret.

Was I the only one Newell hadn't let in on his plans? Surely, he would have consulted me before asking her. After all, I knew her much better. If he did ask her and she accepted, she would move up to Asheville with them. I wouldn't be gaining a daughter-in-law as much as losing a good neighbor. Not that that would be a reason for him not to marry her, but it was enough to let me in on his plans.

I don't think I said a word through most of the meal. Newell and Billie did most of the talking. Some about Penland, some about his paintings, but Newell turned the conversation away from himself, asking about her summer, her pottery, her work, which, like his, was starting back up next week. If they were just now talking about these things, what had they spent two whole weekends talking about?

The boy ate and continued to have a warm, pleased look on his face. My worry gave way to irritation. Why had I been left out of such an important decision? I imagined a FOR SALE sign stabbed in Billie's front yard, the house dark and empty at night. I would eventually have to move into Rolling Hills with Irene, except she would be too busy folding paper cranes to give me the time of day. I would wind up like Decatur Dixon and Mr. Greathouse, except I couldn't even play the harmonica.

"I'd rather be dead," I heard myself say.

And the conversation came to a halt.

"What's that, Daddy?" Newell asked.

"I'd rather be dead than stuck over there at Rolling Hills."

Newell looked at Billie, then back at me. "No one said anything about you going into a nursing home."

"That's where I'll wind up if you marry Billie."

"What?" Billie asked, her face going scarlet and Newell's face flushing a bit, too.

"That ring," I said to Newell. "Isn't that what that's for?"

Newell looked down at his plate, then back up at me. "Not exactly," he said. He pulled out the felt box, looked at it for a minute, looked over at Jackson, who gave him a nod, then handed it to Billie. As she opened it, she put her hand to her chest.

"It's the very one," she said. She turned the box so I could see a small silver ring with a small greenish stone. I recognized it as being made by a Penland jeweler whose studio we had passed. Billie had spent some time admiring his rings and even tried one on.

"A token of our appreciation," Newell said.

"It is beautiful," she said. "Thank you," she said, looking at Newell.

"It was Jackson's idea," Newell said.

Billie walked around the table and gave Jackson a big hug and kissed him on the cheek. And I felt pretty damned foolish for jumping to conclusions, and mumbled an apology, but then Newell said, "Daddy, you do raise a good point."

"I do?" I said.

"The whole question of what kind of ring it is," he said.

"A friendship ring," Billie said quickly.

"Well, Jackson and I were hoping that it might represent a little more than that," Newell said.

"Oh?" she said.

Jackson nodded. "A going-steady ring."

Billie looked at the boy and his father, then frowned down at the ring, which was still in the box. "I've never gone steady before." She took the ring out of the box and held it in her palm like she wasn't sure if she wanted to put it on. "That was a high school thing, wasn't it?" she said, impatiently. She looked at Newell. "I'm not even sure what it means."

"Neither are we," Newell said, looking at Jackson.

"We like the way it sounds," Jackson said.

She looked down at the ring, then back up at Newell. "I'm very flattered, but . . ."

"But?" Newell asked.

"We hardly know each other," she said, sounding maybe more than a little angry at being put on the spot. "I know your father. I know your son."

"You know me by proxy," Newell said. "And we did spend two weekends together."

"I'm not at all sure about this," she said, turning the ring over in her palm.

"You don't have to be," Newell said. "The ring signifies only what you want it to signify."

"Why does this feel coercive?" she asked.

"Because it is," Newell said.

The ring slipped through her fingers, fell to the floor, and rolled under the table at my feet. I bent down to pick it up and started to hand it to her, when she said, "Are you in on this, too, Mr. Marshbanks?"

I looked at Newell and the boy. "I reckon," I said.

She sighed a big sigh, and said, "In that case." She held out her hand to me, and for a minute I didn't understand what she was getting at. Then I did. Newell and the boy were watching me, and I felt that they wanted, maybe even needed me to. So I took her hand, like I took Irene's fifty years ago at Pete's Drive-In, and slid the ring onto her finger.

"Least this time I didn't drop it into the coleslaw," I said.

Newell and Jackson watched her intently as she fingered the ring. She held it up and, sounding surprised, said, "It fits."

The next morning I was up before Newell and Jackson. Jackson had slept upstairs with Newell, so it was easy for me to creep around downstairs and make breakfast without waking them. I hadn't slept that well. I had woken up at four with a headache and a dry mouth.

Reckon it was a hangover, and I couldn't go back to sleep. Newell came down about seven, yawning and scratching his beard. He said Jackson was still asleep. I gave him a cup of coffee, and we sat at the kitchen table. It felt awkward. I didn't have much to say. In a way I wanted them go on home and leave me to sort out what was left.

But after a few minutes, Newell spoke up, "Daddy, I know I have said this, but I really am grateful for all you've done, and now I'm going to do things differently. We're going to visit regularly."

"Don't worry about it."

"I'm not going to worry about it. I'm going to do it," he said. "The other thing is that we want you to come visit. Mama would be all right if you didn't visit her for a week, especially since Billie is willing to go over there."

"Are you serious about that girl?" I asked.

"As serious as she'll let me be," Newell said. "You were there last night. You saw the whole thing."

"I still don't know what happened," I said.

Newell studied me a minute. "I have no idea what the future holds, but let's say at some distant point in time Billie and I do get together, we will not leave you alone in this house." And then he added, "And we won't put you in the nursing home either. You aren't the Rolling Hills type."

"Speaking of Rolling Hills," he said, pulling a folded piece of paper out of his shirt pocket and sliding it across the kitchen table. "I want to help you with that, too."

I picked it up and unfolded it. It was a check, and not for a small amount.

"I can't take this," I said.

"I can't be down here as much as I'd like," he said. "So let me help out in a way that I can."

I looked at the check, then up at my boy. "I don't like taking this," I said.

"I know you don't, Daddy," he said. "I know you don't."

I slid the check into my wallet.

Wasn't long before the boy came down the stairs yawning and rubbing his eyes and dragging Ruddy. I fixed them breakfast but didn't eat much myself. At one point I got up to refill my coffee cup when the boy said, "I'll get it." He set a mug of coffee in front of me, a mug I had never seen before. It was a green-and-blue-glazed mug with little rows of corn plants, tomato plants, and bean plants etched all the way around. There was a hoe propped against a tree, and along the bottom the boy had etched in a neat print, "Gone to Visit Jackson."

"Will you look at this," I said, "Looks like some professional made this mug."

I lifted the mug and took a swallow. "Oh, man," I said, "the coffee even tastes better out of it."

"Really?"

I let Jackson take a sip, but he frowned and said, "Needs more sugar." He handed it back to me. "Billie helped me with the firing. I did everything else."

"You have become quite the potter," Newell said, picking up the mug and turning it around.

After breakfast, they went upstairs and packed while I cleaned up the dishes. I was still thinking about Newell's check in my back pocket. I'd never taken money from anybody. Never needed to.

As I washed Jackson's mug carefully and set it in the dish drain, I realized I didn't have a going-away present for the boy. They were loading the car when I walked outside. Billie had come over and was talking to Newell down the drive. I tried not to look in their direction but I did see that at one point in the conversation, Newell took her hand. I went over to the boy, who was trying to fit the last of his things into the back of the car. I lifted the paintings so he could slide his pack in. The boy kept his face turned away from me. I knew his feelings were hurt, because I didn't have a good-bye present for him. I could have kicked myself.

All of the sudden, he turned around and leaned into me, giving me a tight hug. He didn't say a word, but as I held him, I could hear him sniffle. I pulled him a little away from me and looked at him. His eyes were red.

"What's this all about?" I said.

He looked away. "I like it here," he said.

"But now you get to go home to your own room, your own house."

He wiped his nose on his shirtsleeve.

"Did you forget what you drew on my mug?" I asked. "I'm going to lean my hoe against that very oak, when I come to Asheville to visit." I pulled out my handkerchief for him to blow his nose, but as I did, my pocketknife came out with it and clattered to the ground.

The boy picked it up and started to hand it to me.

I knew what I needed to do. I closed his fingers over it. "It's yours."

The boy looked at me. "You've had this knife forever."

"Nearly fifty years," I said, "When I come up, I'll show you how to clean it and sharpen it and keep it oiled."

Jackson raced down the drive to show Newell.

"Daddy, are you sure you want to do this?" Newell asked, coming back up the drive with Billie. "You had that knife as long as I've known you."

"Longer," I said.

"Are you sure about giving it to him?"

"I thought I would give it to the person I want to have it before I take permanent leave of my senses." I patted the boy's shoulder.

Jackson opened the knife, fingered the blade, turned it over and over, and then closed it against his hip like I had taught him. He kept looking at the knife. Even after Billie hugged him and he got in the car, he was looking at the knife.

"I thought we would drop by Rolling Hills on our way out of town," Newell said.

"Irene will like that," I said.

"I'd stay longer," he said, "but I have course descriptions to write, and I need to prepare for a faculty meeting first thing to-morrow morning."

I looked him in the eye. "Thank you for the check."

Newell smiled. "Think about when you would like to come up. Maybe in mid-October when the leaves are changing."

"I don't give a damned about the leaves," I said.

Newell gave me a hug, said good-bye to Billie, who had been standing to the side, then they drove off. They were gone. Just like that. My summer with the boy was over.

"Can I come inside with you and have a cup of coffee?" Billie asked.

"You don't have to do this," I said.

"You've got it all wrong," she said, as we started back up the drive.

We went on inside and sat together at the kitchen table drink-ing coffee and talking about Jackson and Newell. At some point in our conversation, I found myself thinking about our time together like a doorway I was looking back through.

That evening as I got ready for bed, I was about to pull back the covers when I noticed the boy's stuffed dog at the head of the bed.

"Oh, hell, he's gone and left Rudy," I said aloud, "Jackson won't sleep tonight." I was surprised Newell hadn't called me about it. I

had never seen the boy go anywhere without Rudy, at least anywhere overnight. I picked up the old stuffed dog and noticed a sheet
of folded notebook paper under him. The note in the boy's hand-
writing read, *Rudy wanted to stay. Don't worry, he doesn't eat near as
much as the cats.*

Seventeen

Traveler's

It was overcast and cool, a right fallish day as I drove out to Rolling Hills. There was hardly any traffic since it was a Sunday afternoon. It had been a month since Jackson had left with Newell, and, although I didn't miss him as much as I had when he first left, I still wasn't used to riding out to the nursing home alone. Even if he hadn't ever been all that talkative, he had been better company than I realized. To fill the silence, I had been turning on the radio on my drive out there, and one day they played that old song about "Don't it always seem to go, you don't know what you got till it's gone?" And while the song was a little too easy in its message, I couldn't get the words out of my mind.

That was how I had been feeling about the boy. My summer with him had been over before I knew what I had. You would have thought I would have learned my lesson with Irene. She had been with me for fifty years, but I hadn't fully loved her till she was gone from me. Lately, I had found myself looking around at my life or the remnants of it, wondering who or what I was going to miss next. It seemed that every presence was an absence waiting to happen. And the question that kept coming to me was this: Was there a way to really know what you had before it was gone? I doubted it.

I had thought I would take Irene to ride this afternoon if I could tear her away from bingo. We hadn't been to ride in a while. I wasn't sure I could manage it on my own anymore. Lately, I had been feeling less certain of myself, a little older, a little weaker, a little more drained. Today my legs were sore from the long walk I had gone on yesterday.

Two weeks ago when Chandler was at Rolling Hills checking on Irene, he looked up at me and said, "When was the last time you had a physical, Mr. Marshbanks?"

"Year before last? Or has it been three years?"

I promised him I would make an appointment. He said, "Why don't I trust you?" So he took out his cell phone and called his office, setting up an appointment for me for the following week. My blood pressure was up, he said, after the exam. He thought it was stress-related.

"I've seen it many many times," he said. "The caretaker is so busy looking after their loved one, that they neglect themselves." Then he looked at me. "Mr. Marshbanks, if you don't take care of yourself, you can't take care of Mrs. Marshbanks."

He asked if I exercised. I laughed. He said he was serious.

I thought about it a moment. "I work in the garden most every day."

"That's not enough."

"Painting houses used to be a real workout, but of course I don't do that anymore."

"I want you to take up walking," Chandler said.

"I've been walking all my life," I said.

"I want you to go for a good long walk around your neighbor-hood every day."

"What about my ankle?"

"It might actually improve it if you can strengthen your leg mus-cles," he said. "I want you to go to the shoe store, buy yourself some comfortable walking shoes," he said, frowning down at my lace-up work boots, "and start going for at least a mile walk every day."

"You can't be serious."

"Serious as a heart attack," he said, looking at me over his glasses.

"Can't you put me on some blood pressure medication?" I asked.

"It's not bad enough for that yet, but it might get that way unless you do as I tell you. Regular exercise will also improve your mood."

"Are you saying there's something wrong with my mood?"

He tried not to smile. "All I'm saying is that you need to take some time for yourself every day, and with exercise, you're doing that and you're taking care of yourself, too."

I left his office in a deep funk, and not because of the news about my blood pressure. It was the idea of walking that galled me. I used to shake my head at all these smug fit people who jogged or walked past our house in their little jogging outfits, sipping from their water bottles or pumping their hand weights. I used to think if they had a real job where they had to do real work, they wouldn't need all that nonsense. Now, I was about to become one of the ridiculous. And I had felt pretty damned ridiculous yesterday on my first long walk, parading around the neighborhood in the bright boats the salesman had called walking shoes.

I was surprised to find Irene sitting in her room, looking out the window.

"I thought you would be in the game room," I said.

She looked at me like she was trying to place me.

"I'm Prate," I said. I often had to remind her who I was these days. "Your husband."

"I see," she said.

"Why didn't you play bingo today?"

She looked back out the window at the courtyard. There were several families out there with the residents, it being not insufferably hot as it had been in the summer. She looked sad, and I hadn't seen her look sad in several weeks. I had to wonder if one of her many medications was wearing off. Chandler had said they might become less effective over time.

"You feel okay?" I said, putting my hand to her forehead. A virus had been going around the nursing home, and Irene had managed to avoid it so far. What I hadn't known about nursing homes was that they were breeding grounds for all sorts of bugs because of all the infirm residents living in such close quarters.

I pulled up a chair beside her. "What's wrong then?" I asked, taking her hand.

"I miss Newell," she said.

"You mean the boy?"

She nodded.

"He's Jackson."

"He hasn't come in a long time," she said. "Has he?"

"Not in a while," I said.

She had asked for the boy every day since he had gone back, and each day she seemed more depressed, almost like it had taken her a month to really know he was gone.

"He's up in Asheville with Newell, but they're coming this weekend." Newell had been so busy with his classes starting that he hadn't had time to visit, but he had called two or three times a week, and sometimes the boy would get on the phone, too.

"You want to go to ride?" I asked Irene.

"I wish we could all be . . . in the same place," she said.

"Why don't we go for a ride," I said, getting her sweater out of the closet.

"What are families for if not to be to . . . if not to be assembled in the same vicinity?" she asked.

"We haven't gone for a ride in a while. It's nice out. Not near as hot as it has been."

She shrugged.

"It'll do you good," I said, unfolding her wheelchair. "I'll even ride you out to the car."

Irene had been getting around under her own steam, but when she was depressed she had a harder time walking. As I rolled her down the hall, we passed the dining room lady who looked at us, then at her watch and said in a cheery but warning tone, "Not long before dinner."

"Irene will not be eating supper here tonight," I said, surprising myself.

"Now, Mr. Marshbanks, you know very well you are supposed to notify the staff first thing in the morning if a resident isn't eating supper with us. We require twelve hours' notice."

"Consider yourself notified," I said, then pushed Irene on down the hall, leaving the woman watching us. "Irene will be dining out with me," I called back loud enough so that several of the residents turned to look at us.

I rolled Irene on out to the van, wondering what I had just committed myself to. I had only planned to take Irene for a little ride, not out to eat. I hadn't taken her out to eat by myself in months.

I must have overdone the walking, because my legs ached as I pushed Irene out to the van. After I helped her in, I put the wheelchair in the back and climbed into the driver's seat. When I did, Irene was looking at me, like, what have we gotten ourselves into?

I drove past the developments until we were out in the countryside, going down some of the very roads I had got us lost on back in April. We drove along the same big pastures, where the very same cows grazed that had been grazing when I had pulled over and waited out the storm.

Today the clouds were even and settled in, not like the dark thunderheads that had descended on us that afternoon. These clouds didn't even look like clouds, but more like an endless gray ceiling that made the pasture and the bordering trees almost too green to look at. I pulled over in what must have been about the same place we had pulled over before. I turned off the car and rolled down my window. It was coolish, and I was glad I had remembered to put a sweater on Irene before we had left.

"Why are we stopping?" Irene asked almost in a panic, looking around, feeling for the door handle, which wasn't there, then clutching her sweater around her neck. "Are we . . . not where we know we are?"

"We're not lost," I said.

"Why are we stopping?"

"I thought it might be nice," I said, taking her hand.

She looked at her hand in mine, then at my arm, my shoulder, and finally into my face. Seeming satisfied, she looked outside. A breeze lifted wisps of her white hair, and as she studied the landscape, her face emptied of all expression. It had done that often lately, as if she had wandered off on some lonely path in the wilderness of her mind. And I did not know what to do except to wait for her to wander back. Of course, I knew that one day she would not find her way back.

"I don't remember this place," she said after a little while. She turned to me. "But I should, shouldn't I?"

"We've only been here once before," I said. "When we were lost one time."

"But we're not lost now," she said.

"No, we're not."

"I see," she said, looking out at the pasture as if thinking something over. I watched her watch the pasture, and we sat there for quite some time. "It's very pretty," she said cautiously, like there was something she didn't want to tell me, something she was doing her level best to protect me from.

"But . . . ?" I said.

"But . . ." She sighed, looked me right in the eye, and said with great feeling, "I'm hungry."

"Well damn!" I said, laughing.

She looked perplexed, then grinned a little, like a child who knows she has said something funny but is not sure what.

How we ended up at Traveler's Restaurant, a diner over in Traveler's Rest, I'm not quite sure. All I know is that I had not been able to bring myself to drive back in the direction of Rolling Hills. Instead I had driven north, away from the developments and deeper into farm country, till I found Old Buncombe Highway, then followed it until it emptied into Traveler's Rest, a little town that stood at the fork of two highways. Right took you up Highway 25 to Hendersonville, then Asheville. Left up Highway 276 to Jones Gap, then Caesar's Head and Brevard.

I don't know what got into me. It wasn't something I had planned. It was like the van was an old horse finding its way back to the barn or in this case, to a diner Irene, Newell, and I had often eaten at after our Sunday afternoon rides up into the mountains. We hadn't been here in at least fifteen years.

I couldn't believe Traveler's was still in business. A low little brick building with big glass windows, it only had a few cars and a couple of pickups parked outside. In the old days the place used to be packed most every night. A lot of fast-food places, as well as a steak house and a fish house had opened up around it, and judging from all the cars parked in front of them, it appeared they had siphoned off Traveler's business.

Irene was able to manage the walk into the diner with a little help from me. The waitress, who must have been about Irene's age and who I recognized from years back, didn't remember us. I was disappointed, but I reminded myself how many thousands of customers she had waited on over the years.

Still, she was friendly and led us to a booth beside the window, which, after we sat down, I remembered was the very same booth we always used to ask for, and when I looked up at the waitress she had a twinkle in her eye.

"I was right, wasn't I?" she asked. "This was y'all's booth, wasn't it?"

She had remembered us, down to the booth we sat in. She told us Gene, the owner, had died of a heart attack five years back. There was a big picture of him in the back of the restaurant, memorializing him. She nodded back toward the kitchen and said Gene's wife, Dora, had done all the cooking ever since.

"I'll be right back with your iced teas," she said. "Yours sweet and your wife's unsweet, right?"

"That's right," I said, watching her walk back to get the drinks, astonished at the woman's memory.

I looked around and there wasn't anybody in the place but old folks—two couples looked to be at least our age if not older in booths behind us, and then a vaguely familiar old woman sitting across from us, eating soup and crackers and reading *Reader's Digest*. And no one in the place was saying a word to anybody. All you could hear was the sound of the old lady sipping her soup.

When the waitress came with our teas, Irene and I ordered our usual vegetable plates, or rather I ordered Irene's vegetable plate for her after she looked shyly up from the menu, and asked me, "What do I like?"

The waitress smiled, but not as if amused by Irene, but that she understood her, understood what had happened to her in the fifteen years she hadn't seen her. The waitress walked through the swinging kitchen door one minute and walked back out with our food the next, like Gene's wife was standing at the ready, serving spoon in hand.

Irene started in on the food, but I kept looking around the place, watching the old couples. It was eerie. How they ate without saying one word to each other. And I thought, *Why is that? Why haven't I noticed that before?* I began thinking about all the old married couples I had ever seen eat together and how they always kept their heads down, eyes on their food, like whatever pleasure they took from the person sitting across from them had died decades ago. I looked at the old woman by herself, buttering a cracker, and thought she's not a bit more alone than the couples. In fact, in the easy way she ate, the comfortable way she held her *Reader's Digest,* she looked like her own best companion.

As I watched the couples, I had to wonder if this was how Irene and I used to eat supper together before her illness. The thing that shook me up was that I couldn't remember, as if I had not even been at the supper table all those years. Had I passed precious decades with my wife, eating with head down, mind on nothing but the next bite? And if we did talk, what had we talked about? I couldn't say. The memory wasn't there. I thought for a minute and calculated that I had eaten nigh on twenty thousand suppers with Irene and could hardly remember a one.

"Your food is getting . . . away," Irene said, taking a shaky sip of tea and looking at my untouched plate. She meant it was getting cold.

"Oh, right," I said, taking a bite of mashed potatoes and gravy. They were the best mashed potatoes I had put in my mouth in ages. Nothing like the dry grainy instant glop they served over at Rolling Hills. In fact, the green beans, the coleslaw, and the creamed corn all tasted better than any food I had had in a long long time.

"This food reminds me of your cooking," I said.

"Was I a good cook?"

"A very good cook," I said. I ate with my eyes on Irene, who would turn every now and then and look at me.

"Is something wrong with my hair?" she asked, touching the back of her neck.

"Your hair is fine," I said, "I just like looking at you."

"Oh," she said, actually blushing.

"Can I butter you a corn muffin?"

"If you would be so kind," she said.

I took a corn muffin out of the little basket of bread the waitress had brought, slit it with a knife and, peeling the wax paper off the butter pat, slid it inside to melt, and then set it on her plate.

"Thank you," she said, taking a bite.

Then I buttered me one, and we ate in silence, but I kept watching her, and she would glance up at me now and then and smile shyly like we were on a first date. And with the Alzheimer's we were always on a first date.

The waitress came back, asking if we wanted dessert. The old lady across from us was finishing up a piece of apple pie with ice cream.

"Is the pie homemade?" I asked the waitress.

"Dora's mother made it yesterday."

"It's very good," the old lady said, looking up at us. "If I do say so myself."

"Dora's mother," the waitress said.

The old lady nodded but went back to her *Reader's Digest.*

"Would you like some apple pie?" I asked Irene.

"Indeed," Irene said.

The waitress smiled again in what seemed shorthand for I know what this is. I have been around it. I have lived with it. I am comfortable with it. My husband had it. My brother had it. My mother. My sister. My father. Hell, I may have it. We're all in this together.

I ordered us a piece of apple pie with ice cream and two decaf coffees, which she brought right out. She brought us two forks so we could split the pie. Irene and I took turns forking up bites. Irene was too shaky with the coffee, trying to lift it on her own a couple of times, then having to set it back down.

I had lifted the cup to her lips to help her drink, when in walked Old Man Gudger from the little store up in Jones Gap. He had a pretty young woman on his arm, who must have been in her late fifties, early sixties. Young in relation to him anyhow. Young in relation to everyone else in the place. I didn't remember him saying anything about a daughter.

The old man spotted me as the waitress was taking them to a booth across the room. I got up and shook his hand. "And this is my friend, Lois Turner," he said. "She delivers my newspapers." I could tell by the lightness of the old man's step, the lilt in his voice, and the emphasis he put on the word "friend" that she delivered more than papers.

Lois Turner shook my hand firmly and looked me right in the eye. "Pleased to meet you, Mr. Marshbanks," she said with a deep mountain accent. Nothing sleazy or fast about this woman. I liked her.

"You remember Irene, Mr. Gudger," I said, turning to Irene, who was looking up at us quizzically, like the crowd of us baffled her.

Mr. Gudger took Irene's hand the way he used to when he talked her up in his store. "It's wonderful to see you again, Mrs. Marshbanks. You look as beautiful as ever." Then he whispered to me, "I thought she was in a nursing home."

"I decided to take her out for supper."

His eyes slid down to Irene's legs. "Still as pretty as ever."

"Good to meet you," Lois Turner said, taking Irene's hand.

"Yes," Irene said.

Mr. Gudger was still fawning over Irene the way he always used to, when Lois gently took his arm and led him over to the booth across the room. "Nice to meet y'all," she said.

"Same here," I said.

"Come fishing soon," the old man said over his shoulder. "I've got a new shipment of night crawlers."

The old man and Lois slid into the booth the same way Irene and I had, sitting on one side together. Mr. Gudger was all smiles, and I noticed Lois's hand resting on his thigh. I don't think I had ever seen the old man outside of his little store. Watching him now, I thought he looked and behaved like a new man. I couldn't help wondering what a younger woman like that would see in him. Perhaps she was after his money, although I had gathered he didn't have much more than the little store, which wouldn't have been worth this woman's time. Maybe she had a thing for older men. I took another look at the aged Mr. Gudger. Maybe she had a thing for parchment.

The waitress brought us our check and saw me looking over at Gudger. "Some people say it's disgraceful for an old man to carry on with her," she said, keeping her voice low. "But I say more power to him. Happiness doesn't have an expiration date." Then she looked at Irene, who seemed to have gone off in her head somewhere.

"I have always thought your wife was a lovely woman," the waitress said. "And she's more lovely than ever." Then she said a little quieter, "My husband had this, but if you're like me, everybody gives you their war stories, so I'll save you mine. But I will say this—it wasn't all bad."

"What happened to him?" I asked.

"He died last year," she said, looking away. I handed her back the check with a ten and a five-dollar bill and told her to keep the change. She said for us to come back soon, then she went over to take Mr. Gudger's order.

Irene leaned her head against me and yawned. It caught me off guard—the tender weight of her head on my shoulder. I couldn't remember when she had leaned against me like that.

"Tired?" I asked, taking her hand.

She yawned again. "Do we need to get back, Daddy?"

I paused, not sure I could speak. "In a little while," I finally said. And then I said, "I wish I could take you home with me, Irene."

She sat up, frowning at me. "We are home," she said, searching my face with clear eyes. Then seeming satisfied with what she found there, laid her head against me. And for the longest time, I did not move.